REBUILDING THE
CROWN

REBUILDING THE
CROWN

TIMOTHY C.J. MURPHY

authorHOUSE®

AuthorHouse™
1663 Liberty Drive
Bloomington, IN 47403
www.authorhouse.com
Phone: 1-800-839-8640

Published by AuthorHouse   12/11/2012

ISBN: 978-1-4772-4987-1 (sc)
ISBN: 978-1-4772-4988-8 (e)

Library of Congress Control Number: 2012922808

CHAPTER 1

ONE OF MICK Joyce's earliest experiences in life was when he was about five years old. It must have probably been early summer in 1938. A letter had arrived from the United States from Mick's auntie Mary in Boston with an envelope full of American dollars. It was sent home to get a dress for Aine for the First communion. Madge and Paddy, his mother and father had been preparing all day that Friday for something important. He sensed that they were going on a trip as the filling for sandwiches was on the strong oak kitchen table, some hairy bacon, (unshaven of course) and a small bit of chicken left over from the dinner on Thursday. Shep the faithful family working dog for the sheep sat at the door sniffing for the fresh meat on the table even though it was out his sight. His seven year old sister Aine was all excited about something and kept asking her mother about where was she going to get her first communion medal. Mick had been in school all but a year and his knowledge of God was only beginning to surface despite the ash plant across his hand when he couldn't remember who made the world. He still realised that this would be a big event as in those days one did not travel far beyond their quaint village of Ballinahowen, perched on the verge of the Atlantic Ocean. Sandwiches were only made for the All Ireland or for a trip to Galway in those days so in May it had to be Galway. The first born son Joe, Mick eldest brother was a sturdy lad of twelve and looked at least fourteen. He worked hard with his father on the land, tending the sheep, looking after the eight cows they had, and had this last year or so gone to sea fishing in the Curragh. The night before they would go fishing the holy water was left on the table for them so that they'd carry the Lord's Blessings with them in the morning.

Ma called Joe and Mick at a quarter to seven. Joe pleaded for another five minutes which was ruled out of order so the two of them got out of the big wrath iron double bed. Mick stood at the washstand and douched his face with the best Connemara spring water that was on offer. He put his chest out and tried his best to emulate his big brother Joe in stature, but he was sorely lacking in both height and width as yet. Aine was already sitting at the table polishing off the remains of her fine bowl of thick porridge awash with a healthy splash of cream. She was all chatter about her First Communion dress, as one would expect, as it was a real dressy affair for a daughter. Joe remembered that when he made his first communion that he was covered from head to toe in a black jumper, an old shirt, a cut down tie, that his grand-mother had made for him, and a short pants, made from an old black blanket that had never been woven, because it had always just been in the house. It had now become smooth and worn enough to make clothes from. All this was rounded off with a span new pair of black hob nailed boots, his first ever piece of footwear. Money was scarce in those days and Paddy Joyce worked hard to feed and keep his wife Madge and their children. There was always a fletch of salted home cured bacon dangling from a big brass hook above the fire which collected, not too much smoke, but just enough, from the open hearth. The wool from the sheep kept their backs warm through each winter as it was knitted into the best quality Aran gansais one could find. Paddy was a solemn man, God fearing, who always lead the rosary each evening after the supper. He and Madge made sure that mass was never missed on Sundays or holy days of obligation, it was their way of life. Life was often tough on the bleak winter eves. The sea sometimes roared for days on end, sheep often went missing over the hill towards the cliffs and Paddy arrived home late many a night from Recess where he would sell turf from door to door with the horse and car and sometimes often giving away a bag away to the more needy cases. Madge would always have the few spuds sprawled across the table with a piece of cod or finny haddock on the plate. A jug of porter would be there to wash down the dinner for her Patsy when she had a few spare pence. Paddy was the love of her life and she took care of him as if it was the first day that she laid eyes on him. He stood six foot three and he had given her three fine children and there was another on the way this coming fall. Each night Madge's last word before the Rosary's end to God was *"May his hand be always be at her side"*. She was discrete about those things but all in the house knew the hand, she was talking about.

Aine always got the window seat on the bus with her mother outside her, across from them Joe was instructed to keep young Mick well hemmed in so he couldn't wander something that had been his nature since he was able to walk. Paddy sat behind them with his strong protective countenance keeping an eye on his family. He sat back and took a pull of the pipe. He felt a serene sense of happiness come over him, the turf sold well this last winter, the fishing seemed to be coming right and he had about 10 lambs to sell in Recess next week. There were two calves starting to feed in the high meadow, life was hard but they all got by. The bus plodded on stopping wherever a lonely sole who had walked miles in some cases to meet it, wanted to get on. It was eleven o'clock when the bus arrived at the bus station. Madge took Joe and Aine with her to the shops while Paddy managed the wanderer. Mick was the one who always put his father laughing. He had the sayings of the old men of the parish, and walked with pigeon toes. He loved to be with his father as he felt safe and enjoyed the knowledge that he picked up from him. Today would be a day he would remember throughout his life. His Da had promised to take him to see his first train, mainly to try and keep him from running off. Mick could feel the mighty grasp of his father's large, rough hand that was a conduit for his gentle relaxed nature to pass between the two of them, as he walked him up and down the platform and explained the workings of the steam engine. Mick developed a love for trains that day that would live with him throughout his life. The gush of steam, the hooter, the size of the green carriages, young Mick stood there with mouth open. It was the first wonder of Mick's world.

The dress was bought by two o'clock so they all met up again as planned on a bench in Eyre's Square to sample the sandwiches washed down with a bottle or two of milk.

Madge's feet were beginning to feel the pressure but she kept it to herself as that was a woman's thing. All the talk from Aine was where she going to get the medal for her dress. Paddy spoke, telling her to be patient and let her mother have a rest. She heeded his word without further comment. Madge looked at him and smiled as he rested his broad hand on her shoulder. As they all sat around Paddy wondered what would become of them all, and another on the way. Some would head for America maybe, where his own two brothers and sister had gone, or maybe to England. There was only a bit of a life on the farm for one and that had to be supplemented by the bog and the fishing each year. The more children they had the more heartache they'd be when they were old enough to leave home. Such was life in Connemara, in 1930s Ireland. It was hard, tough, plenty of tears and a little education. The only children who made it then in school were the sons and daughters of the local school master or the shopkeepers. Yet Ireland now belonged to us again and we would build it bit by bit, but it would take a lot of blood, sweat, and many a tear. Madge and the two eldest took off again to look for the medal, a white rosary beads, shoes and socks, and most importantly, a prayer book. Paddy went across with young Mick to Jack Fahy's pub, ordered a large bottle of Guinness and a bottle of lemonade for the young lad. It was there that Paddy realised that Mick's personality was beginning to form. He sat up on a high stool next to his father and chatted to the bar maid like he had known her all his life. He asked her had she ever been on a train. To which she replied oh many times, as if not to disappoint him. She came outside the bar on one occasion while collecting bottles and glasses and gave him a kiss on the cheek trying to embarrass him, only for him

5

to turn around and give her a kiss back. The whole pub roared with laughter. He was a true showman even then. At five o'clock a tired Madge returned laden with bags and stories of what wonders the shops held, only to find her child sitting on the counter amusing the customers. They all had a cup of tea with the money left over that had been set aside for the trip and a few cuts of home made bread Madge kept since Eyre's Square earlier. The bus was boarded at a quarter to six, the tickets were checked and on the stroke of six they headed for Spiddal and the long road home beyond. They got off the Bus at the top of the boreen as the dark was beginning to fall. Paddy carried a young tired Mick who had long since fallen fast asleep. Shep came up the boreen to greet them all with his tail wagging him with delight, instead of the other way around. They all slept soundly that night except for Paddy as he dwelt on the talk of war in Europe in the Irish Press that day. This Hitler fella in Germany seemed hell bent on causing a stir and upsetting the peace.

That June Aine made her First Communion, she was a picture, dressed in the white of the angels. She knew every prayer in her prayer book. She collected 9s-6d that day from all the relations that were left in the parish. She also got a card from Paddy's sister in Boston with a dollar in it. She was a wealthy young lady. Madge had a double surprise for them all, the second week in August, a bit before her time, when she gave birth to twins even though she had known for some weeks. Two fine healthy girls, a bit premature but nothing a few weeks wouldn't take care of. They were named Niamh and Eilish. That week Aine fussed so much that she completely forgot that she ever made her first holy communion. It was all in the past now as she helped her mother with her two new sisters.

At Christmas Santa called as usual but he hadn't much to give around Aine and Mick were told he hadn't much money, even though to Aine's surprise she got a rag doll that Madge made for her from some old clothes. Mike had got a small timber block with wheels on it, resembling a steam engine it was his pride and joy. He played all over Christmas with it even though he didn't really believe it was a steam engine, but still traveled the length and breath of Ireland with it in his innocent mind. His imagination took him that extra mile as it would do many a time throughout his life. Time passed over the next two years, school, Mass on Sundays, the rounds selling the turf with his Da in the horse and cart in Recess. It was there he learned the cuteness from his Da about how to make a shilling, and better still how to mind it! The evenings on the way home from Recess were often cold and foggy but their laughter drifted into the mountain mist that carried their fun all the way to Paddy's sister over the sea in Boston. Mick loved nothing more than to lounge on the empty turf bags next to his mentor, his icon his Da. Mick loved his Da but Paddy often found it hard to reciprocate his love like many a father did in those days towards a son. Mick always knew even from a very early age that it was the way his father looked at him, with love for him in his eyes and in his soul.

Mick's life in school was fraught with daydreaming, idling, and he found that he got bored easily. He could see the curraghs in his minds eye heading for the open water or the men sitting in the bog under a thatched covering surrounded by old turf and a few scraws left to one side from the skinning, waiting for the mist to lift before cutting the next wipe of turf. Where else in the name of God would a young lad prefer to be? By the time Mick was ten he could write his name, the odd sentence and maybe a composition laced with spatterings of Connemara Irish, say his prayers with an odd prompt, and most important of all, count money. It was many a day that Aine and himself had mitched from school and went walking on the sea shore. It was there he got to know his sister as they developed a friendship that would last into old age. If he fell she was there to lend him a hand. When Ma gave out to her for not feeding the fowl or going for the shopping Mick was there to console her. They used to collect periwinkles and crabs on the rocks down below the pier near the church and the parochial house where the stern Fr. O' Brien lived. Mick didn't care where he was once he was outdoors where the salt dried his hair to the point that it felt like the coat of daisy the cow, coarse and rough. He loved where he grew up and made friends easily with both boys and girls of his own age. At ten he played full back for the under twelves in school. All the talk these days in school was of the war in Europe where it seemed like every country in the world was kicking the lard out of the Germans. This was of no consequence to Mick as he had never learned where Europe was, or for that matter who was kicking the lard out of who. The only way the war effected Mick was that when he went to the bog with his father that the place was full of soldiers cutting turf for the crowd in the towns. When the war was at it height out to sea Mick heard his brother Joe arrange for six curraghs to carry out food and water to German U—Boats off shore. Joe made a lot of money that year dealing with the German U-Boats. All this meant to Mick, was that Aine and the twins got the odd bar of chocolate from the shop in the village. One night Joe and ten others set out west of Innispuffin Island, to meet a German ship. That night when they had done their trading they headed back for the shore but met a squall about two miles out. When it was found in the morning that they hadn't returned a search was started but it was hampered with the strong south westerly wind. All that day the church was full and the school was closed. Fr. O' Brien prayed and comforted the families of those believed lost at sea. That evening around 3 O'clock the remains of Jack Connealy's curragh was washed up on the rocks about a mile down the coast south of the pier. For a boy of ten this was Mick's first experience of fear, fear for his brother Joe's life and his father who had gone looking for him in early afternoon. While the villagers were still in a state of shock at the find an hour before, around the western headland came a flotilla of curraghs and the hardest men that ever caught an oar nursing them back to the pier against the sill roaring Atlantic currents. Everyone started to count the heads from the cliff tops as they headed homeward bound. There were two missing. The women started to cry and the daughters followed suit, but the young fellas led by Mick and his friend Jack ran up the hill to get a better view of the harbour. That evening Mick knew the value of being able to count. He and Jack counted aloud eight, nine, ten, eleven, twelve, thirteen . . . yes all eighteen were in the curraghs with two lying down. No body was lost. Jack's eldest brother Paddy was suffering from the cold and had got torn on the rocks as Joe had helped his friend ashore on Innispuffin where they sheltered overnight in an old bee hive hut, where monks once prayed. Joe himself had two bleeding elbows but had saved all the money they made that night plus a fine leather coat he scavenged for his father from a German officer. A night of celebration and prayer followed, the mothers gave out to the sons who had gone to sea but the fathers all got drunk with them. Paddy brought home Joe that night while singing "The West Awake". Mick thought to himself that everyone in the West that night had to be awake with the singing. Joe woke up the whole house when he fell over the billy can that Madge used for the milk. As Mick came down the narrow stairs from the loft bedroom he rushed to his Da and his brother Joe and hugged them, they were all together once again, safe and well. As Mick melted into a slumber that night he thought to himself there must be and easier way to make a bob. Tearing at turf, up to you neck in cow dung, and trying to sell fish to the fish vans that came out from Galway looking for his father's catch for nothing. Roaming the open range in search of sheep with the tilly lamp giving out for the want of oil. Even in Galway life had to be better.

As the war moved on to the winter of 1944 /45 there was a lot of emigration west of Spiddle and the surrounding area. In late September Paddy, and Joe who was now nineteen, and had been promised the farm headed for the munitions factories of Birmingham to make the price of a tractor for the spring. Madge cried for a week as she thought of her beloved husband and her firstborn take the boat to England. As a young lad of twelve, Mick with help from his mother tackled the horse and cart each evening after school and headed for Recess with a rail of turf. The mare was getting old and she was slowing down that year but with Mick's kindness and gentle persuasion she would always bring him home safely, often with Mick walking alongside her. Mick even got on well with the animals something that would stand to him when he would himself head for good old blighty in the years to come.

That Christmas Niamh and Eilish who were seven since August, were all talk about Santa and had a letter to him made out in early December. Madge read it and sent off a letter herself to Paddy so that he might be able to pick up something nice for them in England before he came home for Christmas. Paddy and Joe arrived home Christmas Eve on the late bus from Galway. They were tired and weary from hard work and traveling. As they took off their long heavy overcoats which were made from army blankets, they unraveled four bicycle tubes from around their waists which were full of the finest tea from India, picked up on the black market in London. It was a welcome sight as it was being rationed at home. Their presence in the house was a sight to behold, two fine men with the brawn of four ordinary men. We had exported our best to aid the King! They all ate well that Christmas as there was an extra bob or two in the house, but three days after Christmas day Paddy and Joe caught the early bus back to Galway and to England. Madge and the girls cried for another week, and Mick's heart felt heavy but he held back the tears as he was now twelve and couldn't be seen to be crying anymore for fear the word would get out in school. The next few months passed quickly as everyone was busy. The girls tended the hens and Mick struck off for Recess four evenings a week with the rail of turf. On the 3rd of June a few weeks after the war was over Paddy and Joe arrived home for good. The evening was fine and the sun glistened across towards Innispuffin as it dipped.

Paddy and Mick went for a walk across the hill above the garden that yielded the food for the table each year. While they stood on the hilltop facing America Paddy handed Mick a five pound note. He had never seen one before. Mick knowing that it was hard earned wouldn't take it from his father until he insisted saying *"You have earned this money well this last winter so take it now son and build your fortune on it in the years ahead"*. As Mick reluctantly clasped the money in his fist he felt six foot tall, he had made his first good wage but most of all his efforts were recognised by his mentor. He was so proud of his father and at last felt he could almost, stand shoulder to shoulder with him, without being aloft the timber butter box that sat beside the hearth.

The following morning Joe caught the bus east to Spiddle where he purchased a four year old second hand "David Brown" tractor. He bargained for over an hour and a half with black Jack and got a rusty bit of a cab thrown in for free. He struck off for home after only a half an hour of a driving lesson from Black Jack up and down the street. Such was life in Galway at the time, no driving license, or insurance, and as for tax weren't we paying enough for everything as it was. Paddy was delighted with the tractor and after a hearty dinner that evening Joe and himself went for porter to Tom's in the village. Paddy thought to himself that they had come along way in the last eight years since the day in Galway, but it was only done with hard work and for the grace of God. With the tractor they might now make a go of the land so that he could pass on something worth while to Joe in time. The following morning Joe went for showing the father how to drive this new contraption. The lesson was slow and comprehensive and when Paddy was ready, as he thought, up he sat and took off in the gate and down into the low field below the house. He drove around in a zig zag fashion for about twenty minutes and then headed back for the yard behind the house. All went well until he tried to back it over near the wall of the shed. It was then disaster stuck, he reversed straight into the wall of the shed and made a huge crack from foundation to roof. Luckily he was not hurt nor did he do any damage to the tractor. Madge ran out into the yard in a fit of panic wiping her hands on her daisy patterned apron. She turned, and laughed as she walked to the back door nodding her head seeing that there was no one hurt. She couldn't ever figure out the devices of men, but realised that they were best left to them, themselves.

CHAPTER 2

—⋙⋘—

Tom Sullivan was the youngest boy of a family of five. He had two brothers, Pat and Andy and two sisters Brid and Margaret. They all lived on the outskirts of Tralee with their mother Rita and their father Con. His life and soul was football and the green and gold jersey of the Kingdom. The year was 1941 and Tom was playing in the under 9s for the Christian Brother's boys team. As he soared for the ball dead centre in mid field he could feel a sharp pang of pain to his side as he plucked the ball from its lofty heights, almost in the clouds. A rush of both pride and pain rampaged through his body as he struck the thick green grass with a thud reminiscent of hitting the street pavement. As he looked up he saw the culprit who fouled him and brought him to the ground. As he sprung to his feet, with the ball still in his grasp, he staggered as if a dagger went through his side, thinking to himself that "defeat was not an option" he had to make his efforts count. The ball left his right leg and gained height as it left his boot, the direction was perfect. Everyone held their breath, as the ball hopped once, and then twice into the parallelogram over the head of the goalie and deep into the back of the net. A loud cheer rang out from the sideline. Such playing was reminiscent of the newest crop of young footballers in the Kingdom each year. He fell to his knees in pain until he regained his composure. Without much fuss he got up rubbing his side and set his sights on Tony Dineen, he was now a marked man. The game was hard and the pressure on his young legs was even harder as he approached the final seven minutes. Dineen ran for the ball but Tom headed him off and drove him completely off the ball with a shoulder and a good dig to accompany it. As it headed for the 14 yard line Tom chipped it into his hand and broke into a solo passing it to Donie O'Neill to his left, he hopped it once, soloed and chipped it dead centre over the bar. As the ball passed between the uprights Tom noticed Tony Dineen coming at him with the fists clenched. At the last minute Tom turned and met him with a punch that sent him reeling across the grass. Tom played unopposed for the remaining 4 minutes until he proudly marched up to collect his first football medal having won the match by a goal and two points. As Tom's short fatigued little legs took him home that evening, the feeling of pride in him that day was something, and at eight he couldn't rightly put into words. He knew that winning and the success that came with it meant everything and that there was only one way to do a job, and that was the right way. These were sentiments that became part of his being as he progressed through life. It was to be the first of many accolades Tom would bring home in his life in both football, and in the various jobs that he would work at throughout.

Tom had been brought up as a good living boy with all the right sentiments. His mother Rita bred a sense of kindness and caring into him, that he would one day reciprocate to her in her old age. The bond they had was special in both content and disposition. Con, his father on the other hand instilled a Godly type of devotion in him towards work and the successes that were its rewards. In the evening he would be told to come home to weed the acre of ploughed ground where the vegetables grew that fed the family each year. When this was done it was over to the patch of ground by the rocks that skirted the river Lee to join his pals in a game of football. Life was simple then for them all, enough to eat, houses warmed by two lorries of good black turf from Dromadda, Lyreacrompane, or Keilduff each year. There was always a cake of the best soda bread that was ever made on the table by Rita. Although hailing from the town she had married a hard working countryman whom the soda bread had always been a way of life for. The War was tough on them in other respects, tea and sugar were in short supply and most food was hard got unless you grew your own. The chickens kept coming on stream as did the two pigs that were killed each year for both the pork and the bacon as well as the black and white pudding and the rashers sliced from the side of the fletch of smoked bacon, when needed. The British Queens were always followed by the Kerr Pinks but nothing could compare with the Golden Wonders each year with the turkey for Christmas, they were the best potato ever grown, and from that garden even better than usual. All washed down each Christmas with a good helping of "Nashe's Lemonade".

As sister and brother Brid and Pat were always close, as on the other hand were Margaret, Andy and Tom. In late 1942 Brid left home and traveled to Belfast to work as a secretary for a northern company. She had headed off into the war zone. Rita and Con were worried as it was a fair undertaking at 17yrs of age to make off for the other end of the country, and into enemy territory north of the border. Brid had lived with her aunt Katie in Belfast which was a bastion of everything that was pro Orange and everything that was anti green. She had to keep her mouth shut each day as she went about her business. Before Brid left for the North of Ireland she had lived about a mile from the family home nearer to the town. She educated herself in the arts at the Presentation Convent in playing the piano, and studying music in its finest forms, something which would always bestow pleasure on her throughout her life. She had fostered the love of music from her aunt Bridget who was an accomplished pianist. Pat on the other hand found his calling in the outdoors fishing and shooting. Andy and Tom concentrated on hard work as did Margaret in their early years. The garden was their calling, as feeding the hens was also for Margaret. Their work was always done in an atmosphere of fun and goodwill. When their father would come home in the evening he would praise their efforts as he walked with them into the kitchen where Rita's smile greeted them like a stolen ray of sunshine setting out over Tralee Bay on a fine summer's eve. Con would enquire as to where Pat had gone only to be told, **"To the river".** His reaction to this was always the same, that he had told him to weed the garden with the others. Usually, just before the supper Pat would arrive through the creaking side gate to the rear of the house with a few salmon draped over the bar of the bike with the rust beginning to show on it from the blood of the fish. Con would always scold him for not helping his two younger brothers and sister, but Rita would always protect her firstborn son from such chastisement. As soon as the supper was eaten their thoughts were turned to their homework, something that always received the same commitment as the garden. With the evening sun dipping it was off to the pitch by the rocks and a few kicks around for the last hour of the day.

As Tom reached his twelfth birthday the war was just over. Oil was starting to appear again for the beautifully ornate brass lamp on the table. Rationing was still the order of the day in Tralee but things were slowly coming back to the pre war ways. Tom made his confirmation that year and became the proud owner of his first suit. He looked every bit the young gentleman that he was. The suit was made by his aunt Bridget a seamstress of notoriety in the town whom made a good living from her efforts. He collected 14s 10d which his father rounded off with 5s-2d to make his day's take £1.

That Summer Brid returned from Belfast with all the stories of the soldiers, sailors and airmen of his Majesties Forces and the Yanks that used Northern Ireland as a place of recreation, and were also stationed there protecting the province. As her eyes sparkled with tales of the uniforms and how well the warriors looked in them, Rita would stand at the kitchen sink, roll her eyes to heaven and bless herself saying some of the more lengthily aspirations praying for her soul, and asking God to protect her daughter. Brid was now 20 and left the clutches of her aunt Katie in Belfast to seek her fortune in the business district of London. She was to settle there later that decade and set up a family outpost for those of her kin who would later brave the harsh winters and fog of Great Britain.

Pat left Ireland that summer also and went to sea having trained as a radio / communications officer in the merchant navy. He traveled the world resting his head in every port, drinking every known kind of brew and collected tails by the score to tell when he got home. He even learned to knit while he was bored in his cabin.

Tom started secondary school that fall in the Green School named after the park it was situated in. There he excelled in his studies and learned most of all the great art of self expression. He became skilled at the use of the pen and could tot up an accumulator bet on the horses with such accuracy that on occasion would even outwit the most proficient of bookies clerks and pencil men. His reputation in this area became so well known that he could have very nearly made a living from it by the time he started his second year at secondary school. Right throughout his life he helped the not too well educated in their clerical endeavors. He was not long in secondary before his talents were spotted by the Christian Brothers on the football field. His name soon became etched on every team that was picked in the under sixteens even while still in his fourteenth year. He was small but strong and had it in the shoulders and arms. His ability to turn on the field of play, on what one would describe as a sixpence, outwitted many, a year his senior. The medals flowed in and it wasn't long before his first at the age of eight, all those years ago, was dwarfed and lost in the midst of row after row on his bedroom wall. The fresh mountain south westerly air that swept down from the Sliabh Mish filled his lungs as he covered the four corners of the football pitch, fighting hard for every ball and trying to make every encounter more important than the last, Oh how he loved the sound of the whistle at the games end when his teams name graced the place of pride next to the lead score on the black squares up on the score board that was cut down by one of the Christian Brothers from an old class blackboard. These were the days that put strength in his limbs, across his shoulders and down his back that supported large tracts of muscle. This strength was to be the foundation by which he could get a job anywhere, and carry it out. He always received the best money and praise for jobs well done to a high standard.

Life in Tralee in the 1940s was bleak in both summer and winter, money was in short supply and work was even scarce. It was a small market town on the western seaboard of Ireland. The only reason in those days that anybody knew that Kerry existed was that Killarney was a beauty spot, and that we were winning Football All Irelands frequently. There was no more than a half dozen cars in the town owned by the Old British Ascendancy, the doctors and maybe a communal car for the priests that none of them could drive, but they still tried their best. The bicycle was the common mode of transport, the big black high nelly with the hub brakes' that never worked. In those day the only brakes one had was the steel tips fore and aft affixed to the hobnailed boot that when applied to the road drove sparks into the sky at night that resembled what came out the door of McCowen's Foundry in Edward Street on a busy fair day as the blacksmith fitted the horse with its shoes. Life was simple, it was safe, and what one learned from the sermons in St. John's ruled and guided one along the path of life in a well defined way. For Christmas of 1946 Con bought his first family car, a two year old Ford Prefect, black, as usual with brown leather seats. That Christmas was spent on the road apart from Christmas day which passed eating, drinking and talking rawmeish continiously to the brass lamp on the kitchen table well into the night, even though it never bothered to reply.

As Tom's 14th year rolled into his fifteenth birthday he had sensed a change in the air, that summer was gloomy as if the storm clouds of some great cataclysmic event were looming. That fall Con brought home the two lorries of turf, killed a pig for the winter, gathered all the vegetables from the garden and called to his homestead in Knocknagoshel. The drive out was to be a milestone in all the lives of those who met that day. On the way Tom sat in the back seat with Andy. Margaret, her father's pet sat in the front seat next to her beloved dad. This day would be etched in their hearts for many years to come as it would be the last trip they ever took with their father in the family car. They played as children would, about their grandmother's farmyard. They wondered at the size of the place compared with their home place in Tralee. The hayshed was enormous, the cow house went on forever, and the piggery was denoted by it strong smell. Tom slept that evening as the car rolled homeward. They all stopped at the cousins in Kielduff where they spent another hour and discussed the purchase of a few banks of turf over by the butt of the hill. The deal was done and the banks at the eastern end of the bog were bought. Money changed hands and a handshake sealed the deal, the rest was based on honor and integrity and bound into history. It was dark

that night in late September as the car pulled into the shed
at the rear of the house **"Bell"** Rita's dog greeted them all
at the kitchen door with thirty or forty wags of his tail. As
Rita looked at her husband now in his fifty second year
she though his face gaunt and his features sharp in the
dim yellow lamp light reflecting from its glow on the table.
She wondered as to his state of health. As he greeted her
with a gentle kiss and a hand on her head she lost her
train of thought and got up to get the teapot ready for all
her weary travelers to brew the leafy Indian tea from the
"Home Of Colonial" shop in town which was still being
rationed. As the children retired to bed, Con and Rita
discussed the day in Knocknagoshel and all the news that
Con had brought back with him. She asked him that night
not to return to England that Sunday, three days away.
He assured her that it was his last trip and that when he
returned in the spring he was going to set up a building
and plant hire business and stay at home for good, he
just needed a little extra money to make the start. A tear
flittered across each pupil of Rita's eyes as she thought
of the tough winter months ahead. That winter the snow
stayed on the ground for almost two months bedded in
with the continuous cold icy easterly winds that everyone
said came from Russia. Con arrived home that Christmas
with seven bicycle tubes full of tea strapped to his body
concealed by the finest overcoat that was made from navy
colored blankets belonging to the R.A.F. Con spent three
days at home that Christmas as the work in London was
both demanding and lucrative. He was in pain but brushed
it off with whiskey and sense of denial that he wasn't well.
His strength was diminishing by the week and he could
feel the strain of the tasks he was working at. The night
before he left he went for his last few powers to his favorite

watering hole "The White Lamb" with young Butt as he called Tom. He went with his pal for his company and the glass of Nashe's Lemonade. It was a night he'd remember throughout his life, his last night with his dad! Con never backed from work but only reveled in its challenges. He walked out his hall door the next day and never again returned. As the boat rolled over the waves once more to Blightly Con hoped he would make the trip back in late April, but feared the worst as his pain was tearing through his system now even with Powers whiskey.

That was the last time Con ever saw Margaret, Andy and Tom, he died that April the 18th from Cancer. The three thousand pounds he had saved was lost to another's pocket so with difficulty, he had to be buried under the foreign soil of England like so many had done before him and many would have to do in the years ahead. He was buried in a small cemetery with his daughter Brid son Pat (Who was now settled in London) and Rita in attendance. As the easterly winds passed through Rita's coat she wondered what had become of his fortune and what lay ahead in the wild winter winds of her life for her and her children. Margaret, Andy and Tom who were staying with their aunt Bridget at home all cried themselves to sleep each night that week. Andy even swore he saw his father at the front gate of the family home the evening he was buried. Their anguish was insurmountable, their hearts ached, and there was a feeling of fear fraught with a sense of uncertainty in not knowing for the first time ever, what may lie around the next corner.

As the next few months passed and the space where the turf had been, in the shed, got bigger and bigger Tom wondered what would heat them next winter. Tom reached fifteen less than a month after his father passed away. His brother Andy had started as an apprentice mechanic, and Margaret worked in a shop in town. Rita went to England that August to find work as her widow's pension was too small to get by on for the family. Margaret, Andy and Tom closed up the family home that September and went to live full time with their aunt Bridget. The car was sold to keep the family afloat with food and the bare necessities. With three meager wages and a school boy to feed the four had never known times as hard. The cupboard was often empty and devoid of food. That winter was harsh, with little fuel for the range, and the pangs of hunger raked ones belly. Every week without fail money would arrive in a registered envelope from Rita with a lifeline for the next few days. Tom missed his father's dominance, his defined sense of direction, and his guidance most of all. He missed the love of his mother, her soda bread lying in support of the duck eggs on the breakfast table, her dinners adorned with the best vegetables in Tralee grown in the rich brown earth of its vale. Tom missed suppertime, her smile was nowhere to be seen, the pale yellow light of the brass lamp had long since been extinguished in a flurry of events that started with his fathers death and culminated with the loss of his mother to the St. David cattle boat to England. He had lost both his parents to the two months in the year beginning with an "A", and he never wanted to lay eyes on 1948 again. The only thing that kept his sanity the next two years was his love of football. It kept his mind from being his enemy. His medals were now on a different wall in another house which he now called home which had been in his mother's family for over 30 years. He bonded with his sister Margaret, and his brother Andy over the next few years and looked to them for guidance and support as they suffered hardship after hardship. Their aunt Bridget did her best for them but she wasn't their mother. As Tom grew into the social life that centered round the picture house and the pub in Tralee he dated some of the beauties who lusted after his good looks. The footballer in Kerry was always an icon of wonder by the women so it was only natural that he was in demand. On nights in the house of wonder that was the cinema moans and groans could be heard from those lying on the floor between the rows of seats as they pursued the wicked ways of the flesh so often condemned by the clergy in St. John's church each Sunday at mass. Those who hadn't been floored fornicating on the cigarette tattered boarded floor were laughing themselves into a state of copious congestion as they sat back on the flea ridden seats and they tearing the skin from their bones. It was all in good fun where, the next generation of fleas would populate the picture house and those misfortunes frequenting it. Some of the more innocent of patrons often wondered how two hundred people there could be enthralled in laughter at the sight of four cowboys been chased by hundreds of Indians who were hell bent on scalping them once they were caught. As Tom walked and laughed his way home one night having come from the cinema or some other place of fun he thought to himself if he could ever realize all the ambitions he wanted in the environment in which he lived in. Working now for the last eighteen months in a job he couldn't see any prospects in, he decided to travel to London in search of the bright lights, decent money, and whatever God had placed upon his path in life to experience. That Saturday morning like so many others before him, he bought a ticket for the St.

TIMOTHY C.J. MURPHY

David to sail the following week. Andy who had just got married tried to talk him out of it but to no avail his mind was set and his decision made. In 1952 at the age of nineteen there had to be more in life than Tralee had to offer. All week Tom planned and packed until the realization of his past, present and future hit him. He went back to the old homestead that had now been sold, and felt pangs of deep sadness at the thoughts of what once was, the hot soda bread, shrill of the cockerel at dawn's first light, that last eve his father drove him into the shed before making his hurried departure from both Ireland, and this life. Of the four houses his father built there was but two now left, unoccupied and in disrepair. How his father's hand had been missed, how his mother's love had vanished. Maybe one day if he and his mother lived long enough he may get an opportunity to rebuild some of what had been lost, for now he had to set his sights on the present and the future. He closed his eyes tight as the salted tears began to find their escape from within. The curse of the emigrant had landed at his feet, feet that were never to kick a point or score a goal again. He turned his back on what once was his neighborhood, a neighborhood of joy, happiness and full of fun. The sun didn't shine there anymore, even when it was high in a cloudless sky, because in his minds eye it was always raining. The following day Tom boarded the famous ten to two train for Rosslaire out of Tralee while Margaret and Andy stood transfixed by his departure on the platform. As his gut became twisted with grief at all that was lost he focused on what lay ahead.

Chapter 3

———❦———

M ICK AWOKE TO see the sun filtering through a crack in the wall of the shed; it had been there since his father drove into it with the tractor two years before when the brakes failed. The April sun had a nice feeling that summer was around the corner, which lightened ones heart. Little did he know that the longest winter of his life was about to begin. He had a ticket for the St. David that night from Rosslaire for England.

He had been banished to the shed some months previously by his two younger sisters because he came home drunk from Galway one night and had got sick in the kitchen, he had made a bolt for the round hatch in the range that had swallowed the best part of a thousand tons of turf since he started to walk, but failed to have both the pace and direction and threw up all over it, and the basket of black turf beside it. It was Aine his eldest sister that had looked after him that night. She scraped the range clean for over an hour that night to get it clean as she said with the acid in the puke they'd have no range in the morning if she left it. As he gave a stretch, a yawn, and passed wind Aine came through the shed door, if one could call it that, it was akin to a timber patchwork quilt held together with the odd nail, warped rotting timber and an occasion splash of cow dung near the remains of what once was a weatherboard, with a steaming hot mug of tea. She greeted me with the words "This is the right place for you and you smelling like Tom's bar and his toilet out the back". This, of course was said with her usual sly grin, as that famous ray of sun caught her long golden locks. Mick gulped the first mouthful of tea as she sat on the end of the bed he could see her eyes were starting to well up with tears at the thought of his departure. It was only then he thought of his planned departure later that day. A sore head and alcohol induced sleep and the agony of having to leave home at nineteen; he wondered could he face the journey. How was she going to stick this place when he was gone she thought. Her best buddy gone, but for Mary her long term female friend who lived four miles away. She never missed a dance with her on a Sunday night in Recess. Aine had just turned twenty one and deserved to follow a life of her own.

Mick told her once he got settled he would send her the fare if she wanted to come over across the pond. She looked lonesome as she said "Maybe".

The moment was broken with the sound of Joe coming to collect him in Tom Flynn's car to take him to the train in Galway. Aine told Mick to get up and hurry up to the house. As she left she wiped the sleeve of her blouse across her eyes to mask the fact that she had been crying. As Mick rose out of the bed the nights wind began to escape with the ferocity of ten men on porter for a week. He had to clear himself or he would be hunted from the kitchen. As Mick walked through the back door his brother Joe came through the front one. He poured a mug of tea for the two of them, and handed him a towel to wipe the good Connemara spring water from his face for the last time for quite a while to come. Joe had been aware of his brother's condition since the night before in Tom's pub. As Mick dried his face and had the first good look at the day he noticed his mother looked at him in disbelief, as she thought to herself what did I rear? Good morning Ma, good morning son, as she handed him a bowl of her best porridge. She turned quickly back to the range as her tears began to flow. Nobody noticed but Aine who had always been razor sharp, and would pick up her mother's anguish once Mick had left. mother would you get the money for the messages she said so I can get a lift with the lads to the village on the way. Madge hurried off to her bedroom and tried to stem the flow of tears which were by now out of control. As she sat on the bed where she conceived and gave birth to all her children including Mick she wiped her eyes over and over again but to no avail, with the thought of Mick's departure. Aine warned them all in the kitchen not to follow her into the bedroom. Her mother handed her the money for the messages as she stood up and turned saying here's the list as well. Aine turned her mother around and hugged her tight not looking directly at her in order to preserve her pride and dignity at that moment in time. Madge sobbed hard soaking the shoulder of Aine's Aran cardigan. Aine whispered gently to her to dry her tears only to breakdown herself. They cried themselves out until their eyes were bone dry. You'll miss Mick crater won't you, not half as much as you will, Aine replied. I remember when Mick was two he cried all day the first day you went to school.

Many a brother and sister envied you the way you went everywhere together. Aine said Mick will have to leave soon so we better straighten ourselves out and make an appearance. He is my first child to leave alone from around the hearth, she sobbed again, Aine wiped her tears with her night gown and opened the bedroom door. Mick couldn't eat much as his gut was knotted from Guinness and the heartache of raw loneliness, so all he managed was two cuts of his mother's soda bread and another mug of hot tea. He thought of what his father had said the other night to him as he advised him to stay going to Mass and save his money as if he didn't he'd never return home. Be sure now son keep God in your heart and your hand in your pocket. Mick had his father's fiver that he had given him years back for the winter he spent at home working while he and Joe were in England. As his father had told him, Mick had one ambition and that was to build on it. Joe feeling that everyone was getting too nostalgic for his liking and said right we better hit the road, are you coming Aine? As Joe and Aine led Niamh and Eilish outside through the front door they also began to cry. Mick turned to his father and thanked him for all he did for him over the years, and for being the best of the west when it came to a dad. As he turned to his mother he lost all sense of composure melting into her arms, something he hadn't done for quite a while. She told him to take care of himself, make his money and get out of that place as soon as he could; and come back home with a plan in mind. He assured her he would. It was that moment that kept him focused many a day and night in the coming years.

As the car slipped on the cow dung and slid down the boreen Aine asked Joe did he mind if she went to Galway with them. Maybe it would be better if you went home to Ma as she will be feeling a bit rough today. Yerrah I suppose Da will be with her on their own once the twins are gone to school. Sure come on with us, a Cailin ! He wondered which of their hearts was the heaviest at that moment. They were all silent as far as Spiddle and the trip to Galway was uneventful apart from the Ford Prefect boiling only twice. The radiator was leaking for the last three months but a fill up of water from the nearest dyke was much cheaper than a reconditioned one yet it was the only car he could get for the trip. They arrived in Eyre's Square with three quarters of an hour to spare. Joe went off to get bullets for his father's rifle if for no other reason than to leave the two together for a while. As soon as I get established I'll send you the money for the fare and if you want to come over you can. Oh! Mick I don't know if I could ever live anywhere else only Ballinahowen. What kind of a life will you have there, poor marriage prospects, a squad of kids, one good outfit and a car with a leaking radiator. She laughed, as was Mick intention. I'll think about it, maybe I might go back after Christmas with you. Do, as once we make some money we can come back home and make a good life for ourselves. The twenty five minutes passed quickly until Joe arrived back. As they all walked to the train Joe teasing his young brother, and having been in England, told him to be careful of the women and the drink. Aine smiled saying well lover boy they'll be lining up for you drunk or sober. "Take care Mick" Joe said, as he shook his brother's huge hand the hand that would see him right in Blighty. Aine's eyes welled up with tears as she told him

31

"Look after yourself my friend". He kissed her on the cheek and bid them both his good byes. He turned then and quickly to boarded the train. The whistle sounded like it did the day with his father all those years ago on that same platform. As the steam gushed from the engine Mick waved at Joe and Aine as they disappeared into its fog.

He found a seat and tried to settle down a bit as the day so far had been fraught with the anguish of an immigrant's departure. He was now on his own out into the world to make a living. The train rattled and meandered around every bend in the track picking its way towards Rosslaire. The farther east he went the land got better to the point it almost made him envious. The herds of sheep began to disappear and the herds of prime cattle started to take over. He wished that he'd been born east of the Shannon but he thought he'd never have survived to nineteen without the Atlantic breeze in his nostrils. As the train crossed the Shannon at Athlone the sun moved around to the left hand window which bathed Mick in its morning warmth. As the counties glided by Mick in his sun kissed slumber dreamt of almost all of his life up until then. The trips from Recess the nights with the lads in Tom's, it all seemed so real. He awoke to the sound of the timber door being pulled across in the compartment as the ticket man asked for his ticket and told him that the next stop was Limerick Junction. Mick thought to himself that there was no going back he was a long way from Ballinahowen now. He was starting to feel that empty feeling in the pit of his stomach again, the emptiness that went across the pond to England with so many from nineteen fifties Ireland, not knowing would they ever really return.

As the station sign for "Limerick Junction" glided past the window Mick caught the eye of one of the most beautiful women on the platform he had ever seen. His eyes followed her as she made her way towards where the door was. After what seem like an eternity she opened the door to his compartment and politely asked were the seats free. As Mick tried to swallow his spit, he barely got out "they all are". As she tried to put up her case on the brown netting rack over her head Mick got up and said "let me do that for you" to which the raven haired beauty, with the sapphire eyes replied, thank you so much, as she smiled in appreciation. Mick instantly detected a touch of an English accent, but only a hint. He was so taken in by her looks that he became lock jawed and all he could do though he knew it to be bad manners, was stare at her whenever she looked elsewhere. After about five minutes of looking everywhere there eyes met and she opened the conversation by introducing herself as Kate Collins from Adare to which Mick duly reciprocated and introduced himself also. They both chatted all the way to Mallow without almost taking a breath. She had a nice homely way of putting him at ease and drawing the words out of him. Kate had just buried her mother whom had been sick since last November. She had been in London working prior to that for 5 years at the "Lancaster Gate Hotel" since she had been seventeen. Kate turned to Mick and said "now that my mother is gone I wonder if I'll ever see Adare again". Ah you will of course was his reply. As if to suppress her thoughts she said "Well Mick and why are you going to London"? There is nothing in Connemara only rocks, bad land, and even the fishing had been bad this last year or two. He told Kate he'd miss Aine, and the pint of Guinness in Tom's pub, he is supposed to pull the best pint west of the Shannon. She wondered to herself who was Aine? When I make my fortune he said I'll go home and buy a small place maybe near Galway City as I really love the place, and I have good memories of it, as a child. Kate prying said "how long have you been courting Aine". Mick laughed detecting the loaded question and said that his mother would never let him marry Aine anyway. Kate quizzing looked and asked "Why So". Oh never, because she's my older sister ". They both laughed as Kate felt such a fool having being caught out by the cute hooooor from Galway. When it came to cuteness Mick Joyce would leave the best of them in the halfpenny place, and that he build a nest in your ear for you while you were looking around the next twist in the road.

As the train tore its way over the tracks at Mallow Station Mick took down Kate's case and his canvas hold all as they had to change trains for Rosslaire. It was now nearly mid afternoon and the scoraveen wind was rising as they both stood on the platform waiting for the train from Tralee. As a station porter passed Mick asked him how long would the Tralee train be, to which he replied "about five hundred yards boybawn". Seeing that Mick wasn't amused at his smart Cork comment he said "I'm only kidding it'll be along in about forty minutes". As Mick turned around he caught Kate smiling at the porter's joke. They both burst out laughing as Mick steered Kate to the café on the platform and a good hot cup of tea. The pangs of hunger were beginning to attack Mick's belly so he ordered three beef sandwiches and a large pot of hot tea. Kate had a ham sandwich and a piece of fruit cake. The forty minutes passed quickly as the conversation was good until they heard the Tralee train pull up at the platform.

They boarded the train and found a compartment with only one other man. They both greeted him as he did them. It was their first encounter with Tom Sullivan.

The hot pot of tea, the rail of sandwiches and the clatter of the wheels on the tracks soon had both Kate and Mick sound asleep as the train went east for Rosslaire. Tom wondered what lay ahead, he had left a secure, but dead end employment in Tralee but the lure of good money and a good time in London was a magnet to a young lad from rural Ireland. Kate's beauty caught Tom's attention as she sat across from him. He wondered if they were together or had just met traveling, whatever if the occasion arose she was fair game without a wedding ring. He also thought where he was going even a wedding ring wouldn't matter once she wasn't married to some fella of six foot eight that weighed 24 stone. He thought of the broken hearts he had left behind and of all he would probably shatter in England too. There were hungry days left behind now and maybe more to come but the jar of Brillcream was a necessity to enhance his head of dark shiny hair. As the last night in Tralee and the good creamy pints of Guinness in the White Lamb started to catch up with him he soon drifted into a slumber following the example of his two traveling companions. The odd jolt of the train broke their dreams of the home comforts that they had left behind. The station Master's whistles shrieked out like the Devil's last calls as he shouted "All Aboard" in every village and town along the way. As the night sky came to meet, and caressed, the green fields the lonely shadows of the train's occupants filled the black windows with the ghostly figures of the Irish immigrant. The condensation dripping like the lost tears of those whom were left in the coffin ships

35

of the 1840s. Ireland was still in her teens growing and grasping at the knowledge of how to build their nation. It had been a hard climb since 1922 but Lady Lavery was the only thing that would put our beautiful land on its feet now. So as the train chugged on for the South East its occupant's dreams turned not anymore to the West but to the greenback that would one day bring them all back home. With a violent shudder and the clattering of the points on the track Tom, Mick and Kate awoke to the shout from the ticket collector, "end of the line ladies and gentlemen and don't forget to take all your belongings with ye". As Tom awoke he saw that the three had been joined with another half starved grey faced man with the longest arms he had ever seen and hands like the old rusty shovel outside the kitchen door at home. Tom being a man of many a witty remark thought to himself, "Holy Jasus he must have been made in a hayshed" as he smirked to his own reflection in the window. The new arrival greeted the other three with "where are ye heddin for like". All three remarked London in total unison and then burst out laughing. The new arrival told the others, as they all got up to go that he was Jack Barry from Bere Island down in West Cork. But he didn't really have to tell them where he was from they all kind of knew like. All four left the train in a blast of white foggy like steam the nights cold went through all their bones as they thought of the turf fires at home, something that would soon become another distant memory. As they all headed for the ship down the dusty coal laden pier Kate said protectively "cover yeer eyes lads as the coal dust will blind you otherwise". As the breeze lashed out with a vengeance they could all feel the grit scourge their faces with the ferocity of a Sahara sand storm? After what seemed like an age they reached the gangplank and headed up along leaving Kate, the expert, lead the way. Tom followed as he caressed her shapely legs with his eyes. As they entered the ship the St David a wall of warm air met them mixed with a sour stench of stale vomit that was left by the homecoming passengers they tried to put their mind to the south westerly breeze as they all made for the seats. Having secured a place of rest for the next few hours Tom and Mick stood up and offered to by a drink. Money being tight Mick said he'd get a drink for Kate and Tom bought for Jack. As all the strangers sat down and drank sparingly the stories of whence they had come, began to flow from their lips. Jack had left his wife and three children abroad in Bere Island with his aged mother and father who was trying to make a living from a tiny holding. He was the oldest of them at 32 years old and had one objective and that was to make a fast thousand or two to put the place at home on a firm footing having been promised it by the father some months earlier. Kate told them all of her recent loss and was appropriately sympathized with and consoled. She told them that she would like to go home some day but there was not much in Limerick at the moment only the promise of a factory being built soon. Mick complained of having to head east as the west was definitely asleep right now although his ambition was to go home one day and fire a bit of money into a few tourist ideas he had in his head. Tom was the only one to have left a job behind and did so for the lure of the King's currency and a good time.

He had known only misery since his father had passed and he was out now to have a good time and see what life was like on the other side of the fence. There was a loud bang of metal to metal as they heard the door close and the fog horn was sounded. They all knew there was no going back now. With a heavy heart they swallowed their spit as Mick said "Ar aidghe leat Naoimh Daithi". They all smiled as they toasted their new found friendship, something that would hold them together as friends over the years ahead. As Kate warmed her hands from a hot mug of Fry's coco her eyes turned to glass as she watched the flicker of the lighthouse grow more faint with each wall of rain as its salty soul washed the dark glass. As the night grew older and the wind swept up, the waves lashed the decks as if to make the ghostly travelers pay for the sins of their fore fathers. As Naoimh Dathai cast aside his sainthood he rolled up and down the hilly waves over and over again until the brown paper bags became both popular and necessary. As they were used they became the companion of the litter drums placed every few yards for the passenger's convenience. Tom had never seen such a patriotic bunch, as the crowd sported their green faces. Hell was breaking loose on the good saint with a vengeance unlike was not see since Our Lord himself was crucified. Despite the scarcity of money all four took a small brandy neat to settle their stomachs. Kate having only drank the coco, lightened their demise of the Guinness Warriors with a comment "I wonder how old was that pig that they made the sandwich out of was in Mallow". As they neared the shores of Fishguard it the port lights started to illuminate the clear dawn sky. The storm had passed with their arrival pier side as the clouds shimmered with an orange flakeyness onto the soft green hills of South Wales. Jack Barry asked Kate was it far to London to which she said oh it is a good few hours but we can rest along the way and it will give our stomachs time to heal. As they got on the train and Tom led the way and commandeered a compartment in one of the carriages and shouted to the rest to hurry up before some other one came into it. One thing he knew for sure he was not standing the whole fucken way to London. As the brandies took hold so did yet another doze and they all slept soundly. Mick awoke with the shout of the ticket collector saying "Tickets Please". He gave his to the ticket collector and nudged the other three with him. As he wiped his eyes he saw his first black man and woman sitting down in front of him across the compartment. He stared, and looked away, and then stared again as they all did. They all felt much better after the sleep as they began to chat among themselves once more. Mick could not contain himself and eventually asked the black man opposite himself if he was from Africa to which he replied "No mate I am from Bath" in the best Queen's English. Mick said "Oh I see". Knowing he had made a pure amadan of himself he went a bright shade of red on both sides of his nose. Tom then said to Kate and Jack under his breath, "if he is from Bath he could have spent longer in the fucken thing and used the soap too". Kate went purple, Jack went white, and hearing the tail end of it, Mick went a brighter shade of red yet again. The man across the way remained black. He and his wife got up and he smiled at Mick realizing he was very embarrassed at his comment and that he was of course Irish, and got off at the next stop. As he left the train there was a session of uncontrollable laughter started and the joke carried them all the way to Paddington Railway Station in the heart of London. As the four landed on the platform each with their bag in hand Kate turned to the three lads from home and told them that they could find her at the "Lancaster Gate Hotel" opposite Hyde Park and if they were ever stuck in London to give her a call.

She also warned them to stay in touch paying attention to Mick in particular as she gave him a sly kind of eye, telling them all as well to let her know where they were as soon as they got settled in. She had the makings of a real mother hen. As they all walked up the platform little did they realise how their lives would unfold and merge, in time. History was now in the making.

Chapter 4

⚬⚬⚬

BERTIE'S FACE LIT up like the traditional Irish Christmas Candle when he saw Tom's black head of glossed hair approaching him in the crowd. Bertie and Tom had grown up in the neighborhood since they were both in short pants. They shared the same family name but were no relation. They played football together. They had often set their sights on the same girl growing up and said may the best man win. He had left for London a few months earlier and was working in the buildings. His mother Gracie had cried her eyes out for a week after he had left her side for the first time.

They grasped each other's right hand and as Tom felt Bertie's hand he realised he was now a man with a strong firm hand that had the toils of labour from wrist to fingertip upon it. Bertie enquired as to how all the people of the neighborhood were, and of course asked for the true account of how his mother and father were. Tom said they were all fine and that he had a currant cake of bread in his bag from his Ma. As Tom and Bertie exited the door of the

famous Paddington Station Tom got the feeling of what
is was to be a Paddy in London. His suit was 2 years old
and a little grubby and tattered around the cuffs, where
around him were suits that were well cut and tailored
to perfection. Tom turned to Mick, Jack and Kate and
introduced them to Bertie. They bid their goodbyes and
went off in search of a warm bed. Tom had a Job got in a
shipping firm which was arranged by his sister's husband
and he was due to start the following Monday, four days
time. Tom and Bertie made off a Greek Café near Camden
Town, a place he would often eat in the years ahead as the
huge Greek obviously knew how to feed both a Greek and
also and Irish man. As they sat and ate to their delight,
as Tom's stomach had now settled, Bertie told Tom he
was a fool to go working in an office when he could make
twice as much in the buildings. As if to fend him off, Tom
said he'd have to give it a try for a few weeks to keep the
sister happy but who knows he might like it too. At that
Bertie produced a pocket of money that covered half the
table like wallpaper festooned in the King's head. See that
he said I made almost twenty pounds last week with a
little overtime worked and said "I think you are crazy to
go in to a fucken office". They ate their fill and washed
it down with the best of Ceylon tea. Bertie paid for the
grub being a man of money and being delighted to see
his old school buddy with him at last. They talked about
who had got married at home and those that should have,
as they had children about to be born out of wedlock.
Bertie laughed and said Jesus they will all be dammed
and excommunicated.

Bertie had lined up a Place for Tom to stay near the
street where he would be working. It was clean, cheap,

comfortable and at the top of a three story house. It was looking out onto a string or roofs, chimneys, and one back garden so small and hidden that the sun never really shone there. It was home for now he had a job and prospects. He was lucky that he was well educated by the Christian Brothers who though him to appreciate all he had and work for all that he needed and to never sleep far from his rosary beads. Whenever times would be hard he would reach for them and confide in the blessed virgin and her kind gentle heart.

As Tom finished unpacking Bertie got up from the dusty armchair and lifted a thousand dust mites with him that shimmered in the evening light as it began to dim through the filthy window. Tom handed him his mother's cake of currant bread. Bertie had paid his first two weeks rent for him to help him get started. As Tom left the room with Bertie he locked the door behind him to secure all he owned. As the went down the stairs they met 2 Indian men, a Jamaican, a black man who was blacker than even the man on the train, and two Irish fellas filled to the gills inside the hall door. As they hit the streets the lights came on and evening started to turn to night. They hopped on a bus and Bertie took Tom to a pub where he said the women were all like film stars. As they got off the bus Tom phoned his sister who was coming to London on Saturday with a suit and 5 starched white shirts and a few ties and some shoes for him.

She greeted him with hello boy how was your trip. He said it was alright but very long and they got sick on the boat. I suppose you were drinking with a gang on the journey, to which he replied to the bantam mother hen that she

43

was. "Oh Christ I was not as money is tight" he replied. She knew he was spinning a tale like long ago at home. She asked for his address and said she'd see him Saturday about 10am and that she was looking forward to seeing her kid brother. Being anxious for a pint and watching Bertie throw his hands up in the air telling him to come on he said he'd see her Saturday for the third time.

As they entered the pub Tom was hit with a huge culture shock, there was carpet on the floor, seats that you could seat half the town of Tralee on in comfort and yes it was a place of warm refuge in from the night air. They drank till closing time and fell up the road till they got the smell of fish and chips where they ordered a good feed of the very English dish. They stood at the counter and tried to read the handwritten menu. The bear behind the counter seemed to roar "What will it be mate". Bertie ordered two fine lashings of cod and a decent wipe of chips for them both. Tom's thoughts went back to Mrs Boylan's auld green mushy ball bearings on the way home in Tralee before he left. They were slapped on the counter as the bear shouted here you are Paddy and go easy on the salt and vinegar. As Tom picked his food up he said "Ok Boy Bawn" and flooded the chips in vinegar and plastered them in salt. After all what were chips with out the salt and vinegar.

Bertie had taken that Thursday and Friday off to show Tom around and help him to get settled. He had to go to collect his pay packet for the three days work that week the following evening. On Friday morning Bertie showed Tom the building where he'd be working down Llyod's Avenue and how to find his way back to his room. They both reminisced all that day about home and their wishes for the future. They laughed about school, they almost cried about the hunger many a night going to bed and the heart broken fillies they had so callously left behind never telling them that they were heading for good old blighty. As they walked around Regent's Park they both thought of their own football pitch over by the rocks in Ballymullen and whished that they were back five years soloing through center field with a goal in mind and not a back in life to stop them. They were simple times and times where Tom could come in and look his father straight in the eye and feel secure in the knowledge that he would always be there, but alas he was now gone and all the hopes and aspirations as he was now adrift in a foreign land wondering what was around the next corner. At the tender age of fourteen he was quite a loss to him. That Friday was all about learning where the streets were, and how Tom could find his way back home after work. Bertie brought too him to a rough fella on a street corner who seemed to appear out of nowhere and was able to vanish again as quickly. He went by the name of John, had what appeared to be an Irish accent though not familiar to either Bertie of Tom geographically. Bertie introduced Tom to him and told him that this was where you got your monthly bus ticket and also the one for the tube. Tom handed over a few pound for the month and they moved off quickly in case someone may be watching. Tom had his first introduction to how things were done with the Irish in London. One never paid the full amount for anything with the exception of drink in the pub. If you wanted the hard stuff (Spirits) they could be got in a few of the markets on a Saturday usually for half price. One golden rule was no one ever asked where the stuff came from. The cigarettes in London were controlled by two brothers from Northern Ireland, the Jews ran the rag trade, the English ran the markets and the Paddies took care of everything else. Even some of the lads that were getting married whether by choice or design had access to the rings and the clobber for the day. Nothing was ever to big a problem.

As the sun dipped over Regents Park, the two warriors headed up Hampstead Road for Camden town. There was nothing good in their heads. As they crossed the railway bridge the fumes of alcohol hit their nose as they picked up the pace and trying to avoid the late autumn chill. The first pint of Guinness was something that would stop Arthur's heart. The second tasted a little better and by the third they were both almost back in the "White Lamb" in Tralee. They drank late into the night at a house party, smiled at two Ladies one from Cork and the other from Laois. The two even threw in breakfast on Saturday morning with some of the finest black pudding they had eaten in months or maybe years. At half eight Tom jumped out of bed with a dart and tried to explain to the lassie from Cork that he had to meet his sister down the city at 10am. He got a good helping of cold tongue from her as he searched for his clothes on the floor. Bertie told him he'd meet him about 6pm at the Black Cap pub, as he made for the door putting his tie in his jacket pocket. He ran at first, then walked, and then ran again for a while. He found the bus stop Bertie had told him about and hopped on the first bus he could get down to the kip. Yes the bus ticket worked a dream! He got into his room and cleaned up a bit but he was reeking of drink and stale Players cigarettes. He knew Brid would go mad when she arrived but what the hell she was a settled married woman at this stage.

As Tom was getting dressed having got out of the shower he heard Brid at the front door giving out about the place and that it should be condemned. Her voice had a way of traveling through a building like anyone of a thousand men going through Kilburn heading for the pub after work on a Friday evening. As Tom belted his trousers and ran a comb through his hair she knocked hard on the door of his room. He opened the door to see his eldest sister standing in front of him with her husband Tony and the two kids. His delight in seeing them all was somewhat short lived as she immediately started to give out about the state of the house and also about the stale smell of drink and fags from his breath. His heart sank as he thought a hello would have been nice. Her husband Tony delivered a strong warm handshake as was customary from this fine Polish gentleman, as the two children stood shyly to one side behind their father's legs. Brid enquired of Tom as to how he found this place. He said that Bertie had got it for him as it was close to the office and it would save him money on bus and tube fares. She disapprovingly said I see, but could not disagree with its proximity to the office. She did however have another salvo up her sleeve as she said "He certainly made a fine job of you last night"; saying something about a drunkard under her breath. Finally they all sat down and she quizzed Tom about everything of news and importance from home and of course asked about her favorite aunt Bridget. Tony produced two fine tailored suits and a box of well starched white shirts, shoes and few pairs of sock. He was also furnished with a tin of black polish and a pair of brushes one to polish and the other to shine with. Tony who got him the job at the shipping firm of "Hull and Blythe & Co. Ltd." in his usual polite way suggested that he not be late for work on Monday and that he could show him where the firm had their office at Llyod's Avenue. Tom said that he had already found it and that he would be able to get there on Monday without any trouble, and thanked him for his offer of assistance. Brid of course came in low and hard again from the left like a hardy corner back, though out of concern for her kid brother, saying "and stay away from Bertie tomorrow night". Tom smiled, but agreed. He knew he would have to be ship shape going to work in a shipping firm. After they all had gone through all the important issues Tony suggested they all go to lunch in a nearby restaurant where he frequented as he also worked nearby in shipping. The lunch was up market and the food was good and as the afternoon progressed the children opened up a little more to their new Uncle. They were witty and cute, but then again they were a chip off the old block. Coleen and Tony were the pride and joy of their father and mother. As the afternoon drew to a close Tom went back to his kip and tried to get some sleep before the session in the Black Cap got underway. A few more of the lads from home would be there and the craic should be good. The last he knew was the clock striking 3pm.

He awoke at half five and making a bolt out of the bed dragging half the blankets with him trailing across the dusty floor. With a splash of cold water and a rub of the towel he was dressed and out the door. A bus and two tubes and he was heading for the "Black Cap", in Camden Town which was one of the great Irish strongholds of London, and yes the forged tickets worked once more. As he went through the door to a rousing Tralee welcome he laughed while thinking he was touring London at the King's pleasure almost for free. As he started to shake

48

the hands of welcome he thought again to himself that he could get to like this place. Tom was nearly broke all but for ten pounds Brid slipped him as she left and a few more pounds he had put aside until he got his first wage. Down in the corner there was a group of rugged looking hoors clad in Aran sweaters and working clothes who were well know in the building circles. They stuck to themselves a lot, and it was said that they had to, as their knowledge of the English language was somewhat limited. They were known as the Twelve Apostles and hailed from Connemara and all native Irish speakers. After leaving the bars at closing time they would disappear into the night and no one ever knew where they lived. It was rumored amongst the inner circles of building fraternity that they maybe lived in one of the bombed out mansions north of Regents Park. More said they lived in the trees in the park behind the zoo as they were often seen eating the food in the early morning sun in one of the band stands. The slagging was hard and fast that night and drink or no drink one had to be fast and witty to keep abreast of the hop balls. It was plain to see that the Irish builders were a true and solid family. For now Tom and Bertie said nothing about he going to work in an office, there would be time enough for that. Some of the English brickies and the tradesmen mixed with the Irish as they enjoyed the laughs and the slagging although it took them time to blend usually to the Irish habits and phraseology. However they would still laugh when everyone else did half the time not having a clue what was said. In the Irish pubs it was often said that more black market dealing went on than down in Petticoat Lane on a Sunday morning. That made sure that the plain clothes tecs of Scotland Yard often frequented the Irish underworld and often drank side by side with some of the cutest people Ireland ever bred. There was a warning code for everyone when they walked in one would see the Paddies stroke the right Lapel on their jackets. Once that was done the whole shop clammed up and no more would be said. They were often known to empty a pub much to the demise of the owner who would always have to place a free few drinks for them on the counter. At about 10pm Mick Joyce and Jack Barry sailed in and tied up at the end of the counter where the Connemara headhunters were camped. As the two green horns invaded County Galway they were blessed with about eight dirty looks from them so as they got their two pints they moved carefully away. Mick mentioned to Jack that they we speaking Conemara Irish so they must be in the right place. The next they knew was Tom the Kerryman saying hello as he enquired how they were. They both turned around and smiled broadly at Tom as they asked had he got a job yet. He said he had and was starting on Monday morning but had not said where he was working. Mick asked who he got the start with and asked what the wage was like. Tom said he was fixed up on a new site that he didn't know the name of yet and that the pay was about £14 for the flat week. He changed the subject and asked about Kate and how she was. Mick said he called her about 8pm and she said that she and a shot of Irish girls from the hotel were going dancing at 11pm at the Galtymore Dance Hall in Cricklewood. So it was settled that is where they would all go as soon as the pints were floored. Bertie and the Tralee lad we going there too as it was a regular on Saturday nights.

As they queued outside the Galtymore it started to rain and the crowd started jeering to hurry up to the door men. The two on the door had to be related to the bear in the chipper, as they were two fair animals. They were both at least 6' 6" in their bare feet as to look at them there wasn't a place in London where you could get them a pair of shoes anyway. It wasn't long before Mick caught Kate's eyes and when he did they lit up, but Mick being so boozed didn't really notice the way she looked at him. It was a look that would lead them down many a road together. She looked her best in a respectful black dress with a little embroidery across the front of it and down the arms. Celtic in style, and in it a hint of who she was, and where she came from, a place of mourning where she had laid her mother to rest. Kate and Mick spent the night dancing until she sobered him back into a gentleman or better again maybe a Connemara man. He walked her home to the hotel that night and kissed her on the cheek as he shook with nerves from head to foot. Mick Joyce was a man of work and hard labour and had not much experience with the ladies. Mick's sister Aine had often tried to talk to him about girls only to hear him say "I am a way to young for girls yet a Chailin". Not knowing his way home she showed him to a spare room out in the staff quarters of the hotel where her friend used to stay at times when she spent the weekend in London. Usually she went to see her boyfriend at the weekends in Reading. The pillow was reeking of the girl's perfume which contributed to one hell of a dream about a lady in a black dress, but he couldn't' see her face. As he recounted the dream at mass the following morning more than once, he tried his hardest to see her face but in vain. Maybe it was Kate's mother he though nervously to himself trying to keep him away from her she still being in mourning. After all, it was our way of life at home. Tom and Bertie met the two ladies again, the Lassies from Cork and Laois. The Laois lady

came right over to Bertie but the missy from Cork was
so cool that when she opened her mouth to say hello to
Tom a light came on inside like the new fridges that you'd
see in the posh houses in these days. Having traded him
a fine dirty look, and a sneer, she said, her friend having
gone out dancing "Hi boy are you taking me out dancing"
As they both glided up the hall the air got a lot cooler,
kind of like scaling Mt Everest. Until at last she said
"Well how is your sister" to which Tom replied "She's fine
Thanks" dancing on with a bit of a smirk and changing the
subject. Most of the lads in the company shifted that night
or moved as the boys up the west used to call it. One of
Kate's friends who worked with her in the hotel was from
Dublin got hitched up with a fella by the name of O'Brien
from the Banner County. Julie Fitzmaurice seemed kind
of quiet and timid and didn't really realise she was in the
arms of one the biggest rakes in London. Ignatius O'Brien
lived in a blue van on a building site, showered with the
site hose winter and summer, had hands like iron and was
known as "the Bone" because of the hundreds of girls he
had made women of overnight. Jack Barry tagged along
that night wishing the missus was with him as the younger
lads around him had fun. It was his last weekend out with
them as he worked every day and all the weekends nearly
for the next two years. Needless to say he too acquired a
nickname he became known as "The Slave" On a Saturday
evening he'd head off on his own to the Greek restaurant
to inhale a 36ozs steak or to devour a wipe of bacon and
cabbage, usually to order, supported with a half bucket of
spuds. He and the Greek became the best of friends. They
chatted well into Saturday night about their families and
all they wished for the future also. They were both men
of modest backgrounds that had come up the hard way in

their own land. They had both come to England to make a pound or two on the backs of the war and the way Hitler had destroyed good old blighty. It was, for now, their cash crop and they aimed to bring in a good harvest.

As Brid had instructed, Tom went to mass on Sunday, where he met Mick and Jack. Mick said Kate was working and had been to the early Mass. Bertie was missing. The Bone walked up the middle isle for Communion with a smile and his eyes half closed. Tom was also warned by Brid not to dare go on the booze on Sunday. He thought it the better option so he and Jack called to the Greek for an ordered feed of bacon and cabbage. The chatted all afternoon about home and went for a long walk sheltering periodically under the trees that skirted the footpaths in the soft summer sun, from the showers. Jack was home sick for the wife and children and missed the salty air drifting ashore on to Bere Island. Through long moments of silence they thought of home, the wholesome food, the cake of soda and currant bread on the griddle and the butter from the churn that melted through the piping hot loaf. Tom stood in his mind's eye next to his father's leg he must have been a bit with five or six as he gazed up and up to his broad shoulders. He was gone now to the ravages of disease and all his money and dreams went with him the day he died. At half five Jack said he'd head for the kip and write a letter to herself and the kids and get an early night before the new job in the morning. Jack and Mick had a start got out the East End of London on a huge housing development and there was loads of work up there. A flat week would put £15.00 in their paws and with an odd Saturday at time and a half and sometimes a Sunday on the double they would scrape twenty.

Tom had no one at home to write to but his mother Rita and his aunt Bridget so after penning a few lines to them to let them know he had arrived safe and sound he turned into his bed as the clock snaked past twenty past ten. He awoke with a dart at ten past seven and thought he was late for work until he saw the clock almost smiling or half laughing at him. He was going out the door for a quarter past eight and was dressed like an English gentleman, while wondering to himself, was there any such thing. They were a nation of snobs, conquerors, and shopkeepers who couldn't see the wood for the trees when doing business with the cute hooooors from across the water. As he turned the corner and went down Llyod's Avenue he felt the butterflies do a Siege of Ennis up one side of his belly and down the other, chris crossing in true traditional form. He was wondering what he would be put doing in the offices of "Hull & Blythe". As He went in the door he licked his lips and watered his mouth just in case he was put licking stamps. He walked up to the girl at the reception and told her who he was. She smiled at his broad accent and said yes please take a seat, Mr Blythe will be with you in a minute. Tom again looked at the time on his Gloriosa watch that his mother had bought for his First Holy Communion it read twelve minutes to nine. The door opened and he saw this huge gentleman approach him saying as he walked towards with hand out stretched good morning Tom you are very welcome to "Hull and Blythe". I like a man that is punctual and committed to his work. The rest is abstract anyone can do his job once his heart is in it. Tom agreed as he walked the long mahogany clad corridor festooned with the many photographs of employees over the years, to what would be his office, shared with two other people. Mr Blythe introduced them to Tom the man to his left was Scottish and the lady at the desk next to him was also from Ireland and from Dublin. They both showed him what to do and he settled in well to his tasks with pen in hand and a sense of relaxation now in his heart. He had started to earn.

Tom worked like a dog for the summer mastering the tasks that were demanded of him in the shipping world, but alas by mid August he was feeling restless and had an itch to move on. The days outside all that summer had been warm and sunny and he missed the crack with his own kind down the town. He missed the warriors and the wit, the blackguarding and the skulduggery that was a feature of the weekends and besides the pay was double what he drew at "Hull and Blythe". If he stayed he would be stuck in a smoky office on Llyod's Ave for the next 45 years. On Friday the 15th of August 1952 Tom gave in his one weeks notice to Mr Blythe and said he would be leaving the following Friday the 22nd. The Following Friday he walked out the front door cards in hand and never looked back. Brid heard a week later and was furious but she knew Tom was a man of conviction and that when he got something into his head that was that.

He started work with Jack and Mick the following Monday morning the 25th down the East End.

Chapter 5

Kate worked hard that Sunday in the dining room of the Lancaster Gate Hotel. There was a rally in Hyde Park and they got a huge overflow from the crowd for meals. Her legs were aching as she had got a little soft while at home since the previous November. She managed the dining room well and had the world of experience well built up there over the last few years. Amid her aches and pains that day her mind was on Mick and what a fine gentleman he was. It was hard she thought to find an Irish gentleman in London at times. The buildings had attracted the more rugged type of Irishman in those days. She thought about how shy he was when he kissed her on the cheek and almost broke out in a cold sweat. As she smiled inwardly she whipped off the wear off another table and headed off again for the kitchen. As she closed her eyes for a second she asked her mother to bless him and take care of him, she once again felt his lips on her cheek. As she turned and again headed for the dining room she gathered a table cloth and setup the table that she had just cleared. She was the manager in the dining room but always led by good example and carried her weight well, throughout the day, something that earned her the respect of the other girls under her and also the hotel management. Many a time the assistant manager called her aside and in his best English accent said "you don't have to work in the dining room you know you are now part of management Kate". She always made the fine Gentleman the same reply . . . "sure Mr Parks I'd go mad if I was only walking around and giving out to the girls". She knew that one picture painted a thousand words and preferred to lead from the front. At about half six the crowd eased in the dining room and the pace slowed. She said to half the dining room staff to take a break and have a bite to eat in the staff room. She and the other few girls cleared the remaining tables and prepared them for the morning. As she closed and locked the dining room doors she hoped that one day she would do this in her own place maybe back at home where the profits of the day could be her own. She knew the trade and had learned from the best when it came to manners, efficiency and perfection few would hold a candle to Kate in the catering trade. As the girls headed for the staff quarters the agony of the days work fell heavy on their bones. Their legs and backs ached, bed and a good nights rest was the only antidote. As Kate hit the pillow she thought of her mother's hand on her brow as a little girl at home in Adare as they listened to the stories on Radio Eireann on the cold winter's evenings. A home that was now empty and lost in both memories and in the ivy that adorned its plaster shedding walls. The windows had been draftee this last winter and Kate could not help thinking did the cold hasten her mother's departure from this cruel world. As the turf glowed in the old black range in the kitchen in her mind's eyes she gave into total exhaustion and melted into a deep slumber.

Tuesday morning that week was much the same but far quieter, they had 24 guests for breakfast and then the dining room has to be cleaned from top to bottom after the day before. Lunches were easy going that day also with people coming in dribs and drabs. A few ex military in civilian attire also dropped by as the house had a good name for a well done steak and those that served the British Empire always got a twenty percent reduction. You could spot them a mile away, they always flirted with the girls no matter what age they were and always had their shoes polished. Once they knew that most of the dining room staff was Irish they always became more interested, some having Irish backgrounds themselves. Kate was finished early that evening at half four and the assistant manager took over in the dining room. She went to her flat had a shower and lay down on the bed. She must have drifted to sleep as she awoke with a fright to hear her phone ring from the reception. The girl on the desk said "Kate there is a call for you". There was some clicking and a few silent moments then she heard Mick Joyce at the other end. He spoke in a firm strong Irish accent and said . . .

"Conas a ta tu a Chailin Aileann". Knowing full well what he meant, even if it was Connemara Irish, she blushed at the fact that he referred to her as beautiful, and delighted in the sound of his voice. She greeted him with "hello Mick how is the job working out for you". "Yerrah the work is handy I was only barrowing cement all day and we had some craic with the lads, they are a great bunch". He asked how she was doing and was she busy. She told him that Monday was wicked busy but that day was easy enough. He asked her was she off that night, and if so would she join him for a drink or a bite to eat. His heart pounded while she paused and said she didn't usually go out during the week and she felt a bit guilty about still being in mourning. However being a quick thinker, and knowing if she said no, he might not ask her out again. She said alright but would he mind if they went for a cup of tea instead of a drink and that she'd meet him in a café nearby at what time. He said I'll be there for a quarter past seven. See you then Kate. As she rose off the bed she could hear her heart pound like a bass drum, thinking to herself what would she wear? She opened the window to test the evening air. It was warm and dry. Before she closed it she had decided she'd wear her red floral dress and her red cardigan. She arrived at the café just escaping a light autumn shower. She took a seat for two inside the window as a waitress approached. Just as she was about to order a cup of tea Mick jumped off the bus and followed her in. The waitress left them to decide what to order. Kate ordered a cup of tea and a tea cake as she had eaten earlier at the hotel. Mick ordered a mixed grill, a half yard of brown bread for himself not having eaten and a pot of tea for them both. As the waitress laid the plate before Mick she wondered how any man could attempt to eat so much, she smiled inwardly. This time Kate saw Mick in his sober senses and he also saw her in a different light. The more of each other they saw the more they liked as they chatted about work, home, their wishes for the future and to one day go home and settle down and raise a few god fearing kids, and to make sure of one thing that they had a good education so that they would never have to face what they were enduring right now. As they shared their thoughts Mick wondered was it God that sent this kind and wonderful lass his way. Kate could not take her eyes off of his they were a sparkling blue from the Atlantic mists that had reared him. The haze of alcohol had lifted from them since they had last met. His hands were strong and coated in a kind of boyish fur that had not yet matured into hair. His shoulders were broad and he stood over six feet two or three and most importantly of all yes, he was a gentleman. He talked about Aine a lot and asked Kate would she be able to fix her up a job anywhere maybe after Christmas if she returned with him. She said she'd do what she could and she would ask the hotel manager if he could take her on. Kate kind of looked on Mick Joyce's request as one that was kind of long term and maybe meant he would be sticking around her for a while. Even if not, the thought was nice anyway. As it was now passed quarter to eleven Mick paid the bill and they left. As they walked outside he shyly remarked that she was wearing a gorgeous dress and said he liked her in red. She blushed as if to complement what she was wearing. He walked her back to the hotel and said on the way back that he was not much of a man for the ladies and didn't know much about kissing. He said this while looking away and with his head down. He didn't want to loose her as he liked her and loved her dark curls. It was then she said to him that he was the first gentleman she had met in London using a lower tone of voice which caused a flood of sensitivity in his direction. You are a nice man Mick Joyce and I hope we can see more of each other. As he looked at her warm eyes he kind of trembled as he said "I'd Like that too". Suddenly as they arrived at the entrance gate at the back of the hotel he felt it was no longer a problem to kiss her. Their lips met and melted into each others. She held him close and in her mind she made him hers that night. It was a night they would never forget.

The clock blasted Kate out of a wonderful dream, out of her bed and back to reality. She was no longer standing in her mother's kitchen some months earlier with her before she passed away. She still pined for her kind face and her hand on her shoulder. This had been the first time she had left home without that gesture from her.

It was busy that day but Kate carried a spring in her step all through her chores thinking of the lovely night she had the night before with Mick Joyce. He was all that a simple Irish girl wished for in a man. As she went down her list she ticked all the good points off and as she hit the end she was not left with any place to put an X. She smiled to herself as she ripped through the kitchen door again with another tray of ware to be washed. As she swept out for the dining room once more with four tablecloths she met Mr Parks the assistant manager with a firm good morning. He asked her to accompany him to his office. He gestured her as he always did to a seat and then sat himself behind the desk. She sensed a serious discussion. He picked up a folder of papers with the hotel crest and heading on them and said Kate the board of directors have decided to create a position in the hotel of a junior assistant manager and they have decided to offer you the position first. If you wish to accept the position you will have full control over the dining room staff, the kitchen staff, and the responsibility for ordering the entire consignment of food for the hotel. You will have the choice of hiring your replacement for the dining room and you will be assigned a personal assistant also to help you with the stocking of the larder and the cold rooms. He stopped talking and stared at her in the eye and said "You have been a very valued member of our staff since you came to work at the Lancaster Gate and we feel you are the most qualified for the job ". If you accept you will assist in training in the new staff and you will also have three months to learn your new job. He then told her that until January the 1st he would oversee that process. Being a humble girl as she was reared to be, but also assertive when the situation demanded it, she asked about the wage. Well he told her my dear you would be on a salary then and you would be in receipt of the sum of £25.00 per week from January the 1st. After 3 years in that position your salary would then rise to £30.00 per week. Your meals would be taken care of in the hotel and you would move upstairs to the management's quarters. You will have 3 weeks vacation every year and will work eight hours per day. Mr Parks said I know you will want to think about the position but we will need to know by Monday week. She asked him was that all, to which he replied yes. She said she would think it over and get back to him as soon as possible and thanked him for the offer of the position. She said she'd better get back to the dining room as they were very busy today. He stood up and shook hands with her as he smiled at her flawless level of commitment to the hotel.

As Kate walked down the hall she felt like skipping, like she used to across the school yard in Adare, her wage would be going up from £14.00pw to a handsome £25.00. As it was now she was saving £10.00pw and she could save £20 if she took the job. It was yet an added nest egg for going home one day. She also though of fixing up Mick's sister Aine if she wanted to come over after Christmas.

She'd have to start in the kitchen washing up of course and the rest would be up to her. She knew the money was good but the responsibilities would be very demanding. Her brain would never stop planning she thought but she would not have to start work till either 9 or 10am like Mr Parks. And she would have a bit of time to herself in the evenings without being exhausted having been on her feet every day. She knew she would miss the girls in the dining room and the kitchen but she would still see them a good bit anyway.

She met her friend Julie in the dining room as she again entered what must have been the busiest place in London that day. She said to her "keep this evening free after work I have something to talk to you about". They kept their minds applied to what they were doing and parted their ways. They slaved up until ten minutes to seven that evening without a breath but then closed the double doors to the dining room behind then and headed for their quarters. Kate kept Julie in suspense until they went up the road to the café where herself and Mick had gone the previous night. Kate ordered a pot of tea and they both had apple tart and cream. Julie said to her "Christ girl this looks like a celebration, what's up did that fella from Galway ask you to marry him or what". Kate gave a coy snigger and replied are you crazy "I only know him a week, but he is awful nice". She asked her how she got on with the O'Brien fella last Saturday night. Julie laughed as she said she could see how he got a job on the buildings as he had about four hands and was as strong as an ox. He has lips like leather and a pair of ears like two side plates. The only thing that saved me was when I told him to stop he did, because if he didn't I don't know what I would have done. Anyway, Kate said as she stopped her and held her hand I have something to tell you Julie. Promise me you won't breathe a word about this to a soul. Julie crossed her heart and said on my father's soul, I promise.

Kate related the details of the meeting she had with Mr Parks that morning and asked her what she thought. Julie being a year older than her and equally as steady she said if it was me I would go for it but it would be damn hard work but the hours would be good and the money was the big attraction of course, and three weeks holidays. Well that's settled then I just wanted your blessing as I will recommend you for my position in the dining room and you will be rising from £9.00pw to £14.00 and moving to my flat where you will have your own room and bathroom. As they worked the weeks ahead mum was the word.

Kate met Mr Parks and the Manager Mr Shellswell on Friday morning by appointment and told them that she would take the job. They were delighted with her acceptance and immediately went for the bottles in the mahogany cabinet across the room. Mr parks poured her a small Jameson and then one for Mr Shellwell and himself. All three toasted the raven haired lady from Adare as they said the position was well deserved as she was a great addition to the hotel.

As she walked past the office that would soon be hers she began to think to herself was her mother working miracles up above. This had been the best week she had ever had in England. She had met a nice fella and had just got the job that she hoped would be her ticket home some day soon. She also had a mild sense of happiness in her heart, and light of foot as she saw Mick's eyes in front of her every step down the long winding stairs to the lobby. How she wished she could write to her mother that night to tell her the good news but, ah sure she probably knew it before she did herself. That Friday evening was quiet and they all got to knock off at twenty past six. They were all meeting up that night in the "Black Cap" so off she went for a rest and a shower. Julie and Kate got the bus up to Camden Town at eight O'clock where they would meet all the lads and lassies from the Auld Sod. Mick Joyce called the reception at five past eight but the receptionist told him he had just missed her and that she was gone out for the night. His heart sank.

Chapter 6

⚯

THE 25TH OF August 1952 was a day to remember, a six o'clock rise a good sturdy saucepan of porridge caressed with a drop of milk that the fella on the milk cart called cream, cream my fuck. A fellow would find more cream on a hound's tit that just had a litter of pups. A few cuts of home made bread wit a shot of Irish butter, got in the corner shop and all washed down with a mug of strong tea. Hopefully it would get him to the tea break.

He shut the door behind him and made down the stairs for the front door. He caught the bus about a mile up the road where The Bone was waiting to pick up a few to head for the site. His house was turned into a taxi during the day and a place of unadulterated passion at night. As Tom got off the bus The Bone shouted at him to "hurry the fuck up or we'll all be late". As Tom sat in the back on a steel milk crate a waft of stale drink, sweat, socks, and perhaps even some human body parts hit him straight in the nose. Between two fellas across from him he saw a woman's knickers next to a bolster chisel and a 4 lb lump hammer. He smiled as he thought to himself she must have been some woman if it took the hammer and chisel to get her underwear off. Before they rounded another street corner he noticed two rubbers in the corner near the back door. Suddenly the treat of being killed on the building site, became secondary, he was much more likely to die of a disease before alighting from the van.

They travelled for about forty five minutes out into the urban unknown until they all arrived at a hub of activity where some would leave their blood, their sweat, and most their tears at one time or another. Tom caught the door handle out through the broken window and turned it until the door swung open. As he got out he took the rubbers with him on his boots and buried them between the 4" limestone trunking on the service road to the site. It was 14 minutes to eight and this unknown destination was for now the centre of the universe. All the new men were taken aside and set to work. Most were sent to the mixers to harden them up. The ones with the broader backs such a Mick Joyce and Jack Barry, who had come in another van, were put behind the barrows. Tom was put on the mixer next to a ten ton load of building gravel and 2 ton of cement under a green and brown ex army camouflage cover. A relic of the war years standing next to six jerry cans full of fuel for the mixers during the day. Tom knew he would be tested on the shovel that day, but like his father and elder brother Andy had thought him growing up keep the head down and think about what his job of work was and dive into it. As the site horn blasted the mixer was started and the donkey jacket was thrown on to forty gallon oil barrel. As the sleeves of his shirt were rolled up to his biceps a foreman passed by and shouted over the din of the mixer I want an even five to wan mix all day long so count them hard and fast, and keep it dry. He walked on to all the other lads on the mixers and gave them all their instructions.

After what seemed like two lifetimes for Tom they all stopped at 11 o'clock for the tea and a nosh up for a half an hour. Toms back ached from the pit of his neck to the ravine at the end of his back where a river of pure sweat flowed freely into the brown corduroy pants he was wearing. He stood upright slowly as he cautiously looked around making sure that no one was looking in his direction. He felt the aches as he walked upright to the dining area which consisted of two nine by three planks clasped together like lovers bonding for the first time. Whatever would support a man's arse was used as a seat. The hard work was over, it was now the real craic started. A five foot long fire was started, the shovels were sprayed under the hose, and the rashers started to sizzle on them with a bit of suet got from the butchers down the road. Everyone chipped in two shillings and they ate their fill of rashers, sausages, a few eggs and brown bread. Just as the tea was coming to the boil in a bucket at the end of the fire Henry arrived with the milk cart and handed out the usual crate of milk that had to be stolen from somewhere as it only cost the lads the standard two shillings for the twenty four bottles. Two bottles were emptied into the bucket of tea as the foreman roared out a two to wan mix this time. They all laughed as the tea was stirred with a piece of two by wan. If you wanted sugar you added it from a small sack on the ground that was bought by The Bone in the markets every Saturday. Henry then sat down and was treated to his full Irish straight off the shovel. His plate was a timber off cut that one of the lads slyly wiped across the side of his Aran jumper that the cement had been blowing into all morning. Just before the siren sounded a chippie from Tipperary blasted a pall of wind down into an empty metal oil drum he was sitting on and said that's it lads all back to work. As he finished his sentence the siren sounded and all went back to his place of work with a smile on their face. It was the comradeship that kept the boat afloat, the laughs, and the greenbacks at the weeks end. The work was hard and the hours long but by Jaysus when the weekend came did the Paddy know how to paint London red. Tom was pounding the mixer wan, two, three, four, five of gravel and wan heaped shovel of cement and a splash of water. Over and over he filled the mixers and heaped the barrows to the brim as he turned the wheel. As that famous Monday evening came to an end Tom's back locked while sitting on the milk crate on the way home. He closed his eyes both from fatigue and sorrow as he thought of all that he had lost and of all that his father had wanted, not just for him but the entire family. He was now on a one way ticket to nowhere with an aching back, and a lot of long lost memories as he carried what all the other thousands of Paddies who graced the King's shores did, helping to rebuild his domain. He felt like laughing again and again as he thought of the day's jokes, hop balls, slagging matches and he having devoured his breakfast from a shovel, and his dinner from a galvanized bucket. If only his mother and aunt at home could see him now. The smiles that skipped through his mind kept his thoughts off the pains as they galloped through his aching body.

As the week evolved Tom pondered and worked, till both his body and mind ached.

That first week Tom's ribs and muscles were sore with work and laughter. He laughed so much he didn't know whether he was sick or sore. Every day he ate a strong Irish stew out of a bucket as the site siren sounded at one. The bone flung everything he could find in the line of meat and vegetables into the bucket and left it all simmer and waft across the site from eleven each morning. As Tom lined up one day with a war helmet for a bowl he got a glimpse of something resembling the "Loch Ness Monster" surface and dive between the bubbles and vegetables in the large metal bucket. As the soup bones, vegetables, pork, lamb, beef, and shafts of pig that hadn't been even shaved were hurled into the helmets the Loch Ness Monster splashed and flapped in the end of the bucket and made it clear to all that had lined up to feed that is was no more than a good solid length of a pigs tail. Thinking back on The Bone's van Tom was relieved when he though of what he could have seen floating in the end of the famous dinner bucket. Jack Barry died a few times that week suffering from constipation brought on most likely the lads said by the spoon of cement the Bone put into the stew. Nobody knew if they were only having the crack or telling the truth. Only time would tell. Each evening and morning, that week Jack arrived and left with a bloated belly and a face like Churchill himself. He drank more milk of magnesia that week than the factory could churn out. By weeks end on the Friday at the tea break he was so hungry that he ate the breakfast and the Bone gave him a mug of fat off the shovels from the fry and told him to drink it straight down and it would fix him. All eyes were on Jack for the next hour, it was like waiting for a woman to give birth. At ten to one Jack ran from his barrow and left it full on the plank leading up to one of the foundations for a house. He scaled a mound of earth like a man possessed fearful of what way he may rearrange his corduroy trousers. As the crowd gathered for the dinner The Bone said "you think that is bad just wait till ye hear the roar". He hardly had the words uttered when Jack left out an insane roar that was more akin to a madhouse than even to an Irish building site. The farting machine then sat on his usual bin for effect as he took to his dinner of boiled cod and spuds with a fist of peas in support said to the rest "I wonder is a boy or a girl". The next roar was one of loud and uncontrollable laughter, some spitting peas into the air six feet away. They all ate a hearty feed of fish and spuds, well it was Friday and that was the Irish way of celebrating the ways of the Lord. Even the pagans, protestants and Presbyterians all ate the Lords meal on a Friday. While the bones were separated from the cod, all eyes remained on the hilltop that Jack had scaled. At twenty one minutes past one his head of black curls were seen negotiating the top of the hill. His belly he had left behind as he walked down the mound of earth. He wiped the tears from his streaming eyes as he headed for the last bit of cod. He fished it out of the bucket of boiling water and grabbed the last jacketed spud from the base of the spud bucket it surely measured five inches long by about three inches wide. The peas we all taken but he thought maybe he'd be better off without them. Jack had obviously missed his wife's stable home cooking and was finding it more difficult to adjust to The Bone's Cuisine de Site, or as some called it Cuisine de shite.

At half four that Saturday the foreman told them all to wash the shovels and trowels and knock off an hour before the time as they had worked hard that week and had done well.

With the smell of porter in the air, the site gates were closed within ten minutes and the gangers were in the passion wagon and heading for civilisation. As they all drove back for the City of London the Bone gave strict instruction to be on time Monday morning and to clear the back of the van as he didn't want their rubbish in his home over the weekend. All the rubbish was heaped inside the back windowless door of the van and bit by bit it was hurtled out through the back window where the glass was missing, paper, the ends of sandwiches, stale milk and orange bottles, a rubber or two and the pink knickers that had camped out a whole week in the van. They left the bolster chisel and the 4lb club hammer, as he may need it as a weapon of war or passion over the weekend.

As arranged Bertie and Tom met up at "The Brighton Pub" at nine o'clock. As he walked up the street to Tom he shouted well lets see those working hands young fella.

Tom had four good blisters on each hand and he proudly displayed them to his good friend intent on earning his respect as a hard tough working man. Come on let me buy you a pint he said as they both whipped through the front door of the pub. There was no more coding the boys Tom thought, he was now a builder like the rest of them. Bertie asked Tom had he met Toss that he was supposed to be in London and was seen with one of the Tralee lads during the week in Cricklewood. They had another two pints and headed off for the "Black Cap". As the door opened Bertie and Tom saw all the usual fellas on board. The twelve Apostles lined out on the back line in a fine human wall. Slate Lath and Purlin two lads from Donegal lined out in mid field and as Tom looked to the right he saw Toss and

Pa lined out in with Mick Joyce. Julie and Kate were in goals smiling at their new found success during the week and celebrating with a pair of whiskeys. When Toss saw Tom he left out a shout "How is going Sull" and grabbed his hand. He came over with Pa for a few weeks. Two weeks that lasted for a string of months.

Toss Cournane, Bertie and Tom grew up across the road from one another and ate the same brown bread and kicked the same footballs when they were able to collect the price of one. Pa Moynihan came from up the road and came from fine farming stock and was as hard as the nails he drove into timber as a chippie. They thought with the same brain, played with the one set of legs on the football pitch, and at times dated the same girls, some they made women of in the blink of an eye. Mick Joyce was throwing the odd shape at Kate through an alcoholic haze as she and Julie whispered in the corner and planned the whole future of the Lancaster Gate Hotel in their minds flooded by now with double Jamesons. The Bone fell in the door at twenty to ten and collapsed on the floor. Kate teased Julie saying to her "You better look after your husband". They both fell asunder with the laughing. He had obviously come straight from work as he smelled like a sack of stale socks soaked in stale drink and sour milk. The governor went to call an ambulance but Saint John, one of the Twelve Apostles, held down the receiver gluing it to the telephone with an iron fist, saying in savage broken English that came out something like this "A Voukill lig do skhee, we take care of our own". Even though the Gov' was a bear of a man he had no intension of taking on the entire western Catholic Hierarchy in one fell swoop. The Bone was carried aloft by the lads out to a side lane and brought around with a hose pipe after splashing water on him for 20 minutes. It wasn't just that he was so drunk, but he showered with the site hose every day, and the cold water didn't now have any hope of bringing him around that quickly. He was dispatched in a taxi to a particular building site nearby where the famous blue van was parked for the night.

Jack Barry never appeared that night after the Bone's mug of thick fat and his reaction to it. Mick Joyce approached Kate Collins at closing time and asked her could he walk her home. She took his hand and told him that would be grand but she wasn't sure how far she could walk. His place was closer so they waddled off there that night after a healthy feed of fish and chips with lashings of vinegar and wipe of salt. As they hit Mick's flat at the top of the road he made four attempts to find the keyhole but failed. The fifth time he found it and in they went. They opened a bottle of whiskey from the market and drank till the dawn sometimes repeating the same things over and over again. They drifted into the traditional London fog that made them doze till noon. Kate woke up on the bed with a fine hairy blanket covering her. Mick had taken care of her before he made the couch his resting place. She smiled at his kindness and care as she felt her head pound like a stampeding herd of cows going to the fair at home. She missed mass but would get it Sunday evening if she could stand up. She managed to roll off the bed and made Mick a good wholesome breakfast of porridge, brown bread and a fine helping of rashers and eggs. As she was wetting the tea she felt his arms encircle her waist as he kissed her neck. She felt a sense of passion race through her body wanting him more than anything, but she was Irish and wanted to wait for Michael Joyce till the time was right. Mick and Kate had breakfast and went for a walk down by the Thames that afternoon and shared many a heart warming thought. As Mick Joyce walked into mass that Sunday evening with Kate he stopped turned and said to her. I want you to be my girlfriend forever. She smiled as she walked in the door looking back at her man and said "Yes I'd love that"

Tom, Toss, Pa and Bertie met four girls that night from the "Cumberland Hotel" where nearly every Irish girl worked in London at one time or another. They went off to a party in Ponsard Road up in Kilburn that night where they all remained till Monday evening. It was a wipe out weekend that nobody remembered. The Bone was found in his van on Monday afternoon, with some saying, that over two million flies were perched on his pants. More said it was only a rumour but most of the lads knew better. Julie went off with the Slate Lath from Donegal who she later said was a really nice guy who only kissed her once or twice on the cheek. To be quite honest she didn't know how many times he kissed her with her brain soaked in Jameson. Purlin was arrested by a bobby in the lane where the Bone was brought, for hosing down a wall with the hose God gave him at birth.

He was fined thirty bob in court on Monday morning after enjoying the King's accommodation over the weekend.

The Twelve Apostles headed off to Regents Park around midnight and were seen half marching and half staggering across the park to their bombed out mansion. They shared the building with four Jews who were all displaced in

Europe during the war. All carried the tattoos of a Polish death camp on their forearms which earned them the respect of all that knew them. They were in the rag trade and made the finest suits in London. They got all the black market business and even some of the shops were starting to deal with them too. They occupied four huge rooms at the top of the house and cut from dawn till dusk often selling a suit past midnight, but that was business. Nobody ever got to find out their names that they had long forgotten and some said that they hadn't any now, only numbers. The Apostles christened them "Mathew, Mark, Luke and John" and this was not done in jest but in a way that brought the four out of the abyss they had lived in for three years in western Poland. It was a time in their lives they were never heard speaking of. The Connemara men were tough, boat riggers, and animals to work God bless them but when it came to christening the four Jews nothing was more important to them. They were sacred to them and were the closest thing to Jesus that they knew. The Twelve Apostles occupied the rest of the stately home. They had running water and a stolen light connection from a nearby factory. They had more than the home comforts ever had to offer at home but in the western sky each evening as the sun set over the West End the south westerly breeze brazenly beckoned the holy men home. The winters were harsh in this foreign land, the snow fell deep sometimes even before Christmas as their bones stiffened with the harsh cold. The soft Gulf Stream was not there to heal their ills just a foggy artic wind each night that sliced their hearts in two.

Mick Joyce prayed for Eilish and Niamh his two pets at home and thought of Aine still heading for the dance on

Sunday night. Joe had done well with his Da Paddy on the farm that summer, and it had been a great year for the turf. Mick's prayed for his mother Madge as she had a hard life on the western seaboard. Kate always thought of her mother and father when on her knees and often wondered what became of her brother in America who had not written home in years. There was twelve years between them and he left the year she made her First Holy Communion. Her mother said years after that it had been over a girl but never elaborated before she died. Kate prayed for guidance and hope for the future and placed an each way bet on Mick Joyce the gentle Galway man, with the man above. They stood for the blessing as they both left the church to face the cool autumn chill. They walked all the way back to the Hotel slowly. As they walked through Hyde Park the sun dipped as they sat on a bench. She thanked him for the respect he had shown her the previous night and said to him catching his huge hand in hers "I will make it all up to you one day". She nestled on his shoulder as he thanked her for a breakfast that morning that would have kept the Twelve Apostles happy. He thought to himself, this cailin knows the way to a man's heart. As he saw her in that night she melted into his arms and kissed him in a way that left him know for sure she was his.

At seven o'clock The Bone was missing and there was four men waiting to be collected. They were just about to give up when along arrived Purlin and Slate Lath with a van. They all piled in after the usual few fucks telling them to hurry up. They raced to the site getting there for twenty to eight. They passed two black mariahs on the way and Purlin was heard to say "We're all shagged now we're Fucken caught". They all got out of the van in a nearby car park and walked a short distance to the site. Jack Barry, who was once again walking straight and upright asked Purlin where he bought the van at seven in the morning with a rye smirk on his face. Purlin said we don't ask those kinds of questions in London, and besides I never said I bought it.

It was as well The Bone arrived that Monday evening to collect the lads. They all Fucked him out of it over not being there that morning and told him never again tell them to hurry the Fuck up. As they passed the car park where they had left the van that morning, on the way home that evening, the place was alive with tecs from the yard watching to see if a Paddy would take a ride back in the morning transport. The trip home was stinking in the van as usual there was a corduroy pants tied on to the roof rack on top of the van to dry. The flies were still trying to catch up but only a few made it at the traffic lights. Tom and the other Tralee lads spent the day on the beer and got completely floored. They all went to the Greek that evening for a feed of steak and chips with a half acre of onions. The smell that night was so bad in Toms flat that if anyone lit a fag the place would have gone up in a gush of flame like one of Hitler's bombs. They all passed out that night where they sat. The toilet was frequented for what could only be described as prolonged hosing sessions throughout the night. Toss was found in the bath in the morning but his father being a plumber he probably felt at home there as he was serving his time with him that year. Tom hunted them out before work that Tuesday Morning as he was hell bent on going before he got the sack. They spent a few hours walking the park and sat in the morning sun next to a huge oak tree.

Chapter 7

⎯⎯∞∞∞⎯⎯

ALL THE TALK that September was about the All Ireland Hurling final between Cork and Dublin. There were bets flying in all directions during the lead up to it that week. In the pubs, on the building sites, during the grub and the slop ups. Three Paddies from Cork opened up a mobile betting shop in a red van for the month of September to take care of both the Hurling and the Football also. There were times that it was rumoured that there was more money in that van than above in the Westminster Bank. Cork won the hurling the first Sunday in September they beat Dublin 2-14 to 0-7. There wasn't a Cork man or woman at work in London that week, they painted the City of London red and white.

Later in the month Cavan beat Meath 0-9 to 0-5 in the All Ireland football Final. The Cavan crowd didn't win much as they didn't bet too much in the first place, such was, and still is their gra for the money. The Cork bookies paid out their bets in full and honoured ever pound. They all bought new suits and a new second hand van was also bought by them. They setup a long term business after that and years after all went home and setup bookies shops in Cork city.

On the run up to Christmas that year the craic was never ending and the all their jaws were sore from laughing day and night. Tom, Mick Joyce, and Jack Barry stayed working with the crew up the East End. Toss and Pa's fortnight went into Christmas that year as they got a job working with the lads up the East End. There was more drink flowed through Camden Town and Cricklewood at the weekends than water went out the mouth of the Thames. It was common place to see a bunch of the lads drink a pub dry on a Saturday and Sunday when the weather was bad. The Bone made a fortune on Cork in the Hurling and bought himself a new blue van. He kept it well for a few weeks and sheeted the floor with three quarter ply. There were even two windows in the back doors. He had his mattress strapped to the inside of the van but there was always a rush for the other side as the floral pattern was often seen to move as they travelled to work. One of the Lads drew the body outline of a woman on the floor of the van the second week he had it with a piece of chalk. She became everyone's dream date until after a few days she got covered in mud from the boots that traversed the site. The Bone saw the funny side in what the artist did but he still fucked the lads out of it, but just to show them who was boss.

The slop ups were still a howl all the way to Christmas . . . One Monday they all gathered to be collected at Kiburn Park Road outside St Agustine's Church. Ten past seven came and there was no sign of The Bone. Quarter past came and still no sign of him. As it headed for twenty past around the corner came the famous Bone. He had been on an early morning mission to a nearby butcher's shop he was a fella from Tipperary and well known for the best meat in North London. The role was reversed that morning it was the Bone who got the fucking as the lads were always hounded by him. They asked where he was. Some slagged him about the chalk doll on the floor who was now almost faded. More asked was he with Drezna the Russian. He smiled but made no reply. When it came to Drezna he never kissed and told. Drezna was the closest thing God ever made to a human female bear. In her bare feet she stood 6ft 2ins, more said when she lay down she stretched out to 6ft 4ins. Even more again said she was awful fond of the Bone and was known to get jealous when he would disappear off with any other semi normal female, but that was between them. As they rounded a corner at speed the van nearly went over as they all gave a loud cheer. Tom, Toss and Pa's heads nearly burst from the barrel they put away Sunday night, and the lack of fresh air and methane gas in the back didn't help matters either. As the van straightened again, and barely staying upright a pigs head slipped out of a soggy wet sack and rolled down the full length of the van smiling with that wild homely look on his face at all the revellers as he passed them by. Hahahaha the cat was out of the bag or should they say the pig. No sooner had the pigs head slid down the floor than two more followed in quick succession, leaving traces of their well known intelligent grey matter strewn across the faded chalk lover that was now almost gone forever. Still no one could say that before she went forever she got a rub of a true Irish relic.

A fine lump of a 10 Gal oil drum was taken out of the van at the start of the tea break and the three pigs heads were slapped and punched into the drum to make them fit. It was filled with water and a ripped head of raw cabbage. As the morning passed they came up for air periodically and quickly dived again as the scorching bubbles singed their ears. As the fire raged on and as the lads began to sober up from Sunday night and strangely wondered where the fuck they were, the siren for the dinner sounded. They all lined up in front of the fire for a good homely meal of pigs head, cabbage and a generous helping of spuds. Some or the gangers got more spuds, some got too much cabbage, and more got too much of pigs brains hidden in under the cabbage, but then the fellas in question probably needed them. They winged and moaned about everything that day but as it started to rain, they all ran for the big black metal container across from the fire and sat where they found a spot to accommodate their size forty corduroy trousers. Some were so hammered after the weekend that they ate the eyes as well and didn't give them a second thought as for some it was the only meal that they had since Friday on the site. The few that ate the eyes that day shall remain nameless but it was often said afterwards that they could see around corners. They didn't know at the times if foresight, insight or foreskin was the most important, but anyway all three were treasured much the same.

As they left the site that evening and travelled back to their beds whenever the lads belched you could smell the oil from the drum, in the air in the back of the van from the food. Some of the lads whom were more akin to half shouting seemed to speak that evening with a somewhat smoother voice as if their voice had never broken at all.

As the months rolled on to Christmas Kate confided in Mick Joyce about her promotion and he took her out to a posh restaurant to celebrate the event. They both got 8 days off for Christmas that year and Mick insisted in taking Kate home to Ballinahowen to meet the family as he put it, but it was really because he didn't want her to be alone in London that Christmas and thinking, of not being with her mother. Kate got the tickets the first week in December and started to pick up the odd Christmas present for Mick's family in London before she left or got cramped with work. Right up to the 20th of December Kate was attending courses for her new position and Mick as usual was working his fingers to the bone as each day brought in another biting easterly wind from, as the English fellas would say, the Russian steppes. All Mick thought about that December was heading home for Christmas with a lady whom had become very special to him and to also get his mother's opinion on her. After all that was how it was done at home and the mother's advice was usually taken. They both boarded the train at Paddington at seven on the evening of the 23rd of December and shunted out for Fishguard. Jack Barry went too with a case full of purties for the children and few trinkets for the missus and the parents. Toss went home that Christmas and served out his time as a plumber with the father and went into business with him, in Tralee.

The Bone haunted the Christmas markets that Tuesday morning the 23rd, bought a 5lb porter cake, a turkey, a bag of spuds, and an assortment of vegetables. He also bought a brown paper carrier bag full of broken chocolate and a few flowers but kept them under wraps in case anyone saw him with them. Drezna had for the first time given him her address and invited him up for Christmas. They spent Wednesday morning sitting down by a small river on a weir peeling the vegetables for the dinner next day. Drezna lived in a house that was bombed during the war with two other Russian girls and 6 Russian men who everyone mistook for Connemara men, girls included. The only running water in the building was in two toilet bowls one was used for natural reasons and the other for hygiene purposes so the food was prepared out down by the river at the back of the house. On Christmas morning the Bone and two other Russian fellas set up a big table made from scaffold planks the Bone FOUND in a nearby building site. The girls cooked a fine Russian dinner that you'd think came straight out of a kitchen in either Kenmare or Castlebar. A sack of Vodka and seventy pint bottles of Guinness were used to wash the food down. They all got washed out on a mixture of Vodka and Guinness that they called Vodness. They all laughed at the same joke that Christmas day over and over again. Russian song and dance was the order of celebration and the Bone even tried to teach them how to dance a Siege of Ennis but after several attempts he decided to call a halt before they all ended up with broken legs. They all fell fast asleep on four huge sofas in front of a roaring fire of timber off cuts supplied by the Bone from the site, as they ripped and tore out the springs and horse hair for the bowls of them with frequent serenades from the neither reaches of their bodies. The Bone woke up at 2am in the morning cold and looking into the broken down fireplace where the mound of timber had reduced to a smouldering heap of grey ash. He wandered out to the latrine half way down the blown up corridor only to find one of the male Russian Giants passed out naked, half way in and half way out of it in the

84

doorway lying face down. He sat down and dispelled with the day's food and drink intake while he stared down at the Russians head on the floor next to his over grown toe nails on his feet. After a long sitting he introduced several pages of the Christmas edition of the Daily Mirror to his rear end, repositioned his corduroy pants and went to leave. As headed off for the sofa again and being the hooor he was hatched a plan fraught with some Irish skulduggery. He rummaged in the dark for the carrier bag and found two pieces of broken chocolate and headed off again down the black corridor. Finding his comatose Russian still in the same position he gently placed the two pieces on top of his hairy arse, being careful not to awaken the sleeping colossus. As he walked back up the corridor he felt a huge hand grab his arm and heard a voice say "Where do you thinks you are goingk" it was Drezna. Four hours of wild wicked semi-sober, seasonal sensuality followed as they romped in a flea ridden bed like the High King of Ireland and The Czarina of mother Russia. The large metal bed hammered out its own version of Morse code against the half shattered plastered wall intermittently for hours on end. Drezna kept telling The Bone "I love you My Paddy man". There was no response but maybe the Vodka had deadened his vocal cords. Vasiley was found at sunrise by one of the other girls as she went to the toilet still on the floor lying face down and still passed out. The sun rays had shone where they were supposed to and coupled with his extreme body heat from almost a gallon of vodka the chocolate had melted all over his arse creating wan hell of a suggested mess. The smell of the toilet in that area contributed to the overall reality of the situation. Drezna's friend shouted out for help. Two of his friends came running with Drezna and The Bone as he tried to pull up his pants. Vasiley was ice cold and they all thought he was dead. The two Russians lifted him up into a standing position and kept slapping his face until he came around while they kept shouting at him in Russian. The two Russian Girls were relieved and also smiled at how well endowed he was. The Bone found out that morning what it was like to feel hopelessly inadequate.

Slate Lath and Purlin spent the Christmas in their bed sit and cooked a few pairs of crubeens and some spuds with a bit of turkey they got from the Greek. They went through five bottles of Paddy and passed out until the 27th of December missing the dance at the Galtymore in Cricklewood on St. Stephen's night or boxing night as it was called over here.

Mick Joyce and Kate parted with Jack Barry in Wexford and took the train for Dublin and then on to Galway. Jack Barry didn't make it back to Castletownbere and Bere Island until late evening on the 24th. His father came to the slipway in Castletown with his eldest young lad Johnny. The reunion was emotional as Jack could see his father was looking haggard from trying to keep things going on the rugged farm that caressed the hills of the island. Jack took the oars as he had done many a time and gave his father a rest as his huge hands and gruesome arms carved the journey home to the island to pieces.

Johnny stared at the mighty draw of his father's arms on the oars as he heart leapt for joy at the thought of walking the land with him that evening. Mary his wife was on the strand as the keel of the boat tore over the stones, she had the two little ones with her one buy the hand and the other in her arms and young Maureen who was just gone four had the tilly lamp in her little hand. Jack lifted Johnny out of the boat and grabbed his case with his left hand as he pulled the punt ashore with his right hand. As he neared Mary and the young ones her eyes welled up with tears at the sight of her man. His arms were bigger, his back broader, and he had filled out since he left home last April. They hugged one another for what seemed like a week as his father went off with his case and walked the children up the track to the house playfully teasing them along the way about Santa the following day.

Jack and Mary followed the light from the tilly lamp as they kissed and hugged their way home. Mary said to Jack "I don't know if I can get my arms around you anymore", giving him one of her roguish gazes. He smiled as he told her he'd show her how later. They laughed their way back to the house in each others arms. Jack's mother was waiting at the gate for them all to return. Eileen's eyes came alive when she once again laid her eyes on her Jack.

Mick Joyce and Kate Collins had a two hour wait in Dublin before they caught the train west. Kate had a good hot mug of Bovril and Mick was thinking of a hot Powers but thought no as he didn't want to face his mother with a smell of the good stuff on his breath. After all he wasn't yet twenty and had to show respect. As they trudged on for Galway the train broke down twice and as a result they did not hit Eyre Square until ten past five. The evening was cold as they got off the train and there was a hint of a south westerly squall dragging the salty wind in off the Atlantic. Mick stood for a moment and said to Kate as he tasted his lips. "Do you taste the salt in the air a chailin we're home I think". Kate Collins knew that moment that she would one day have to live in Galway if Mick Joyce was to choose her as his woman. But that seemed like a lifetime away now, but maybe it wasn't? Mick picked up the two large cases and with the sweet Limerick lady at his side as he headed up the platform. Like the first train he saw there all those years ago now this one too left off a huge gush of steam as it shut down the boiler. As they neared the door out Mick saw Joe's imposing manly figure approach with Aine by his side. Kate's heart was pounding with joy and fright not knowing, if a Limerick lass would be accepted in the mid west but there was no going back now. Mick downed the two cases and hugged his elder sister and grasped his brother's hand which made his brother say "be Jasus you went away a boy and you have come back a man". This of course was delivered in their native tongue. Aine hugged Kate saying "You must be Kate you are welcome to Galway I have heard a lot about you in Mick's letters and I am finally glad to meet you". As they all headed for the car Joe told him that he had bought his own that October as the harvest brought in a bit of extra money. Mick slagged saying "well we might get home for midnight then" turning to Kate saying "this fella learned to drive on a Tractor you know". As they cleared the city for the long road west Kate and Aine settled in well to a conversation in the back seat full of woman talk and questions from Aine about the style in London. Mick enquired as to what was the true status of the parent's health and how were the twins. All reports were good and they were so excited about seeing him and meeting Kate. Kate overheard that bit from Joe and it eased her panic somewhat. They turned in the boreen at twenty five to eight as Joe's new car held up handsomely. Kate's heart started to pound as she thought the other three in the car had to hear it.

As the lights of the car shone into the yards Niamh and Eilish came to the front door with Madge wiping her hands in her navy floral apron. Mick's heart jumped with delight as he saw his mother for the first time in over eight months. She looked well he thought and thanked God for keeping the cornerstone of the home safe and sound. Mick got out and brought his seat forward for Kate and Aine and then turned to his mother. As he hugged her he felt like he was six years old all over again hugging her as he left for on one of those stormy mornings for school. Her eyes welled up with tears as she said "how are you my Son". Mick answered with another hug and a kiss to her cheek as he said "I am grand Ma and how are you" "Yerrah boy I'm fine son, now introduce me to this beautiful lady please". Madge outstretched her hands to Kate and gave her a warm western welcome. She complemented her on her dark beautiful appearance and said you are a pretty one. Kate responded, sweetly addressing her as Mrs Joyce and thanked her for having her over for the Christmas. Joe headed into the house and dropped the cases in the kitchen and came back out as he was heading up the village for a pint and to meet his intended. As they were all about to enter the house Paddy appeared out of the hay shed having heard all the commotion in the yard. He, being the man he was, followed shyly into the house after the crowd. Once in the kitchen Mick turned and gave his father a strong grasp of his hand as he asked how he was. It was the first time he caught Mick's hand with such a manly grip. He felt so proud of him but it was not his way to show it with other than a look. "How are you Da" Mick asked. I am fine my Son and you look well also. Now tell me, who is this lovely girl? Kate had never blushed as much with such and adoring audience. "I am pleased to meet you Mr Joyce" she said as he responded, "oh please call me Paddy girleen". Niamh then said Ma calls Da Patsy at which everyone laughed. It was then Madge's turn to blush as she went a nice shade of rose pink.

They all sat down to the large oak table and dined on a feed of the best golden wonders that year, carrots and turnip from the garden and a large fresh fillet of salmon was doled out. Mick said to his Ma that it was a pleasure to have a plate for his food instead of a timber off cut. Madge was horrified that he would say such a thing in front of Kate, but his Da knew exactly what he was talking about and gave him a sly private smile as he put his hands together to say the grace before meals. Grace was the tradition in the Joyce household as indeed the rosary was also after the wash up, after dinner. They all settled into a good warm welcome bowl of homemade vegetable soup and a freshly baked loaf of Madge's brown soda bread. As Kate downed the first few spoons of the thick country vegetable soup she said you have to give me this recipe Mrs Joyce it would go down well in the hotel where I work in London. Mick gave one of his usual comments as he said "Ma's soup is the only soup west of the river Shannon that a fella could walk across". Paddy joined in the joke saying as he looked at his one true love "I'd much prefer to eat it though". The chatter continued with lots of questions from Aine about London both of her brother and also the sweet Limerick lady. Both she and Aine had got on so well Mick thought since they met they have never stopped talking in the car all the way from Galway and it continued at the table also. Niamh and the quieter Eilish sat shyly by listening to all that that was said taking in what life in London was like. As Mick sat across from Kate he couldn't stop staring at her. She was still in black as her mother was not passed a year yet, but how beautiful she was he thought. The sharp eyes of both his mother and father noticed how he looked at and how he adored this sweet lady. They both thought in their own way as to how their son had turned into a fine man. He would be twenty soon but had the sense of a man of forty years. His father noticed his broad shoulders and his large hands and he had developed a chest that would soon, he thought, put his elder brother's to shame, although Joe was a fine cut of a man also. Madge, Kate and Aine kept the chatter and talk going over a desert of the finest home made apple pie laced with cloves and a hint of cinnamon. Kate again asked for its recipe. Madge and Aine were all questions about the hotel and how she liked working in London. Kate and Aine were one age and found out that night that they were only born a week apart in nineteen thirty one. Mick was listening and heard what Kate's birthday was something he made a mental note of. The wash up was done by Aine and the twins as Madge and Paddy caught up with what the travellers had to say. At half nine the front door opened and Joe and Mary Conneally came into the living room. When Paddy saw his son Joe walk in he stood up and said "hello Mary dear how are you and a happy Christmas to you". As Aine and the Twins came back in from the kitchen Madge went for her rosary beads and suggested they say the Christmas rosary. The family all settled to their knees and made the sign of the cross. Kate felt a lump in her throat as she remembered the cold evenings in Adare doing the same with her dear mother. She missed the beauty that was her life growing up before she left for London at the tender age of only sixteen to earn a living. She felt that night as she pledged the rosary to her mother that she was slowly becoming a part of a very beautiful family. Their welcome was majestic and warm and she was greeted with a real "Cead Mile Failte". As all the deceased relations were prayed for and the Christmas blessing were both sought and bestowed on others Madge noticed Joe and Mary smile roguishly at each other. It was then she noticed the engagement ring on Mary's ring finger. Her heart leapt as she tried to attract Paddy's attention but he was too engrossed in standing up while blessing himself. Madge was speechless as she caught Aine's eye and gestured to her ring finger while looking at Mary. At the very moment Joe announced the good news and there was a second celebration held in the house on Christmas night. Young Eilish lit the Christmas Candle being the youngest and as they all blessed themselves again. Joe and Mary were congratulated over and over again and the ring was the source of everyone's attention. Mick and Aine produced four bottles of Power's between them and the glasses were placed on the hand embroidered Christmas table cloth that had been in the family for over forty years. Mary's two brothers and a few more friends arrived soon after and the uilleann pipes and fiddles were played well past midnight. Aine picked her tin whistle off the dresser and they all settled into a night of song and dance across the flagstone kitchen floor. Mick took the Bodhrain off the top of the dresser and Kate asked Aine had she another tin whistle. It was then that Mick Joyce knew he has met a true western cailin. She sailed through the reels and gigs with the expertise that Aine had displayed since a child of nine.

Kate and Aine kept the show on the road with beautiful music while the jugs of porter were downed by the lads on the pipes and fiddles. They played the "Immigrants Lament" twice that night which made Madge's tears flow for her son Mick as she knew he would have to travel again in a few days. But at least he had a good girl at his side now and hopefully he would have the good sense to mind her.

Mick handed his mother and father a roll of notes Christmas morning after they all got back from mass, and told them to have a nice day in Galway after Christmas. Needless they didn't want to take it but he insisted and said, "there will be more coming so get used to it". Privately he took out the folded fiver his Da had given him the time he returned from England years back and said "Da I still have it and I am adding to it". That Christmas in Ballinahowen was like a western fairytale as the sparkling stars graced the western sky those sharp frosty winter nights like a diamond encrusted coat on a princes back. Kate and Mick walked the Cliffs as they looked out the sea many times that Christmas giving her a taste of what he grew up with. The Atlantic mist glazed her beautiful eyes so often that Mick thought for sure she was the woman for him, forever. Joe and Mary spent a similar Christmas and hatched plans to get married that June in the local church down near the pier. Kate told them to come to London for the Honeymoon and she'd put them up in the hotel as a present from Mick and herself something they decided on Christmas Eve. They were delighted, and gladly agreed.

Aine made up her mind on St. Stephen's day that she'd go back to London with Kate and Mick on the 29th but she didn't want to tell Ma and Da for another day or two, she told them. Kate had a job provisionally lined up for her just in case she decided to go back with them. Her life there in Ballinahowen was hard and the social life was the same for the last hundred years with a Ceili in the hall on a Sunday night. Aine sat down with Madge and Paddy two days later and told them of her plans while Kate and Mick went to the village with the twins. Madge's eyes fell lonesome and Paddy's heart ached at the thought of his eldest girleen striking for that pagan land across the water. He would sooner see her go to America to his sister in Boston rather than to a place without a Hail Mary or an Our father.

All three took the bus south to Limerick and on to Adare on the 29th as Mick wanted to see where Kate grew up. That summer had put its mark on the hedges and grass around the house. They were all over grown. Mick spent the day on the scythe and cut all the grass and clipped the hedges afterwards. The house was musty and damp and there was an emptiness there that almost tore Kate heart out of her chest. They all went up to her mother's grave as it got close to the time for the bus to Limerick. Mick set a little shrub on the grave for Kate and they said a decade of the rosary and left. Kate's heart was heavy and she decided that evening she would sell the house at it would not survive another year. She put it on the market that January and it sold in February for the princely sum of four hundred and eighty pounds. She got the cheque from the Solicitor on the 16th of March and put a twenty pound note with it and put it into her savings account in the bank. Kate's brother still had not written home and maybe she thought he didn't know his mother had even passed.

The Bus and train ride to Mallow and on to the boat that night was cold and miserable. Kate became a true friend of Aine's that night as they cried a lot, one for leaving a home she had and the other for leaving a home that she had lost. Mick tried to console them both as he hugged them from time to time, but sure he was only a young fella what would he know, they both thought, and besides he was a man.

Bertie Tom and Pa ended up in Bertie's sister's house that Christmas somewhere up in North London. The landed up to Cait and her husband on Christmass Eve in the afternoon with a four stone sack of spuds carried by Tom, Bertie had another sack with a collection of Vegetables, and Pa of course brought the drink in a sack also but in a pram he found out at the back of off license. The child's bottle he found in it and the blankets were left up on a dustbin. Cait got the fright of her life when she saw the pram as she thought she was maybe an aunt. They emptied the pram and gave it a nudge down the hill from the house and all went inside dying with the laughing thinking about where the pram may end up.

They drank to the dead of the morning and all found it hard to stand up to go to bed. Tom told Cait that he'd put on the turkey in the morning for her and to stay in bed. She made some incoherent comment something about eight o'clock. Tom's clock blasted him out of an alcoholic haze at ten to eight and he staggered to the kitchen to put the beast into the oven. He headed back to bed not really having woken up at all. He got up again and went to the bathroom a couple of hours later and found Bertie in the bath with his face all scrapes and a dirty cut to his head. The hoooor had

95

fallen into the bath during the night. As Tom tried to get him out he fell in on top of him. After a struggle he finally got him out and walked him to the kitchen where he tidied him up a bit before everyone got up. Tom started a bit of breakfast for the household as Cait was still hammered in bed. When he was half way through the fry Pa appeared around the door from the hallway in only his underpants which was hanging low from his skimpy arse saying "Fuck it I'm feeling awful queasy is there anything there for the stomach". Bertie was laughing at his patriotic green face as he staggered across the kitchen. Pa seeing Tom at the breakfast decided to cut some bread. He asked Tom did he see the bread knife but he hadn't so Pa went out to the hall and came back in with his saw, from his tool bag. He took off cutting the bread with the saw and did a fine job. As he was nearing the end of the loaf in walked Cait in her dressing gown and said "Oh Jesus Christ" cutting the bread with a saw in your underpants and fell in an intoxicated heap with the laughing. They all ate a hearty breakfast and went off to twelve mass over in Kilburn. Pa said on the way over to keep away from the gas works in case they would ignite the place with the smell of drink. They all ate a fine Tralee Christmas dinner that day and drank out Cait by tea time. Pa and Tom went off later and arrived back with a pram full of liquor which took them all up to the 27th in a state of total inebriation. That Christmas would remain largely a blur for the rest of their unnatural lives.

CHAPTER 8

———— ⚬⚭⚬ ————

THAT JANUARY WAS cold and bleak and Regents Park looked like some place in Siberia. All the Paddies had emigrated into every bombed out building in London it was no time for the outdoors or indeed for living in motor homes like The Bone. He camped out with Her Royal Highness the Czarina that January and February in her winter palace with the other Russian women and fellas. The building sites were hard going and everywhere the ground had to be dug, a jackhammer had to be used. Brandy was the drink that winter for the lads and the bucket of stew at dinner time was always welcome. Nobody knew for sure what went into the bucket those months but no one cared either. The soup and meat lined their stomachs and kept their bodies going that January and February. The big black container on the site for the tools was kept tidy as all the dining was done indoors while the snow, hailstone, and occasional downpour pitted the roof. The weather got so cold that winter that The Bone stopped showering completely the water being icy cold every day. Laying bricks had to stop those weeks as the plaster was turning to a soft kind of jelly and most of the work had to be done indoors, the carpenters had more helpers that they ever imagined.

Jack Barry turned up like the rest of us, back on the job, on the 5th of January. He was down and out and hardly spoke to anyone. He missed the wife and kids leaving on the Saturday and drank his way back to London. Tom asked him what boat did he catch but he hadn't a notion, all he said was that it was dark when it got on board.

Tom, Bertie and Pa sobered up around the first Saturday in January suffering from a dose of the shakes, or as the Tralee fellas called it the wrigers, from how they had hacked themselves over the Christmas. The entire holiday was a complete wipe out and the last thing they remembered was Pa with his pram load of drink heading for Cait's place on Christmas Eve.

Slate Lath and Purlin went in and out of an alcoholic stupor periodically visiting consciousness and intermittently being aware of the fact that they were perched in London right up until the day before going back to work. The whites of their eyes were stitched together with red thread from being so bloodshot. They were physical and mental wrecks and spent all that week walking around the site outdoors trying to keep their heads and bodies cool with the bitter easterly winds. It was their way of de-toxing cold turkey 1950s style and it worked. They had spent the festive season supping cheap whiskey from the markets.

Kate Collins had her last shift in the dining room of the Lancaster Gate Hotel dealing with the crowd celebrating

New Years Eve on the 31st. It was a busy night and Mick called in around midnight to wish her a Happy New Year. He slipped her a rose and discretely as he kissed her flushed cheek. Two minutes past twelve and she was flat out once again attending to the needs of the fat cats that chose the hotel for ringing in the New Year. Mick also went around to the open back door of the kitchen to wish Aine a Happy New Year, and to enquire was she getting on alright. As Mick strolled back to his flat the first fall of snow started to colour his dark overcoat. He put up the collar, drove his hands deep into his coat pockets and picked up the pace to generate a bit more body heat. As he walked back up Kilburn High road he threw his mind back to Christmas in Connemara and the wonderful time all the family had together. Being with Kate in Ballinahowen was special, Joe and Mary getting engaged, and he seeing his mother and father again in good health.

Aine spent her first few days in Julies flat at the back of the hotel and started work in the kitchen of the Lancaster Gate at 12 noon for the lunches. Kate being around her that day showed her where to work and what to do. She settled in there if she had been there for years. Her heart ached like the hearts of all young Irish girls that went abroad that time but for now it was her only place to earn a shilling. She slowly gulped two breaths and carried on washing every dish that came her weary way. Suddenly Ballinahowen became a nice place to have grown up and like her brother when he first left she missed home and its comforts. Aine went to her knees that night as she had always done and prayed for all the family at home. She also prayed for guidance also that Our Blessed Lady would keep life on track for her in the years ahead.

With Kate's promotion on the 1st of January she moved up to the top floor in the hotel proper and had a fine luxury apartment a short walk up the corridor from her new office. She put all her belonging away and felt at home straight away. She folded up her old suit she had to wear in the dining room and laid out the other she was to wear from that day on. At eleven that morning she breezed into the dining room meeting Julie and congratulating her on her new appointment. Kate interviewed four people that afternoon for the position for her office and catering assistant. All four, three girls and a man were well qualified but in her final analysis she chose the man as he appeared to have an excellent personality and was, she felt a good man to strike a bargain something she would need in her assistant when out buying produce for the hotel. He was 25 years old, Polish, and had come to England towards the end of the war after escaping Nazi Germany with 3 other friends across Europe. He came across to her as resilient, defined about what he wanted out of life and he was studying for a business degree at night. His name was Stefan Woychek and was a perfect gentleman. Kate felt the hotel was on a winner with him and she could see in him the support she would need in her new position. Julie took over Kate's old apartment that evening after the cleaners had finished, and Aine moved in with two other girls into Julie's old apartment.

As January came to a close the weather was still severe and hard on the hands, the chippies were flat out that month and Pa found the going tough at times but being hardy and wiry he tore through his work to earn the few bob to keep him afloat on a lake of pure alcohol with the lads. Tom and Bertie took to the brandy while the weather was cold and kind of even got to like it a bit more than they should have. While they were all sitting down around the fire one morning in February during a break in the snow Purlin complained that he was loosing his hair the last week or so. Pa asked him had he got a dog at home. Coming from a farm Pa knew about these things. Slate Lath said that they had one in the bed sit the last few weeks as it was too cold to let the poor hooor outside.

Pa immediately said ah sure that's your problem you have a slight touch of the mange. He said he knew a doctor that would give him a few tablets for it that evening on the way home. Pa, being Pa stayed totally serious of course. That evening on the way home we went into the vets to get a few tablets for the complaint. Mr Thorne the vet gave him a course of tablets and charged him five bob. Next day he sold the tablets to Purlin for seven and six and made a half crown profit on the deal. When he completed the course and all was well Pa told him where he got them in a slagging match while they were all eating the dinner. Purlin went raving mad and fucked him from a height and tipped the remains of a bucket of stew over him. Pa shouted out "What the Fuck is wrong with you? didn't it cure the mange, all you have to do now is be careful of being out on the road licking your balls when a car is coming or marking your territory at every street corner on the way home from the pub". A big row ensued and they had to be tore off one another roaring and balling and fists flying in all direction. The laughing was mighty, the cold was animal, and everyone forgot for a while that they were in trying to work in sub zero conditions.

Sunday the 1st of March rained all day and every heap of sand and gravel in London thawed. The Paddies spent that Sunday on the beer drinking pubs dry all over London as they always did on a wet day. Monday morning early The Bone appeared around the corner near St. Agustine's Church. The exhaust was gone off the van an there was a roar like a lorry from it. Bertie said, "Drezna must be using it for a Pipe", another big howl of laughter to get the month of March underway was had. The first thing The Bone did that morning was to strip to his God given finery behind the hut and hose himself back to a state of human tolerance and cleanliness, and by Jaysus he needed it, for when they all boarded the van that morning they didn't know if he had a dead body in it or not. At least a thousand scales of dead flesh went into Jack Barry's mixer that day from the bodies of Drezna and the Bone. The bricks that the mortar bonded that day would surely stand for a thousand years. They all dined that day on a feed of sheep's liver, rashers and ten chopped onions in a make shift frying pan which was a cut off from a cleaned Tar barrel with a handle welded on to it. The usual bucket of spuds was put down and a catering tin of Heinz beans had the top cleared off it and they were left to heat in the fire also. The smell of the food wafted around the site from noon onwards and had the gangers so hungry by the time they sat down for the feed they didn't really care what animal or human the liver might have been extracted from. As they all waded through the fried onions they picked bits of rust out from between their teeth and complained to The Bone, but kept eating. The back doors of the Bone's van had to be held open that evening going home as the gangers serenaded each other on a diet of liver, onions and Heinz's beans.

Occasionally Bertie was heard to shout out "For Fuck's sake lads don't destroy the leather upholstery", referring to the bone's galvanized milk crates that they all rested upon.

Purlin's hair grew back and covered his head well and he hadn't been lifted by any of the London Bobbies for pissing in any public place. He was slagged through March and the lads kept telling him that the tablets he took were fucking horse tablets and that Pa wanted to enter him in the Grand National in Aintree that year. Slate Lath, his buddy, even joined in occasionally in the smart comments.

Once the cold weather lifted a bit the spirits came with it, liquid ones, and the ghostly ones were also seen to wander in an out of the famous Regents Park close to midnight and even sometimes well after that ungodly hour. Everything rambled on to St. Patrick's Day as usual the craic on the Saturday nights, the fun around the tea in the morning and the dinner on the site. The boss being Irish on the site suggested that the lads could work Saturday and Sunday before the Tuesday, which was our Patron Saint's feast day and that the lads could have the Monday and Tuesday off. They agreed to work the Saturday as a compromise and get the Tuesday off and the boss had to take his chances after that. Needless to say most of the Irish went abroad that week, not to the rolling green hills of the Emerald Isle but to the "Black Cap" and "The Brighton" pubs. The Paddies drank the places dry from mass time on the Tuesday till closing time. Few turned up for work on the Wednesday and the gra for the few bob brought in a few more on Thursday and Friday to collect whatever pay they could get their hands on for the week. When all was said and done it would have be difficult to get St. Patrick himself to work in London that week.

Tom's sister was getting married on the 7th of April 1953 so he booked the ticket the end of March in case he went on a bender with the money. He had a new suit made by either Mathew, or Mark the two Jewish tailors and by God did it fit well. He filled the pockets with a shot of tenners on the 3rd of April and headed for the train at Paddington Railway Station. He made it home the following day around lunch time and sat down with his mother Rita and aunt Bridget to a fine home cooked meal of real bacon and cabbage, not like the rubber they had to eat in London, this was the real deal it was home cured. Margaret called in just as he was getting up from the table and gave him a big hug and thanked him for making it home for the wedding. He handed her an envelope with her wedding present in it and wished her the best. Margaret was marrying Ted Murphy a fine upstanding man from just up the road from where she had lived in Ballymullen. It was said by many at the time that the made a fine good looking couple. Tom lined out the morning of the 7th of April for the wedding in his new well cut Jewish suit that came out of the most notorious bombed out building in the whole of London. As Tom stood for the photograph he smiled inwardly as he thought to himself, what the priest would say to him if he only knew that his suit came from, a Jew, and he wearing it at a Catholic wedding where the cloth was quite possibly stolen, at the price the suit was sold for, sure it had to be. He'd probably face excommunication on the spot, but if the priest knew what he had been up to in London this last twelve months he'd get the door for sure anyway. As the photographer told them all to smile he stuck out his fine builder's chest and looked the part in his muiti—million pound suit. A great day was had by all, The food was good at the "Manhattan Hotel", as usual, they all drank their fill and danced the night away.

Tom caught the famous ten to two train once again from the Tralee railway station the following Saturday and found a corner where he could put the feet up and go to sleep. Friday night had been a killer in the "White Lamb" pub with all the friends at home. There was a short stop in Mallow that Saturday but no change of train so he kept on sleeping. He awoke somewhere between Mallow and Rosslare. Like the last time, his ghostly immigrant comrades joined him in the darkened windows at dusk and were making the trip again with him tonight, keeping an eye on him once more like they always did when a son of Erin left for the streets of England. The crossing was calm for once and no one got sick. Having slept well on the train all the way from Tralee he took a walk around the St David and also ventured out on deck for a bit of fresh air. It was a beautiful night, a little cool with a slight hint of a light spring frost. As he gazed back at Ireland for the second time he found it hard to believe twelve months was gone since he first left. This time there was no uncertainty, no real pang of pain, or a soft pair of hands. Even though he was battle hardened now with hands of pure rawhide he still thought of his mother Rita and his aunt Bridget at home together alone. He left Rita a wad of money before he left and got a few things she needed. Dawn was not long creeping up on him as he sat inside the window looking out with a pint of mother's milk, the good old pint of Guinness. It was drank by alcoholics, business men, doctors, teachers, and even guards, you name them they drank the pint of porter for nearly 200 years, and yes it was true that the pregnant mothers of Ireland also drank it to build them up for the road ahead. Tom arrived in to Paddington Railway Station mid morning and met Bertie and they headed for a new kip that Bertie and Pa had lined up for the three of them while Tom was at home in Ireland. He cleaned up got his clothes ready for work on Monday morning. They drank a cup of tea and relaxed with the Sunday Papers while they had a bit of dinner on the go. Like Tom always did he studied the horse racing for the next few days ahead and done out a few dockets. The two of them had a fine pair of pork chops and a shot of rooster spuds, surrounded on the plate by about two dozen robust Brussels sprouts. The usual frying pan of onions was left to one side as their stomachs were still a bit raw after the beer the night before. They headed off for the "Old mother Red Cap" pub mid afternoon where the lads used to pitch their tents on a Sunday afternoon.

As Tom and Bertie walked through the front door Tom was glad in a way to be back as the shillings were running scarce. Pa, Mick Joyce, Kate Collins, was there and Jack Barry came in having worked another Sunday shift in his working clothes. While Tom was at home the twelve Apostles had befriended Mick Joyce after hearing he was from their part of the world and also because they heard him speak Irish one night and knew it was their dialect. Jack Barry since his return to England at Christmas was stacking the pounds and had set his date on returning home in April 1954 to get the garden set and get things underway on the farm that summer. He had one year of slavery left and then he was away home. That evening at twenty past six the pub emptied in a matter of a few minutes and the patrons headed off for evening Mass up in Camden Town. Two stops later on the tube to the north and they all got out at Tufnell Park station and headed across the road to mass to the Church of Our Lady help of Christians. No matter how drunk, or hungry, no matter how sad, or lonely the Irish in London were those years, they always made their way to the nearest church for holy mass. In a strange way being in the country that for so long subjugated Ireland it was like making a pilgrimage there to the local mass rock in defiance of the wishes of the crown. That evening was cold and damp and there was the odd shower. The Bone arrived with the usual van load and staggered from the van to the church door. He, as always, was a holy show with drink but still made the weekly journey no matter what. Tom could very clearly see that evening that Kate and Mick had become closer and he was courting her now in a way that was indeed quite serious.

The sermon that evening was all about family values and the power of the rosary within its structure. The priest spoke for what seemed like an hour, Mick sat upright with Kate close. Bertie was spotting a girl that he used to see in the Galtimore but he didn't think she was Irish. Pa was asleep and was sliding a little off from the perpendicular, but still every so often he would give a mighty jerk to stay half upright. As Tom prayed that evening to Our Lady he asked her to guide and protect him in the year ahead. He was happy in a way to be back as there was nothing at home in the line of work and money was almost nonexistent there also. For now, like Andy and his father bred into him, it was a case of the head down to keep

earning the shilling. Bertie, Pa and Tom got the tube back
to Kentish Town where their new house was. The Bone did
the transporting for moving the clobber and he was paid
with a sack of Guinness. As soon as they hit the bed that
night it was all lights out in their head as they thought of
the week ahead rebuilding the crown. Tom's dreams were
shallow and full of Green Fields and the "White Lamb

Pub" at home. As he drifted into a slumber he could even
hear the clatter of the change in the till.

CHAPTER 9

---—⟨∞∞⟩—---

BY THE END of April, and before the real summer rush the management of the Lancaster Gate Hotel had a general meeting. It was Kate's first such meeting and she had to prepare a lot of documentation financial, personnel and work reports. She found Mr Parks very helpful and he told her what she would need for the meeting. Kate and Stefan kept their heads stuck into their paper work for the next few days until they had it all properly prepared and laid out. She found Stefan every bit the asset she knew he would be. He was thorough and finite in everything he compiled. The meeting convened Thursday morning at half past nine on the on the last day of April. The main trust of the meeting went well and Mr Shellswell was very happy with all the reports that Kate had prepared and they concurred with the accountant's assessment of all the financial matters pertaining to her area of management. She gave a number of sighs under her breath, feeling a little worried about her first encounter at this level with senior management. Mr Shellswell complemented Mr Parks on a fine job and was pleased with his continued dedication to the establishment. He also complemented Kate on a job well done in her new role as junior manager and he was very impressed with her continued guidance towards her staff and her new found commitments to her paperwork. Towards the end of the meeting the bottle of Jameson was produced and the all engaged in a little tipple. The firm's accountant arranged a meeting with Kate for after lunch in her office where he discussed a number of issues relating to the dining room and kitchen, he asked her to see if you would be able to source the fish, meat and vegetables at a more reasonable cost. All went well at that meeting after lunch also and by the time Kate saw half five that evening all she wanted to do was down the remainder of Mr Shellswell's bottle of Jameson. She thought back, as she lay on her bed about the times she would walk home from school in the pouring rain up home to a bowl of hot soup and a slice of home made brown bread from her mother with a plaster of butter on it that had to be put on with her father's trowel. Her money was mounting up and her bottom drawer was filling by the week. She was getting on well with management, staff (as usual), and she was finding the paperwork a little over bearing as she was a hands' on kind of lady, but still coped well with it even though she was still only learning.

That night Kate and Mick met at their usual haunt and up the road from the hotel where they had many a pleasant hour together. Mick saw a little trouble in her eyes that evening as they sat down to some apple tart and a pot of tea. He held her hand in his and said "are you alright Kate my dear"? She pondered momentarily and then confided in him thinking from the outset that he couldn't do anything for her anyway. She explained the accountant's concerns that day about procuring the food cheaper. She wanted to do as he asked but didn't wish to in any way compromise the standard's of the hotel. She was so sure he was putting the squeeze on her just because he knew she was Irish and he didn't see why she should have such a prestigious position on the hotel staff. The minute Mick heard what was troubling her he smiled and said I may have a solution for you. It was Kate's turn to smile then, but in her usual kind way keeping his feelings uppermost in her mind. He reminded her of the rough fella that took Julie home last year. Oh yes I remember, the fella with the blue passion wagon as she laughed at his wild looking physique in her mind's eye. Yes that is the fella, well he has some great contacts in the markets and we can ask him if he could setup a good Irish supplier down there. Mick told her that he'd arrange a meeting with him tomorrow night at the "Black Cap Pub" if she liked. Well ok but I hope he wouldn't try anything crazy. Well if he cannot deliver to you maybe you can try somebody else. Ok fair enough she said as she thought she'd give it a try. The both met The Bone as arranged the following night and Kate asked him could he arrange a supplier for her at the hotel for fish, meat and vegetables. No problem girleen rolled off his lips like many a saucepan of Guinness. I know just the man but you will have to kind of grease his paw looking at Mick for support as he started to go down the back alleys of London's underworld. I can arrange for you to meet this fella tomorrow here at say 12 noon. Kate agreed with a little bit of Irish caution but it was worth a try and as Mick said well the fella was Irish, and that we did take care of our own here when it came to getting on in London. The following day Mick and Kate arrived at the "Black Cap" and sat down with a drink and waited. A little after a quarter past twelve in came The Bone with a huge hooor about 6' 6" and approached them in the corner. The Bone introduced him as Frankie Collins from Limerick. Straight away she asked him from where in Limerick saying I'm from Adare myself. He said straight away Oh I'm from out the county, and changed the subject. Collins was a common name in and around Limerick but there was something shifty about his eyes Kate thought, but she couldn't quite put her finger on it. He told Kate that he could supply what ever she needed in the line of fish, meat and vegetables she would need and he said he'd be able to organise her list of stuff for a figure less than half of what she was getting it at the moment. She knew that she could not buy that cheap without causing some suspicion with the accountant and then in turn Mr Shellswell so she would need to discuss the finance in more depth with Mr Collins. She said to Mick to go to the bar with The Bone as she needed to be a bit discrete. Mick smiled and said of course feeling a sense of cuteness and pride in his woman come to the surface, but she was a business woman after all. When she got Mr Collins on her own she really went to work. She pressed him about where he was from again but he wouldn't budge however he said he'd shake first on the price and then they would work out the payment. Kate said that she'd want delivery each Friday morning at eleven o'clock. She also said that she wanted the invoice to show that the price was 35% higher as to not arouse suspicion. That was not a problem either. She would deal with him each Friday and that if she was missing a man by the name of Stefan would deal with him as he was her assistant. He was happy with that and each Saturday she would pay him for the previous week's supplies. He asked for cash as he didn't like dealing in cheques. She said she'd

come back to him on that one on Monday and that if it was
ok she would take delivery of the list next Friday morning.
She would have to run it past accounts first. The final
point and that was not a problem, he was to put the 35%
in an envelope and she would meet him each Saturday at
the Black Cap with it. He smiled and said "that's a deal
Limerick lady". He had one request and asked her if she
could arrange a lunch ever Sunday for him the wife and
four kids at the hotel. It would be a treat for them he told
her. She thought about the difficulties of bringing up Irish
kids in London and agreed but you have to pay and you
can take five pounds ten shilling out of my cut. He said
grand to her spat on his hand, and offered it to her in
true Irish fair day fashion. She took it with the honour in
which it was offered and sealed their deal. He gave her a
phone number for him and said to only call after six in the
evening as he'd be out all day. He also said that Sunday
was his family day and preferred no calls that day. She
smiled and said "Of course" sensing a decent man behind
his rugged dealing façade. They parted with a smile and a
firm shake hands, and as he was about to turn he gave her
a gentle peck on the cheek. I'll call you Monday evening
she told him as he left. Frankie Collins left the pub and
hurriedly went straight to his twin wheeled black Bedford
van across the road. The rain lashed his face as he got in
as he sat back with a heavy sigh, he had just seen his sister
Kate for the first time in 14 years. He wanted to ask her
how his mother was but couldn't he was in pieces and it
did him all he could do to stay steady in front of her. His
heart ached for twenty minutes until he composed himself
again and started the engine. As he turned the steering
wheel he saw Kate and Mick come out of the "Black Cap"
with the Bone. He had to leave before his heart burst wide

open. Kate phoned him Monday evening but he told his wife Peggie to take the call and to take a message. He knew her voice would be too much, his heart had been red raw all weekend. Peggie took the call as he asked knowing he always had a reason for whatever he would do. He was also in a business that paid well and he was shrewd business man. Kate left a message for Frankie and just said to tell him to deliver Friday morning that everything was alright at her end. Peggie said thank you and gave the message to her husband. He thanked her without lifting his head and continued to eat his dinner. Peggie knew he was troubled but he'd confide in her when he was ready she knew, and that would be time enough.

Frankie had left Adare as a young man when Kate was only a child fourteen years back. She had grown into a fine woman and had her mother's looks and cunning. Frankie married the lady he had left in Adare all those years ago as they never lost touch he had sent her the fare after she came to London working and she left straight away for Boston just 2 weeks before war broke out in Europe. They married in early 1940 in Boston and honeymooned in New York City. When she got home to Boston she wrote to her parents to tell them she had married John Collins (Frankie's real first name) and that she was in Boston. They were furious, as it was their wish, that she would not marry him as his family came from the working class. They wrote to her and told her that their door was always open to her but not to her husband. To Peggie that meant that they closed it in her face also and she never again went back. Peggie gave birth to Sean their first born son the day Pearl Harbour was bombed. God sent Padraig 22 months later and Kevin arrived on almost

114

on horseback only 12 months after. Frankie worked in a factory making trucks from1942 until the war was over in September 1945. Peggie had worked making tents and soldier shirts during the war. In mid 1946 they had come to London to follow the boom that was coming and settled in Cricklewood. Young Katie was born in 1947 and she christened their house with their first daughter, she was six that June and a little doll with black curly hair and the picture of her aunt at that age. Frankie picked her up that evening after dinner on to his lap and thought her the six times tables off by heart. That night he and Peggie turned in and he told her the whole story before he slept. She was as stunned that night as she had ever been. It was a chance in 10 million to find Kate in London working. As she held her man Peggie Collins thought of all the trial and tribulations of the immigrant Irish in Boston or in London. She longed to hold the brass knocker on her parents door again too and had never forgot the cold feeling of it in her hand. Her man's heart was aching now but he would find a way through this ache the same way he always did when the time was right.

Kate, Aine and Mick left London on the 3rd of June for Galway for Joe and Mary's wedding the following Saturday the 6th. They landed in Galway at half one on the Thursday and all went for a bit of lunch to a pub Mick knew would fire up a good feed. Joe was to call there with the car to take them home around two. They had a good feed as the sea air had put the hunger on them. All the way to Ballinahowen Mick was instructed by Joe as to the duties of a Best Man while Kate and Aine sniggered in the back seat. Kate occasionally slipped her hand forward to tickle Mick in a teasing way. Each time she did it he would jump and Joe would tell the two in the back to steady up that this is serious. Saturday passed off all right and the entire ceremony was conducted in Irish as Kate sat there in a beautiful peach coloured floral dress obliviously to all that was being said. Irish was never one of her strong points especially when spoke in the Connemara dialect. That Saturday night Joe and Mary left and spent their wedding night in The Great Southern Hotel in Eyre's Square. That Sunday after early mass Aine, Kate and Mick followed on after he gave the mother and father another wad. The trip to London was a huge teasing session by Kate and Aine on Mary while Mick and Joe spoke about what London was like. The Girls teased Mary and asked her how the wedding night went.

She kept tight lipped and never said a word despite getting as red as the red post boxes on the footpaths of London. They all got a taxi to the hotel from Paddington Railway Station. Kate had the honeymoon suite all arranged and setup. Kate had to get back to the office and see how things were doing since she left and Mick had to call home and get ready for work Tuesday morning. Kate found the place in shipshape; after all she had a good man at the helm. As Aine was making her way to her apartment and thinking of a good sleep she met Stefan. He said to her "It is nice to see you back Aine did you have a nice time in Ireland". "Yes Mr Woychek the wedding was lovely and my brother and his wife are booked in to the honeymoon suite for the next two weeks". Yes I was just speaking to Miss Collins and she told me they are booked in and that you all had a lovely Irish wedding. As honeymoon couples sometimes do, Joe and Mary kept their nights for themselves and spent the days' sight seeing and shopping.

Their first weekend in London was a wipe out on drink once it was announced they were on their honeymoon in the "Black Cap" they never bought a drink after that. They were as sick as the proverbial dog when they awoke on Sunday Morning but still managed to get to mass with Mick and Kate. After mass they took the newlyweds out to lunch and they also took them to Regent's Park Zoo in the afternoon. They left for home the following Friday after having the time of their lives. Kate and Mick took care of the bill at the hotel as arranged.

In late June Mick took a few days off and had a surprise planned for Kate. He went shopping to one of the finer parts of London, that Saturday morning and bought her an engagement ring she had admired the previous week. He collected her before lunch that day and they went for a walk around Hyde Park. After he plucked up the courage he went on one knee while they walked around the Serpentine in Hyde Park near the hotel and asked her to be his wife. She knew it was coming but she didn't think it would be that fast. Her eyes melted into his and without batting an eyelid she accepted, knowing she would never meet a better man. Mick placed the diamond engagement ring on her ring finger and pledged himself to her for life. He took her to the hotel with her diamond upon her finger and he told her to get a weekend bag with enough clothes till Tuesday evening. He had left his bag at the reception. They boarded the train for Bournemouth that afternoon and spent the next 3 days by the sea where they both felt so at home enjoying the salty air. It was there they planned their lives and kept on track with money and common sense as if they were to ever get home again they had to take a van load of money with them.

Mick put a deposit on a house up near where Bertie, Tom and Pa were living a few weeks later. It was a fine three story brick house with good windows and a good sound roof. There was a small garden to the front and a good size one to the back and it was the end house on a block of twenty five houses with a side entrance. As he signed for the house he was hatching a plan. There were eight bedrooms he was able to let out and four were double rooms so he could get twelve boarding altogether. All he had to do was buy six beds and he was in business. He kept a room for himself and they all had the use of the kitchen. Mick spent two weeks after the tea each evening painting, papering and organising the furniture. By the time he had the work done he had got all twelve tenants bedded down. He got a loan of five hundred pounds to cover the cost of the place with the money he had saved. With a bit of luck and a bit of hard work he would have it cleared in no time at all.

The last Sunday in July Mick had arranged to meet Kate at eleven mass. When mass was over they went for a drink afterwards and then struck for the hotel for lunch. They had an early lunch and they had planned to head off to the fairground in Battersea Park. Aine came out to them from the kitchen before they left and had a brief chat with them both. As Mick and Kate headed for the lobby and onto the street she stopped dead in her tracks as she noticed Frankie Collins across the road. He had young Katie by the hand and the minute she saw them her mind went back fifteen years to Adare and her father walking her home after mass. She went cold with emotion and caught Mick's arm said "Oh Jesus it's him" as her voice became emotional. Mick replied "who". It was then she said that fella that supplies the stuff to the hotel is my brother. It was Mick's turn to grow cold. Each Saturday they had met, he had sent a chill through her bones because he had had a look of her father, now she knew why. As they reached the footpath Kate stopped, and Mick braced himself. Frankie and his family were half way across the road. She stared at them all and it was then she knew there was no doubt but that he was her bother John and his daughter was the head cut off of her also as a child. As they reached the footpath Kate stood dead in his tracks as he said hello. Kate looked into his eyes and said "hello John and hello Peggie, this is some shock to get." To think Ma thought you were somewhere in America, and that she thought you were in Dublin Peggie all these years. I suppose I have a lot of explaining to do, don't I. How is Ma keeping he asked. She died a year ago last April and I buried her with Da. She turned to Peggie and said your mother was at the funeral. She offered me her condolences but we did not speak beyond that. John eyes welled up with tears as he though of his mother dead in the ground in Adare with his Da. I sold the home place after Christmas this year she told John and got four hundred and eighty pounds for the place which is going to you as it was in Da's will that you were to get it if I ever again met you. Mick suggested that they all go back into the hotel as he anticipated a long drawn out afternoon. Kate invited everyone up to her apartment and ordered dinner and drink for her guests. Once they all arrived into her apartment John introduced his family to their aunt Kate and Kate introduced Mick as her fiancé. There was some sadness, tears by the women and a lot of congratulations all round and of course some almost endless hugs too. Kate was in a state of shock and Mick was somewhat stunned but still so glad to have met Kate's relations as he had always knew it was a tough part of her life to deal with. John explained all that had happened since he left home and the fact that Peggie followed. Kate could openly see that Peggie was a devoted wife to her brother and a warm sensitive lady to their children. Kate inwardly felt like hammering her brother against the mahogany wall in her sitting room as they all sat and had lunch, but this was not a time for recriminations she had just caught up on the last fifteen years of her life. Kate warmed immediately to Padraig who was now ten years old and also young little Katie who had just turned six. It was Mick's first time seeing her with children and he liked a lot what he saw in her that afternoon. They all chatted well into the evening and it became a very memorable Sunday. Peggie invited both Kate and Mick over to their home the following Saturday evening for some food. They all left before seven that evening and Mick poured Kate a strong Jameson and took her by the hand as he led her to the couch. He left her talk a lot that night and sat and listened over and over again about why he never came back. John was strong willed and could be stubborn at times like his father. I suppose he wouldn't go back to Adare without Peggie Mick kept saying to Kate. Eventually she agreed and finally said "I suppose your right". The little sup was beginning to settle her. Mick seeing his chance asked her what did she think about having three nephews and a niece and a sister-in-law as well as her long lost brother back in her life again. Kate was putting away a wad of cash each Saturday now with the deal she had struck with Frankie/John Collins now her brother. He was making good money also for his lovely family and Mick was just about to embark on the venture of his life.

Herself and Mick went up to John and Peggie the following Saturday and spent the day with the family. John opened the door and blocked out the light into the hallway as he stood facing the mid day sun. As Kate walked in the door John pressed another solid envelope full of cash into his sister's little hand as she removed her black gloves, and whispered in her ear there is a few bob extra in that this week and there will be from now on as I'm getting the stuff at a better price. It was John's way of looking after his sister. Seanie and Mick hit it off well and Mick was teaching him some Connemara Irish before the day was out. The pride in the Irish tongue that time in England was a cherished piece of life in a foreign land. Kate spent the day talking with Padraig, Kevin and little Katie wandered from Mick to Kate and then over to her mom and dad. Kate asked Peggie while in the kitchen with her did she think she'd ever go back to Adare with John and the kids to see her parents who were now old. With a far away look in her eye she said "Maybe we will soon who knows, but if I do, I will never walk in that door without my husband at my side". Saying John and I have been through too much together.

While Mick was doing up the house he found an old trapdoor up to the attic that was sealed and seemed to be for years. He decided to open it up and fit a new one. When he went up he found a treasure trove of stuff. There was old swords, jewel crusted daggers, a full chest of document referring to the some of the British colonies dating back over two hundred years. He also found a box of gold sovereigns which looked to be in good condition in the dim candle light of the attic. He gasped a few times and wondered what it all could be worth. He bought

121

another chest and brought all the stuff down to his room and locked everything away safely and tried to calm down. He also found that there was an open attic over the five houses that were next to his place. There were two next to his place unoccupied and the other two were occupied by two old ladies who lived on the ground floor and never ventured up the stairs. Piece by piece he sheeted the entire attic over the five houses with three quarter ply procured by The Bone. The Bone helped him to screw down all the flooring up there and even got a few remnants of carpet for the walkway to help to soundproof it.

That summer there was a huge influx of workers arrived in London to work in the "Isle of Grain" oil refinery that was going up in Kent. Mick had the twelve customers bedded down in the house and he had room for another 30 in the attic at a half crown a night for just the bed. At this rate he would own the street before he was thirty he thought to himself with a loud hearty laugh. The coach that took all the lads to Kent every day stopped at the end of the road. Before long, a precession of Paddies left Mick's house by the side entrance each morning for the coaches that had to come to collect the increased numbers. The crowd that kipped in the attic grubbed in a cafe not too far away.

Kate and Stefan were working in her office one afternoon planning the following week's menus when out of the blue he asked her, who was the nice Irish girl that worked in the kitchen. Kate told him that her name was Aine Joyce and that Aine was the Irish word for Anne. He also enquired did she know if she was seeing anyone. Kate said that she didn't think she was, and being Irish she asked, why. Stefan became a little flustered and passed it of by saying she was a nice lady and she was also a very good worker in the kitchen. Kate enquired no further and gave a coy inward smile. As Stefan and Kate finished their work that evening Kate made a passing remark to Stefan, saying maybe you should ask that Irish lady out on a date. Stefan knowing that Kate, with her cunning mind had him twigged, he said "maybe" smiling as he left and closed the office door. Kate rang the kitchen and Julie answered the phone, she asked to speak to Aine. Aine said hello to Kate and straight away Kate interrupted saying "I think Stefan is going to ask you out". Put down the phone now as he is going down to the kitchen with menus for Julie. They both dropped the phone.

Aine was cleaning up two work benches in the kitchen when Stefan walked in and spoke with Julie he was talking with her to a few minutes and then came directly over towards her and said very shyly "hello Aine". She responded saying "good evening Mr Woychek" He continued to the back door of the hotel that led out to the yard and to his flat. Aine left shortly after and went out to her flat laid down on her bed. The day had been long and busy and all she wanted to do was rest. Her two flatmates had a date that evening and were not long with her. She sat at the small table and wrote home to her mother and father. Just as she sealed the letter a knock came to the door and her heart stopped. She was frozen to the chair, stuck solid. If it was him, what should she do. As there was a second knock up she got and opened the door. It was Kate the colour drained back into her face. Kate asked her to join her for a cup of tea down the road in the café. Off they both went and stayed chatting till gone half eleven about the hotel, life, Kate's relations, and of course men. Being the same age they had a lot in common and now that they were almost family, sure there was no holding them back when they got talking. Aine was all panic about a Polish man asking her out. Kate said sure isn't he a Catholic and he is a real gentleman, and Aine dear they are hard to find in London these days so if he asks you out say yes. Aine smiled wondering to herself, what would her father say if she landed home to Ballinahowen linking a Pole to mass on Sunday?

CHAPTER 10

———∞∞∞———

THAT JULY THERE was a mass exodus out of London for Kent and the Isle of Gain refinery building project. That was where the money was and they were doling it out down there by the wheelbarrow. The Bone changed the van again and was able to get over 20 into it standing up. It was blue of course to go with his eyes. More said he should paint a black stripe on it and it would then look like another part of his body. The site stretched as far as the eye could see and they even erected army billets there to house the Paddies, Jamaicans, Poles, a few Russians, some of their women got jobs in the kitchens and some said that more were working in the trenches with the men also. The Irish lads who stayed in London called it the English Man's version of a concentration camp, although no one ever saw the funny side of that comment. The Bone hired six other Irish fellas from home to do the cooking for the Irish on site. He leased one of the kitchens that was one of three that had been setup in a billet and did taxi morning and evening. His breakfast in the morning between nine and eleven was the talk of the place. Two of the fellas that came over from Ireland were cooks by trade and knew the game. The Bone got a huge frying pan made up by some factory crowd and it was about four feet square. You could line up about seventy rashers at the one time, and they weren't the streaky ones either. Wherever he got the eggs nobody knew, but they were as big as half sized tennis balls in the frying pan. Some said they had to come from Mayo hens as they wore red and green jerseys sometimes. The Bone made sure the crubeens were a must for the breakfast every morning. There was a crowd from Clare that had to have one with the rasher for the breakfast every day. A small lorry pulled in every morning at half eight with about a ton of big long brown soda loaves of bread. Each was eighteen inches around and arrived piping hot. Another lorry arrived around the same time every morning with trays of meat, fish, and about sixty bags of spuds, and at least another thirty bags of vegetables, driven by John Collins from Adare. The departure by the Bone from the shovel to the industrial frying pan was some undertaking he had it up on a huge metal frame and had about 15 gas rings running under it. He was firing out more breakfasts than any other slop team on site. When it came to the dinner it wasn't cooked in a bucket or barrel anymore. The bone had two big vats around six feet in diameter and three feet deep where the bacon, pigs heads, Irish stews, or any other mystery dish got boiled in. He raked in the money every day to the point that he had to be looked after each evening on the way home. His twenty taxi mates looked after him, as nobody would even talk to them as they were one hell of a wild looking bunch.

John Collins did well from his deal with Kate but this deal took the biscuit. The Bone had set it up from him and he was flat out every day fulfilling the orders. He also had to take on a battalion of meet cutters and another few to bag the spuds. There were some nights he did not get home till gone nine and his time with Peggy and the kids was taking a lashing. The money he was raking in was making him shiver with delight each night as Peggie and he would sit down to count it. Night after night she would say to him,

"My God John we have never seen this kind of money not even in Boston". One night in late August she said to him maybe one day we will go home and set up a life for the lads and little Kate and make sure they will never have to do what we had to do. She was sounding the ground with John, he made no answer, but she had stirred a muscle in his heart.

The work down in the "Isle of Grain" was hard, and tough going. There was seven days on offer for anyone who wanted to work each week. Many took on the deal and committed themselves to the slave and save mentality. There was subsistence every day for the lads as they all could not be bedded down near the site. Jack Barry never lifted his head that year only maybe to write home and wire the few pounds to Bere Island to keep the family from starvation.

The new time for the Bone's early morning fucking was six o' clock. He got a room in Mick Joyce's house and they pulled out every morning with a full van filled from Mick's attic. The rest of the travellers headed for the coaches. The trip down was the usual introduction to human gas, sweat, sour socks and, the roughest of handovers aggravated with the usual smell of stale drink sliding onwards to Kent on every burp that was born in the back of the van. The pick and shovel was the best friend the Paddy had there. As they dug deep and threw well back they reshaped the landscape of south east England. The money flowed in and some drank it by weeks end, more saved it with the dream of returning home and more saved to buy the houses around the city as they went up for sale.

The twelve Apostles headed south also and dug like there was no tomorrow. When they put a shovel in their hands they became possessed. Heads down, with broad backs, and flexing mussels as the picks drove deeper with every lunge into God's own clay. They walked off the site every evening like they walked across Regents Park every night as they headed home, labouring to them was second nature and with every few shovels that they flung out of the open trench another pound lined the pockets of their brown corduroy pants.

As they walked off the site on a Friday evening you could hear them make up the money through Irish. Whimpey's were a good crowd to pay and would never try and fiddle you out of a shilling, not like more of the hoors of contractors, quite often Irish, out to do their own. They gave a good wage of fifteen pounds for the five days and a fella could hurl another twelve or thirteen pounds up on that for a Saturday and Sunday and with the two pounds ten shillings subsistence a good man would scrape over the thirty pounds. At home in Ireland that time a man would not make it in two months. The Bone made sure that the food was good and every lease holder of a kitchen got a "hows your father" or a handshake from the contractors to keep the boys happy and well fed. With the money The Bone was making he could have bought a new van every month. He was not seen with Drezna that summer as some said maybe he wasn't able for her, but few would chance saying it to his face.

As the Hurling All Ireland drew close in fifty three the Cork Bookies appeared again moving around the sites and the Isle of Grain was no exception. Christy Ring captained Cork that year and they were heading on for their second win in a row. The tribesmen from Galway were facing them down that year. The Connemara men betted heavily as did the Cork men. There was many a row about who was the better in the canteen for the lunch every day on the run up to the match. The odd bowl of stew was poured over each others heads and the canteen would get wrecked after with the follow up fight. Spuds were plastered into fellas faces and almost ate off them again with a fit of temper. Thousands of pounds changed hands with the Cork bookies who were kind of certain that Cork couldn't loose with Christy Ring lining out for them. It was a hard fought match and Cork beat the tribesmen into submission winning 3-03 to 0-8. The bookies from Cork made a fortune that year as the Galway men licked their salty wounds all the way up to Christmas week that year. Later in the month Kerry clipped Armagh's wings 0-13 to 1-6 Tom Sullivan made over a month's wages that weekend and celebrated into a state of oblivion with Pa and Bertie who also made a killing on the Cork bookies. They had long faces that Monday evening after the match. They met the three lads in the "mother Red Cap" and had to pay each of them out the price of a good car. Reality struck again at five next morning, as they all made off down the road with sick, sore and sorry heads and boarded the Bones passion wagon for The Isle of Grain.

Their breakfast was a welcome sight that morning and a cake of brown bread devoured between the three of them, plastered with a wipe of good creamery butter. The three of them lingered on about twenty minutes after everyone had left the canteen that morning as Pa heard the foreman say he was going up town to order some shuttering for the following days work. On their way out of the canteen Bertie had a look into the kitchen to see if he could get another cut of bread. What he saw stunned even him, he called back Tom and Pa and said "hey lads look at the fucken Bone" they all had a look in the billet door where the kitchen was. There they saw the Bone inside one of the large cooking vats having a bath and having a good scrub down. The three lads from Tralee had a chat with him that evening on their way out the gate about what they saw. The discussion didn't last too long, but all that can be said for now, was they never paid for a meal again while down at the Isle of Grain. It was his way of asking them to keep it quiet. They had many a laugh about it over the next few years. What went on down there was in every way inhuman but all that mattered was having a laugh as what happened on a daily basis kept the hard work easy and of course the money, the porter and the women at the weekend kept everyone coming back to work so their social lives would not be interfered with.

As October opened up a lot of the Paddies came in for the Saturday and some the Sunday too to make a few pound extra for the trip home on the St. David for Christmas. One Saturday morning that month as the line of coaches and vans approached the site a pall of smoke was seen standing firm, like a black thorn stick, in a calm red morning sky. The talk on the bus was that there will be no fucken breakfast as one of the kitchens had to be burned down. The Bone raced in the gate wondering was it his place but he found out, his place was safe and sound. The word at work was that the night before a dozen or so Connemara men were up the town on the beer and when they came back they found out that a black fella had hammered and cut one of their boys with a blade who was singing an Irish song, while drunk in bed. He had told him to shut up but Paddy told him over and over to shut up you black bastard and kept on singing. It was often said that some of the Connemara men's singing even got to the Irish lads at times. In a flash, up jumped "An Fear Gorm" and he bate Paddy to a pulp and slashed his face and body with a knife. As his mates were coming in the gate and heading for the billet they heard what happened as the ambulance passed them on the way out with the siren wailing like a Banshee. Down they went for the hard man that knifed and bate the portered Paddy. He had locked himself into the billet. After numerous attempts to get the hooor out with threats of extreme violence and insults that could not be written for fear the paper would ignite. Eventually it was the billet that was ignited. When the blaze inside and out was like a seen from "Dante's Inferno" there he came tumbling out a window with a pall of smoke as black as himself. He was caught and there was a terrible debt repaid. He was hospitalised for over six weeks and never returned to the site. Despite a crowd of over three hundred watching the event nobody saw anything, as it was late at night and dark and beside the fella was supposed to be black. The Connemara man that got the doing came back to work four weeks later and carried on the Job as if nothing ever happened. No one ever said anything about his singing, to him again.

The Bones pigs heads and crubeans became a huge delight for some of the Russians on the site and all downed it with the usual wipe of ripped cabbage and even sometimes boiled whole and parted after with a hatchet that the Bone used for cutting the meat. The English and Scotch lads would keep well away from the Paddies and Russians when they started to eat the pig's heads and all they contained. They could often be heard to say "Crikey mate did you see the big fucken paddy in the green sweater eating the bloody brains". Even though the Scotch being good able Celts also, and being up for the occasional plate of Haggis, eating the head of a pig and his crubes was something they could never stomach.

To see The Bone doing the stew was in itself nothing short of a pure raw education. A sack of chopped beef or lamb would be flung into one of the large vats of boiling water. About five buckets of marrow bones were then added with ten buckets of chopped carrots and parsnips. Twenty onions would get a slap of the hatchet down the centre and would be tipped in also. A few bags of flower would then be tipped in to thicken the soup and it was left to simmer for a couple of hours, getting the occasional stir with a good big shovel kept strictly for that purpose. Everyone said on a cold day, be they from the far flung corners of the earth or across the Irish Sea, that the Bone's stew was the best and that it put hair on many a boy's chest and made a man of him in no time at all. It heated the body when the cold icy winds hit them that came from across northern Europe.

That November everyone worked the full seven days and the work progressed at lightening speed. The Bone never went home those weeks and got a friend of his to do the taxi work up and down to London. John Collins worked the seven days too but Kate took care of Peggie and the Kids every Sunday at the hotel and usually spent the day with them. By late November Peggie told Kate that John herself and the kids were going to spend the Christmas in Adare as they all needed the break. They had booked into the Dunraven Arms Hotel for a week and were going to call to her parents first on their own and if they were received by her parents she would bring the children the next day. Kate thought it was a great idea and encouraged Peggie to be optimistic about the trip. Peggie asked her had she and Mick made plans for Christmas or were they staying in London. She said they were going to Galway for ten days and were going to spend the last two in Adare as she wanted to visit her parent's grave. Kate and Peggie became much closer as Christmas drew near despite their difference in years. They both came up the hard way and had roughed life in different ways something that had made them really appreciate their men and all they had gathered. Kate often said to herself over and over what a great wife her brother had found in Peggie. The children were looking forward to the trip also but the reason for the visit was being kept quiet as John and Peggie did not want their little hearts maybe opened to grief at such an early age. It was to be their first trip home to Ireland. There was a mass exodus of Irish out of London that Christmas.

Most went back to the Auld Sod as there was plenty of money to make the trip. More went up north to see what Scotland was like and to see if the real Scots could drink as much the Irish. Another forty or fifty struck to France to see what it was like over there and to go mental on cheap French brandy. Some said, some of them never returned or regained a full state of consciousness. More said it was the French women who fell in love with the Paddie's accents.

Peggie and John left the children with an old school friend of hers who was shocked, stunned and surprised to see her. They hadn't seen one another in over fourteen years. As they walked up the gravel covered drive to her father and mother's home with John it took her back to the time he used to walk her home all those years ago. John took her by the hand and said "Everything will be alright my girl". She looked her husband in the eye, feeling his strength enter her body for what lay ahead. Her mother opened the door and stared at them both with a frosty eye. Peggie said "hello mother, how are you"? This is my husband John Collins". Please come in she responded. While standing in the luxurious hallway Peggie could get the scent of tobacco from her father's pipe. He walked out of the conservatory and into the drawing room only to hear Peggie's voice in the hallway. He momentarily hesitated, but continued across the drawing room. As he entered the hallway his wife turned and said "dear we have visitors". Peggie seeing her father said cautiously "hello father". He walked towards her, stern faced, as he always did. Stopped next to his wife and then moved a step further and took Peggie in his arms and said "hello my girl, it has been far too long, I have missed you so much these last years". He stood and faced John and also said "John you are welcome to our home". John responded being the gentleman he was, saying, Thank you very much Sir. Then he said "let us all sit down", Peggie's father suggested knowing they all had lots of questions to be answered. Before the conversation got underway they had tea and cakes. Brian and Margaret Noonan kept a lot to themselves in Adare and enjoyed life on their own. Peggie's elder sister was living in Dublin with her husband and two daughters. Brian and Margaret were never blessed with a son but cherished their daughters dearly as young children and teenagers. When Peggie left home like she did it broke their hearts but then they had reared Peggie like they were themselves to be firm and go after what was their wish in life. It was there she clashed with them. Peggie and John told them of their life in both Boston and London and of the ups and down they had during their years together but now they were getting on well in London. Brian had been in reasonable health these last two years. He was now sixty six and Margaret who was in good health was just gone sixty four since early December. Margaret then asked them had they children, to which Peggie replied "yes mother you are grandparents we have three great boys and a beautiful daughter". Margaret's eyes lit up as she asked "are they with you". John then addressed them both saying we wanted to come and visit first. Brain then said Peggie your mother and I have been unkind to you both and we are sorry for they way we reacted to your marriage and our subsequent comments. We would both wish, that you can see it your way to forgive us for the way we treated you. Thank you, father and mother for your apology. John has always been my one true love, my gentle giant of a man and I cherish him more today than when we were here as a young couple courting. He has been my rock and my support through life and I will always love him. I am glad, now through your apology, that you have accepted my husband as your son-in-law. Peggie then told her parents that we are staying at the Dunraven Arms and if they wished we can call again tomorrow with the children. Margaret said that would be lovely and would you all like to come for lunch maybe tomorrow. John thanked both Brian and Margaret for their hospitality and asked what time would they call the following day. Brian told them to call whatever time they wished but that they dined at 1pm usually. They both left. As Peggie walked down the driveway John took her hand and said to her "didn't I tell you it would be grand". Two tears were gently displaced from under her long pretty eyelashes, which she left dry in the sweet Adare breeze.

The following day a little after noon the Collins Family arrived at "Brook Hall". As they all stood outside the door John explained to the children that this is where your mother grew up and that they were coming to meet their grand-dad and grand-mother. The door opened and there stood Brian and Margaret. Little Katie stood next to her mother's left leg peering out from behind her cherry coloured coat, at the new people in her life. The boys stood erect and confident like their Dad had always thought them to be. As they all entered the hallway and pleasantries were exchanged Peggie's mind went back to the Sunday lunches when she was a young lady and the smell of the roast was all around the house. She missed that life in many ways as a young married lady in Boston but she would have never once have traded her loving husband for that life in Adare. He was truly her soul mate.

Margaret took their coats and Brian showed them all to the sitting room where a beautiful warm seasonal fire sent the room into a gorgeous orange glow that warmed all their hearts from the outset. Brian poured drinks for everyone as Margaret and Peggie went to the kitchen to check on the food. As they both entered the kitchen Margaret turned to Peggie and burst into a flood of tears as she hugged her daughter, her pet, and her favourite. Now, now, mother, the strong willed Peggie said, as she held her close. She told her to dry up her tears as this was a joyous occasion. Peggie took a striped tea cloth and dried her dear mother's flowing tears saying don't let the children see their grandma like this. Brian had Katie sitting on his knee after a few minutes as she appropriately entertained the crowd putting on her own version of a black curly haired Shirley Temple. The boys stood in front of their grand father as Sean bamboozled him with many questions about his hunting exploits around West Limerick over the years. Brian said we must teach you to shoot sometime when you get a little older. The boy's eyes lit up as they all looked at their father for his usual note of approval. They all sat down to lunch shortly after and dined on a luscious free range turkey garnished with all the trimmings. That evening the staff at the Dunraven Arms brought the bags belonging to the Colins family to "Brook Hall" where they all stayed for the remainder of their trip.

Brian and Margaret's days were filled with wonderment for their grand children and the true gentleman qualities their Son-In-Law portrayed towards them both and in particular their daughter, but then John doted over Peggie as much as she did over him. Peggie's elder sister, husband

TIMOTHY C.J. MURPHY

and two daughters paid a surprise two day visit to "Brook Hall" and got to know their new extended family of cousins and relations. Anne and Peggie went for a few long walks with each other and caught up the way women do.

Ballinahowen was awash with celebrations that Christmas also. Mick and Kate were guests of honour as their recent engagement was celebrated in true western fashion on a diet of fresh fish, poultry and all washed down with Guinness and bottles of what the children used to be told was holy water. Kate remarked to one of Mick's friends that his eyes were swimming in the holy water only for him to tell her, sure that's no problem I will be taking them out before I go to bed to wash them anyway. Kate and Mick headed for Adare the Friday, New Years Day with sore heads after ringing in the new year in Ballinahowen. On arrival at the Dunraven Arms Hotel in Adare they found that John, Peggie and the children had left the hotel Christmas Eve. Kate thought the worst had happened with Peggies parents and felt a great sadness. While Mick and Kate were just finishing dinner that evening Peggie and John entered the dining room and fully appraised of how the week went. Next morning early John and Kate went to visit their parent's grave and placed a few flowers on it. It was a special, although sad moment for them, but after all they were now together by a terrible twist of faith. They all left for London afterwards. They met up with Aine in Mallow who had come down that day from Galway and boarded the St. David that night for Fishguard.

Bertie shacked up with a girl from Tipperary that Christmas and had a great time spending his hard earned money. Tom and Pa headed for Tralee and lived it up in their two Jewish suits for the ten days. There wasn't a girl safe in town as they charmed the very birds off the trees with their wild stories of the streets of London. The craic was good in the "White Lamb" and the dances were alive with Christmas cheer also. Before Tom left, the traditional wad was left with his mother Rita and her sister Bridget to get them through the winter and into the early spring. Times were still tough on the Auld Sod but as a race we were getting there, little by little.

Mick and Kate started to make plans for their life that Christmas as they walked the cliff tops across from Ballinahowen. They planned to get married Saturday the 12th of June 1954 maybe in London or in Ballinahowen, as Adare was in her distant past now. Kate knew she would settle in Galway one day soon with her husband, his heart was in its very rocks and boulders that protected Ireland from the Atlantic waves, winds and squalls. Before Mick left that year he bought a small bit of a plot down the road from the home place sheltered from the south westerly winds by a small headland. A neighbour was selling off a few small fields and retiring. Mick felt sad in a way buying the plot as his only two sons had been lost to a grey spring tide some five years back and the dreaded TB had also taken his wife. He lived a lonely life but called to see Paddy and Madge most days for the company and a bit of dinner. The day Mick paid over the money for the scratch of ground Kate sprinkled a drop of holy water in the gate and said "May all who stand in the field have the blessing of Our Lady upon them.

It was back to the grindstone on the 4th of January and to the harsh reality of the London cold and bitter easterly

/ Russian winds. All the boys from the mid west were steeped in the best of Connemara poteen until the end of the month until the case loads they brought back to London ran dry but it kept their bodies warm and staved off the winter cold. Peggie and John returned with a new lease of life in their hearts about the way Christmas in Adare had gone. Jack Barry returned with a new zest in his soul for his last four months in London as he was going home in early April to set the garden on his island farm. Mick and Kate focused their minds and bodies on earning as much as they could to buy a home before their wedding six months hither. Tom, Pa and Bertie continued to dine free at the Bone's slop house in the Isle of Grain.

CHAPTER 11

---∞∞∞---

THE FIRST FEW weeks of January were mild with a little rain falling from time to time. For winter, the construction work down in the Isle of Grain went flat out every day. There wasn't a sign of a snow flake until around the last week in January. Up to then the Twelve Apostles worked like possessed warriors. They all travelled back from Connemara in two vans laden down with poteen for the winter cold and all worked the full seven days on the site on piece work on some of the buildings there. They had struck up a deal with the bosses and had to work to the clock, something they never found any difficulty in doing. They had hatched a major plan but were keeping it all tight to their chest. Mick who knew the Connemara lingo thought he heard them talking one night, while downing a few drinks, say something in Irish about a street of half bombed houses. He though, that maybe themselves and the four evangelists were think of changing residence.

Kate's first day back at work the 4th of January, was marked with a meeting with Mr Shellswell and Mr Parks. This time the Jameson was out as she entered Mr Shellswell's office. This usually signified something to celebrate. In Mr Shellswell's usual mannerly disposition she was offered one of the plush sturdy leather chairs. As she took the seat and a little tipple from Mr Parks the two towering figures stood standing towering over her. As the first drop of dew hit her lips in the shape of the soft Jameson a cold shiver ran down her spine and out from there in all directions. Had the two found out about her dealings with John in the market? Just as she could feel the blood start to rise to her face and start to redden her cheeks they both lifted their well laden tumblers. Mr Shellswell then toasted Kate on an excellent job done with the catering side of the business over the last twelve months. The colour started to drain back into her face but with some caution. She was seeing a roguish look in Mr Shellwell's eye she had not seen before. He then addressed her saying "Kate we have noticed that you are buying the freshest of produce for the kitchen as of late and the accountant has told us that through your dedicated endeavours the hotel has made a handsome profit this last year". Thank you gentlemen Kate muttered in her gentle voice and staring right through both of them, trying to hide all she knew of the endeavours in question. Kate feared a hidden agenda was coming as these two were always scheming as well. Kate was tense and ready for what came next. Mr Shellswell then asked Kate would she take over managing the bar also. Seeing very clearly where this was all going she could see in her mind eyes, The Bone pulling up each week with a van load of whiskey from an unknown source. She was not going there. She hit it straight on the head making it quite clear that she knew absolutely nothing about the bar trade and besides she was very busy keeping track of her staff, kitchen and dining room and also taking on extra paperwork. She respectfully declined the position. They were contented with her reply and then Mr Shellwell handed her the Christmas bonus he had made up for her over the festive season. He also reminded her of her raise in salary as from the 1st of January. Both gentlemen then raised their glasses again and congratulated her on her recent engagement to Mick. As she was leaving the office she turned to say goodbye, while Mr Shellswell told her to keep up the good work. She left the office in a cold sweat while, saying a prayer to her friend the Blessed Virgin. She came to her feet and poured herself another stiff Jameson to moisten her dry mouth. She opened the bonus payment to find in it a double bonus and a little note from Mr Shellswell which read "I hope this will buy your wedding gown for you, regards Humphrey Shellswell". As she was just draining her tumbler a knock came to the door. She invited the visitor in and in walked Stefan. As they both approached one another in true European style he leaned forwarded and kissed her on the cheek while wishing her a very happy new year. As the news was out also about her engagement to Mick he asked her, who was the lucky man? It was then she told him that his name was Mick Joyce a builder from Ireland working in London. She also then told him that he was the brother of Aine Joyce the girl who started last year in the kitchen. "Oh yes the sweet Irish lady" he remarked not looking Kate straight in the face. He then said "I have been meaning to suggest to you that I would like to move her into the dining room as she is a very efficient girl and has a good manner with others, something that would be an asset to her in dealing with people there". Two girls had not come back from Ireland after Christmas and they were short staffed in the

dining room were now in need of hiring two girls as soon
as management sanctioned it. "There are two Polish girls
working in Reading, he continued, in another hotel and
they are anxious to come to work in London". Being open
like he always was, he said he'd vouch for them and knew
one of their bothers. Kate then told Stefan to move Aine
to the dining room the following Monday and to set up
the two interviews as soon as he could with the two Polish
girls. Kate signed off on a few pieces of paperwork that
evening for accounts. Stefan went straight to the kitchen
as Aine was getting ready to finish work. As always she
was the last to leave so he took the opportunity he had
been waiting for. As she went for her coat he picked it off
the peg and offered to put it on for her. She thanked him as
she buttoned it slowly sensing that something was coming.
Aine I have been doing a diploma in business and my course
finishes on the 11th of February and it is being marked with
a Valentine's night ball on the 14th of next month and I was
wondering if you would like to accompany me to the ball.
Aine blushed so badly that Stefan went for an ice bucket
as a way of teasing her. She tried to speak but was tongue
tied. Fearing he may run off if she didn't reply soon she
just blurted out, "That sound's lovely, I will be delighted to
yes Mr Woychek". He thanked her saying "Stefan please".
He looked her straight in the eyes as he said that, which
sent a cold eastern European shiver running recklessly
throughout her body. Oh! Miss Collins said to tell you
that she is starting you in the dining room as from next
Monday. Your pay will be adjusted accordingly also and
please see Miss Fitzmaurice concerning a new uniform for
the dining room. Aine thanked him for the news and also
for asking her to the ball on Valentines night. She tried
to hold her composure as she walked out the rear door to

her flat. She felt like cheering out loud as she thought to herself of this incredibly sexy European man asking her out. If only the girls in Balinahowen could see her now. She waited about thirty minutes for Stefan to leave the hotel and then headed up to Kate's apartment to tell her the news and thank her for the promotion. They chatted to the early hours about all the things that women like to.

Tuesday morning down in the Isle of Grain a new bookie turned up trying to muscle in on the Cork boy's betting ground. Most of the Irish lads knew that there would be trouble when the Cork fellas heard about him. Veins of rock were starting to crawl up to meet the lads that January and February stinging their muscles and almost shattering their bones as the picks hit dead blows right down on to it. It started to slow up the Twelve Apostles also, but being on piece work they were often seen to work up to nine at night with a string of flickering bulbs lightening their paths through the earthen and limestone trenches. They were all back in their mansion in the East End since returning from home as they used to say the billets on site were only dog kennels. They maintained that there were so many fleas in them that there wasn't a hound safe south of fucken Birmingham even though few of them had any idea of where Birmingham was. A new bunch of Mayo lads arrived after Christmas around twenty of them and stone mad for work and making money. Four more came from Dublin and a scatter from along the western seaboard also. The Mayo lads were on a mission and it wasn't to Lourdes either, they were there to make the price of a street of houses and bleed the crowd that owned that big clock, Big Ben, to the bone.

Aine, Kate and Peggie went off shopping the first week in February for a gown, shoes, a purse, and some fake jewellery. Peggie being older and knowing the ways of the modern world, teased and slagged Aine about the fact that she would have to buy some nice underwear also as you know what those sexy European men are like. The very virginal Aine was having none of that though, thinking of the advice her mother had given her the night before she left home for England nearly fourteen months ago now. Peggie still treated her in that regard, although she blushed throughout the purchase. The evening of the February the 14th Aine got ready in Kate's apartment where Mick, Peggie and John called up to after lunch that Sunday with the children. Mick never saw his sister fuss so much long ago about anything, the two women were driving her mad with suggestions and whispers and sniggers. He, John and the boys struck downstairs with a task in mind, young Katie stayed with the girls. Stefan called at eight o'clock sharp, being a good time keeper. Peggie and Katie hid in the bedroom while Stefan was there. Kate wished them both an enjoyable night together. When they were gone Mick, John and the boys returned and both arrived with two large bouquets of roses for the loves of their lives. They all went down to the bar and drank well into the late hours as the children slept soundly on Kate's king size bed. A bit gone half three they all headed for home as work was not far off. As Kate's eyes were drooping a gentle knock came to her door. Aine entered and they chatted to gone five in the morning. She had a wonderful night and Stefan had given her a beautiful bunch of yellow roses with a single red one in the middle. Aine had never received this kind of attention from a man; she was quite stunned at his manners and respect for her as a woman. Kate told her to

keep hold of him he was a good man and they can be hard
to find. He had asked her out the following Friday night
again to go to maybe a film or for a drink, she accepted!
They parted and went to bed.

Jack Barry was back with a vengeance and worked the
seven days non stop right through till the first week in
April when he made for home to Bere Island with a shot
of the Queen's pound notes. The morning he called into
the office for his last pay packet and his cards a call came
through to the site office. It was Mary on the phone from
the post office in Castletownbere. She had bad news for
him. She said "Jack your father passed away last night in
his sleep you better come home". The word went around
the office fast and the lads down the site got wind of it
in the canteen. Over 580 men chipped in a pound a man
that morning at breakfast and Jack was handed it as he
left the site with the foreman in his car for the trip to his
kip for the clobber and then on to Paddington Station.
Every Irishman's heart ached for him there that morning
at the loss of his boss at home. They all knew that news
could come their way at anytime as well. Jack worked
a hard two years and saved almost every penny he had
made, he never missed the post on a Saturday morning
sending home a few bob to keep his family afloat abroad
on the Island, never once missed mass no matter how
flattened he was from the night before either from work
or the occasional scoop of porter. This man was indeed
sculptured in heaven and sent down to do the Lord's
work on earth. He was inoffensive, and by Christ was
he polite for an Irish builder. He hardly ever took the
Lord's name or mentioned the Blessed Virgin outside of
a prayer. He was loyal to Mary and the kids and never

147

left a gaze upon another woman while he was away from his wife. An agonising two years of hard work, and total slavery to the point he took the name "The Slave" with him, from site to site and now this was his reward. He was now travelling home but would never see his father's eyes glance in his direction ever again. That day while feeding on a wipe of stew, spuds and bread Tom and Mick recalled meeting him in Mallow two years ago as they all headed for the cattle boat that night. Do you remember Tom Mick said "the strong Cork accent he had and when he said "like" we all knew for sure where he was from". They laughed with a pang of sadness knowing most likely they had seen the last of Jack Barry. In a word he was the salt of the earth.

Mick was the bearer of bad news that night as he told Kate what had happened she had said her goodbye to him a few nights ago but was so saddened to have heard the news of his father. That night they chatted over a few drinks and rekindled their conversation at Christmas about planning their life in Galway. Kate reminded Mick about trying to get back home and settle down before something may happen to Paddy or Madge. This is no life for the Irish over here she said as she held his hand tight thinking of the loss of her mother the week they both had met. The heartache and the distant loss of a parent at home was a cross every Paddy carried upon his broad back and if he did not loose them he always had the worry of doing, so often in the dead of the night. So often the pain came in a five day old letter when their loved one was already cold and wet in the ground.

The following weekend they started the preparations for their wedding in earnest and getting out the invitations. Aine, Peggie and Kate went off to purchase her wedding dress that she had put her eye on, and paid a deposit on also a few weeks back. It was figure hugging in every respect and adorned her beauty beyond belief. Peggie stood her the shoes and Aine got her garter, underwear and her bag. Mick, John and the children all met up that Saturday at the "Black Cap" and John handed over the usual, discretely to Kate. This week there was a second envelope and John took Kate into the usual corner they frequented. He took her hand and said to her "Kate my sister this is what father and mother would have wanted it is our family tradition that they would pay for their daughter's wedding on their behalf I want you to have this money". Her wedding had been booked by John at the The George Hotel in the square in Pangbourne outside Reading. She and Mick had planned to marry in "St. James's Catholic Church at Forbury Gardens on the 12th, of June. 1954. John handed his sister five hundred pounds that afternoon also towards your honeymoon. Kate and Mick planned to go home for the honeymoon to Ireland and tour the west coast in a rented car stopping off in both Adare and Ballinahowen for a few days in each place. Kate's eyes welled up with tears at the though of her brother's gesture. I have only one request of you he said "that is to give you away on your wedding day". She spat on her hand like the day they struck the deal for the stuff for the hotel, and said "That is a done deal John Collins". He had turned her life around financially and had sent a lot of pounds her way since they first met a little over a year ago. They were all earning well in London from their

TIMOTHY C.J. MURPHY

acquaintance of one another. The under table envelopes
lined many a Paddies pocket and many a girleen's fist also,
those years in London. All one had to be was shrewd and
cunning in true west of Ireland style. It was a case of "Dun
do bheal". (shut your mouth).

Stefan was of great assistance to Kate those weeks and
largely did her work and his at the hotel to allow her the
scope to arrange all she had to. Joe was to be best man to
Mick and Tom groomsman, Julie Fitzmaurice was Kate's
chief bridesmaid and Peggie was her other bridesmaid
or matron of honour. John put Peggie in touch with
two Irish girls down the market who took care of all the
flowers so that was all taken care of also on the cheap,
but yet, they were the best at their job in London. Aine,
who by now had been on several dates with Stefan invited
him to accompany her to her brother's wedding. He was
looking forward to this Irish wedding as he had heard that
they were much like Polish weddings also. His friends
who escaped to England with him after the war were also
invited with their girlfriends. It sure had the makings of
one hell of a "knees up". The twins, Niamh and Eilish,
who were now sixteen, were coming over from Ireland
with Joe and Mary. Paddy and Madge were not feeling
to up to the journey Mick and Kate were told. Niamh and
Eilish were all chat in their letters to Aine these days asking
her so many questions about London and this handsome
Polish man she was courting. Aine remained tight lipped
of course.

The list of guests numbered almost two hundred and they
were some mixed bag of hoors. The music for the wedding
was going to be traditional of course with six from Galway

near Kinvara playing the Uilleann pipes, Bodhrain, 2 fiddles, a tin whistle and a melodeon, or as some called it a mologen! Kate got cold shivers down her spine the weeks leading up to the wedding as the acceptances came back. It looked like every warrior in London would be there. There were nights she though to herself that maybe she should have put in a note with the invitation, to tell the guests that no saws, trowels, or screwdrivers were being allowed at the wedding. She nearly fell in a faint when she heard that The Bone and Drezna were coming also, and that they would be coming in the blue van with about sixteen others. Mick seemed to think that the entire matter was a huge joke and kept saying to Kate "Sure they are only out for the craic", and he'd walk off in his usual cool frame of mind. The troop from Connemara arrived on the Friday about dinner time and all got settled into The George Hotel and kept it dead quiet that Paddy and Madge had also come. It was their surprise for Mick and Aine.

Saturday morning the 12th of June 1954 was a memorable morning the wedding was on at 12 noon at St James's Church in Reading. Mick, Joe and Tom arrived at quarter past eleven met the priest and the fella taking the pictures. Aine was there as she was going to play the "Immigrants Lament" on the tin whistle after the organist played "Here comes the Bride" and before the Mass started. Mick, Joe and Tom sat at the top seat as the guests arrived. At twenty to twelve Mick got a tap on the shoulder and he looked around. There, sat his mother and father smiling at him for coding him about coming to the wedding. His father greeted him saying "Conas a ta tu mo bhuachaill" Oh! m'Aithir ta athas an domhain orm. Paddy and Madge

151

sat proudly thinking of all their son had achieved since leaving home just a short two years ago. He was marrying a fine girl who was a rock of sense and who would make him a good wife. Since she had first come to Ballinahowen she had graced the Joyce family with her beauty, manners, kindness and generosity. In a word Madge thought she would make her son a flawless woman for life and she was Irish and a Catholic. Suddenly as ten minutes past twelve struck there was a fuss at the back of the church Kate and the bridesmaids had arrived and were getting organised. Mick's heart started to thump, he felt a shiver, his head spun once maybe twice, here he was at twenty one marrying the goddess of his thoughts, the Lady of his dreams. As John walked up the aisle with his kid sister he thought of the day he married his Peggie, he thought that it was his Da that should be doing this, and he knew deep down that he could not see a finer young man marry his only sister. As Kate looked at Mick and he at her, in both their minds St. James's emptied and they saw no one else only each other and God before them. Mick Joyce took his raven haired beauty to the kneeler and went on his knees with his soul mate. There were loud cheers, wolf whistles, a few uncouth roars from the back as they lads cheered on Mick. The rest clapped for Kate as her cheeks went a gentle shade of rose pink. Aine then played the "Immigrant's Lament" on the tin whistle. As the mass progressed The Bone and Drezna sat stary eyed down at the back she taking swigs from a vodka bottle and he knocking back a half bottle of Paddy. There were the odd few bursts of human gas from the back and everyone thought it was The Bone but those close by knew it was Drezna without a doubt. The vows were taken and the sermon said all in the Queen's English which made no sense to Paddy Joyce as he was still Irish to the core. He was wondering if they were getting married at all, but Madge who had the coupla focail sasanagh (The Few English Words) assured him it was going to plan. As they walked down the aisle after they signed all they had to, they looked the picture of happiness, a happiness that would last well into their old age and would bless them with many graces as the years went by. As they headed for the door and out into life their eyes fell upon the wildest bunch of men, hard to the core, and built of nothing short of tool steel cheer them on and shake their hands.

John spared no expense at the wedding but as the staff saw the crowd that arrived they became worried and concerned as this was not going to be any ordinary wedding. Some were in jerseys and pants, some in suits, but none with the shirts closed and few ties were in evidence. The table where the sherry and whiskey reception was nearly got knocked over twice as there was a scramble for the free whiskey. When the two hundred glassed were floored one of the managers asked John should he pour another round. John replied you better because if they hear you have the drink and won't give it out you could be in mortal danger. John told him just keep filling the glasses boy bawn and I will pay for it. The meal was eaten by some, devoured by a few more and inhaled by most from the west. The British Queen spuds were just surfacing from the ground and were a bit small. Most of the lads ate between fifteen and thirty of these bloody marbles, skins and all just like at home. At one point on of the waitresses came over to The Bones table with a silver dish of spuds only to have it pulled from her hands and spilled out on the white starched tablecloth. She was handed it back and told by The Bone "here you are girleen go off and fill that saucepan again please". The Poles were hardy types also who had come through the war as young lads a had been hungry many a cold night on the plains and mountains of Europe but no matter how hungry they had ever been they never ate like the Paddies did that day. Farting was the norm and no one took any notice of it, burping was more like a symphony with no other instrument on the go other than the obo. Every table in the hall was laced with such an array of alcohol that it was a wonder how the table legs could hold it all up. The speeches went on for over an hour and all the usual things were said. Paddy Joyce welcomed Kate Joyce into their tribe and it was all translated by his son Mick as he held his strong arm around his father's shoulders. There was great pride in the hall that day, to hear Paddy Joyce deliver a lash of a speech totally in the native tongue. The cake was cut and the bride and groom took to the floor for the first dance. It was a reel and by God they both know how to dance. Aine took out Stefan and tried to teach him how to do a "Siege of Ennis". He tried and eventually mastered it nearly breaking his two legs on several occasions. Before the night was out his friends were all Irish dancing with the greatest of ease. They kept telling everyone that it was a waste of time trying to do Irish dance while sober, you have to be drunk to dance like this. It was plain to see for Paddy and Madge Joyce that they could be soon going to another wedding as Aine and Stefan could not keep their eyes of one another that night. Well at least Paddy said to his good woman "we won't have to travel to the next one". That will be in Ballinahowen for sure he said as they two went off out for the next jig. The bar was drank dry by half twelve and a lorry of drink had to be delivered to the back of the hotel. At half two when all was in full swing again, a wipe of sandwiches sausage, and crubeens were brought out on trays. It was obvious that the hotel staff and the English guests were disgusted at the sight of the Irish and Russians eating pigs feet, but they were ordered by John and that was that. They sucked bones and the knuckles of the pig's trotters which were spat out and disregarded all over the floor and tables. The trays were cleaned while some people looked around them. Fellas filled their pocket with sausages and the crubes were carried around in their hands for fear they be whipped. The next eight trays that were brought out by four girls were knocked out of their hands as they were charged by the crowd, and two were themselves knocked to the ground also. The food was gathered off the ground and consumed before the people were standing again. It was nothing short of a free for all. The four waitresses ran in terror for the safety of the kitchen, while the Celtic feast continued. Mick and Kate Joyce danced till after three in the morning and then made a bolt for their marriage bed, a grand eighteenth century oak four poster in an undisclosed and very private part of The George Hotel. Many of the guests drank till lunch time that Sunday, more slept under tables in the hall, more across seats clasping their women for their dear lives. The music played until a quarter past seven that morning at which time Mike Doran from Kinvara ran clean out of wind in the Uilleann Pipes due to the fact that his elbow had seized up in something that could only be described as an ancient Celtic moan from Cucullain's hound. Aine as a closing piece played the "Immigrant's Lament" once more on her tin whistle. As she finished she passed out in Stefan's arms and they fell fast asleep across a yellow damask covered sofa. At three O'clock that afternoon the newly weds headed off for the boat and home to Ireland where they rented a car and set out on the first few weeks of their life together. The guests turned back into the bar and drank it dry a second time that weekend, and finished all the remaining food that the hotel could serve them. They all wandered back to the city that evening in dribs and drabs to get ready for another week in the trenches lined with British pound notes.

CHAPTER 12

⬦

THE TWO POLISH girls had started in the kitchen of the hotel on Stefan's recommendations. They were quiet, polite, and were still learning English. They were both twenty years old and good workers. Stefan helped them whenever he could with the language, but he was now focused on Aine and they were both starting to really enjoy their time together. He spoke with Aine's mother a little at the wedding and tried to communicate with her father also but it was difficult with the accent and language barrier.

The new lovers Kate and Mick had the time of their lives honeymooning in the Emerald Isle. The hills seemed greener through their eyes as did the sea bluer every time they felt its misty air on their faces. One call they had to make was to Bere Island to see their friend Jack Barry, they had a Mass Card for him for his father. They got lodgings in Castletownbere on a Friday afternoon and then headed out by boat to the stony strand where Jack had gone ashore so many times on his way home. They asked the boatman where the house was and he pointed them to the very house on the hill facing them. As they walked up the grassy boreen where Mary and Jack had courted, Kate and Mick felt so happy with its softness underfoot. It was God's own avenue shrouded by high bushes and trees full of summer bloom. As they neared the Barry homestead Kate and Mick saw an elderly lady in the haggard beside the house with a few children. Kate excused herself and asked was this the Barry household to which she was told "yes it is". Mick and Kate introduced themselves and asked for Jack. The lady said she was Jack's mother and invited them up to the house to meet Mary Jack's wife. She also told them that Jack was gone into Castletownbere to order some cement and timber and that he'd be back in around four o'clock. Kate and Mick shook hands with Mrs Barry as they arrived at the door with her. They were met by Mary who also introduced herself as Jack's wife. Mick and Kate both offered their condolences to both of them for their recent loss of Jack's father. Kate handed Jack's mother a mass card for her husband. Mary said to them that Jack had a kind of a feeling they may turn up while on the honeymoon so he was half expecting ye to maybe call. They all smiled as Kate said and why not sure and we almost passing the door. They heard Jack open the squeaky gate into the farmyard and as he did he shouted out "come out here Mick Joyce you Connemara rogue for sneaking up on me like this. I knew ye'd never pass the door without calling, I was talking to the boatman on the way back and he said you two were on the island and had asked for the house". They met at the front door where two massive right hands clasped each others. Jack then looked beyond Mick and said do I get to kiss the new bride as he approached Kate. "How are you Jack" she said. Mary then said you will have supper with us and stay the night. Kate said we'll sample your brown bread alright but we got lodgings in town before we came over. Jack and Mary said don't worry about that you are staying here tonight and we will get the boatman to bring out your bags later. Kate and Mick spent two of the best days of their honeymoon on the Island with the Barry family and were sad to leave when they went north for Adare. The two men went fishing together which was part of their nature and ate the catch around a family table that evening. They women chatted about the things women talk about like the wicked wild wedding in Reading and the honeymoon so far. The bond of the Irish who worked in London together was immeasurable their doors were always open to one another and there was always a spare bed to lie upon, and no one was ever turned away without a bite of food either. Something in Mick and Kate that day told them it might be a long time, if ever, before they would see their friend Jack again. On they went to Adare stopping in Killarney for a pair of days to see the scenery they all talked about. Kate and Mick made a vow that day that the quicker they could get out of old blighty the better but Mick said we must make a few more bob yet then I will take my girl back home. By the time they reached Ballinahowen Paddy, Madge and the family were all back home. The twins were off school for the summer and had got jobs. Kate had always felt at home in Ballinahowen but this time she felt different, Madge took her for a long walk one day while Paddy, Joe and Mick spent the day in the bog footing the turf. They talked about everything from women to men about life and in particular about life in Galway. She told her that life west of the Shannon was not easy as a wife and farming in particular was a long tough life. Madge said to Kate that day that if ye come

159

back make sure my girl that you have plenty of greenbacks before you return. Kate took her arm and assured her that they had a plan and a good one and they would be home in a few years. The newly weds spent their last two days in Dublin then drove south trough Co. Wicklow, the garden of Ireland, down for Rosslare and boarded the good old St David once more.

Mr and Mrs Joyce were back at work on Monday the 28th of June and Mick moved in with Kate in her apartment at the hotel. Mick put a down payment on two more houses next to the one he had that July and rented them out from top to bottom. He now had three in a row and was doing pretty well ploughing all the rent straight into paying back what he owed on them. Mick was raking in the money now and still left for the Isle of Grain every morning at a quarter past six. The coach trip down with Tom, Bertie, and Pa was always a pure howl of laughter, hearing the exploits of the single men as they wandered from woman to woman, pint to pint, and scam to scam, making the very best of every day they lived and sometimes existed on the streets of London. One morning in late July they arrived in for the nosh up to the canteen and downed a feed of rashers a pair of sausages and a wipe of black pudding and eggs as the Bone's army of helpers lined them out on their plates. In line with their agreement it was all free of course. The lads noticed the English bookie going from table to table taking bets and paying out on more. The two Cork Bookies arrived in and made for him in a slow calculated manner. They meant business as they frowned and closed their fists. Everyone knew there was trouble brewing. Just as one of the Cork lads was drawing on "Liverpool" The Bone and one of his mates stepped in and said take this out side lads, I don't want the canteen wrecked. As the three of them walked for the back door another fella stood up with his tool bag and walked out after Liverpool. He was a chippie called "Dublin". When the four landed outside Dublin put up his hand and said he was owed three hundred and ten pounds by this lad, when I get paid he is yours boys, speaking to the two Cork lads. Dublin approached Liverpool and asked him for his winnings. Liverpool told him that he never got his bet on. Dublin said to him in his strong north side accent. "Hey man that is your bleeden problem I want me money now you fucken runner". He was told again I didn't get your fucken bet on Paddy and I haven't got your three hundred notes. With speed of an ancient Celtic warrior under the command of the "Red Branch Knights" Dublin whipped our his hand saw and gave it to Liverpool down the left side of his face ripping him open from his ear to his chin. Dublin then said "my money now or I will do the other cheek as he whipped the saw in front of his face. Liverpool paid over the winnings in full and ran like a dying rat with a rag up to his face. He was never seen amongst the Irish community again. The building sites could be wild places and there was not a whole lot of regard for the rule of law but if something was right it stayed right and if it was wrong it had to be straightened.

The All Irelands and September crept up again fairly quickly and the Cork bookies had an open door to do business again, and when they lost a bet the always paid up it was a case of honour and that was the Irish way. In the Hurling All Ireland Christy Ring again led Cork to victory again, 1-09 to 1-06 over Wexford. The Cork bookies made a huge killing out of the match that year and they started to put they eyes on some property up in Cricklewood. Meath beat Kerry that year in the football 1-13 to 1-07 and most of the money went on Meath so the bookies lost a good few bob on that match. Tom, Bertie and Pa spent Sunday evening drowning their sorrows after the match. In late September, Mick Joyce, Tom, Pa and Bertie went on piece work like the Twelve Apostles did on the site. The graft was hard but the money was good and Mick Joyce encouraged the lads to come with him on this number. Mick and Kate were going home again this Christmas again to Ballinahowen, and the second trip that year was digging into their savings somewhat. They slaved like dogs that October and November working every hour they could and stacked up the greenbacks. Mick got on the coach one morning and he in stitches. Tom, Bertie and Pa were half cocked from the Sunday night porter session when Mick started to tell them about a Gallagher fella from Mayo who was staying in one of his houses. He told the lads that Gallagher came home the previous Friday night and put his stinking rubber boots under the bed and as usual hung his sock up in front of his open bedroom window. That evening while he was out on the beer the wind rose and drove the stench of socks all over the house. A few of the other Mayo lads came home late about one in the morning and found his socks first and burned them in the sink. They then made for the rubber boots and they all pissed and defecated into the boots. They were put back in under the bed. The following morning Gallagher and the other lads were getting up for work. Gallagher donned a new pair of socks and pulled out the boots from under his bed and drove one of his legs deep into the first rubber boot. The shit and piss hit the ceiling with a squirt, as it all went up like an Icelandic geyser bursting out each side of Gallagher's fresh new socks. When he realised what happened and seeing a certain amount of humour in the lads joke he jumped up and went into their room and flung the other boot full of sewage all over the boys as they were getting out of their beds. The two rooms were like an underground London brick sewer. Patsy Gallagher went back to his bedroom got the boots and rinsed them out got more socks and pulled on the boots and headed off out to work. He was put tidying up that day on the site on his own and The Bone asked him to grub on a plank outside the canteen for fear he'd empty the place. He was known from there till Christmas as the toilet and when everyone would pass him anywhere they would catch their nose.

As December was hatched that year the drive was on and everyone worked the full seven days to make the money for the Christmas be it in England, Ireland or maybe even a place the Paddy never knew where he was. Mick's three housed were doing well and he had his eye on the next two up from there where two old spinsters lived. He and Kate used to look in on one of them some evenings and some weekends as she was a darling. Mick often told Kate she reminded him of his aunt west in Boston. On the run up to Christmas week Tom, Bertie, Mick and the Twelve Apostles were called into the site office and asked to go on piece work doing the concreting on a huge gas tank, one of the first to be done on the site. Pa, Dublin and four other chippies from Cork were brought on side to do the shuttering when the roof had to be done. It had a huge circular concrete base with a deep foundation of hardcore and 30 nt aggregate mix. The side was all welded circular metal panels and the roof was cased for another 30 nt aggregate mix again. If it was completed within a fixed time they picked up a bonus. The first one was important as it was to be a template for the rest, all of which they wanted to start early in January weather permitting. They got stuck in on a Tuesday morning and downed the four inch hardcore and blinded it off with a mixture of two and one inch chips afterwards. They poured the concrete the following morning, at eight o'clock, after an early wipe of breakfast from The Bone. Their backs bent with their sweat dripping of every part of their bodies the crew spread the concrete floating it as they went before the next barrow lined up behind their back. They waved their timber levels in the watery winter sun as they peered through a foggy sky laced with the usual smog as they made sure every inch was levelled dead on to the steel pegs that they had driven for guidance. As the winter darkness started to fall they floated the last seven or eight yards and clocked off. The Thursday morning the steel fitters moved in and started to erect the cage and metal panels to it. They worked all weekend and had it ready for Sunday morning. Pa, Dublin and the Cork chippies moved in and had the lot cased for midnight Sunday Night. The lads never stopped for the dinner that day only worked straight through on a diet of fags and coffee to keep them awake and focused. The concrete was ordered for early the next morning and the got the pumps going to put on the pointed roof on the tank. They slaved all day as the snow fell on their back with nothing but vests to cover the leather skins. They all swore and fucked all day trying to get the job done. The guys on the pumps were the hoors to blame and by God they got the blame. Four, five, six, seven, and eight came as they floated the last three yards from two nine by threes nailed together and suspended up in the snowy sky which had now become a blizzard, by one of the site

cranes. The clocked off at half eight. The numb workers
negotiated triple time for the days work, they all got the
dinner on the bosses say so and they all collected on the
bonus finishing well before the eight o'clock deadline the
following morning. The whole team took the following
day off and downed brandy and hot whiskey all day long
to get the blood moving in their veins again and to make
sure they would be able to stand for the Christmas. They
slaved from there till the 23rd of December when the site
shut down for the season. The fingers were coarse from
concrete, splinters filled the chippies hands and the lads in
the trenches could feel the pick and shovel in their hands
everywhere they went that Christmas, be it in Blighty or
at home in the Auld Sod.

Mr and Mrs Mick Joyce arrived in Ballinahowen late
Christmas Eve after stopping in Galway. They rented
a car from a friend of Joe's in the city and headed west
down the road to Spidal as the winter darkness enveloped
the black Ford Prefect the dim yellow lights of the car
picked yard after yard to the west. They turned in the
boreen as the Paddy's grandfather clock in the kitchen
struck eight o'clock. Mick and Kate were glad to have
reached home as the Atlantic fog had come ashore this
past half hour and driving had become a pure torture on
the twin pane windscreen of Henry Ford's dream car.
The twins encircled Kate and wanted to hear all the news
from London. Mick hugged his ma and shook his father's
right hand with its sturdy grasp. He slipped a wad into his
hand and winked and put his finger to his lips indicating
to him to keep it quiet. Mick brought in the bags from the
car and closed the front door on the haunting immigrant
fog as it tried to follow them into the kitchen. The family

gathered around the table as Mick and Kate cleared a fine plate of the finest Irish stew west of the Shannon. The big news was that Mary, Joes wife, was pregnant this last three month and she was doing well. Paddy said that the turf sold well that year and that there was a great crop of golden wonder spuds. It had been a great year also for the fishing and there had been a lot of catches that had laden down the curraghs many an eve on the way east to the pier. Joe and Mary called up just before ten and they all sat around the dimly lit kitchen, lit with the brass oil lamp that Madge had been passed down to her from her mother. The women of the house enjoyed a nice hot pot of tea while the three men downed a few drops of the local holy water brew. At half eleven they closed the front door and walked the half mile to the village and to Midnight Mass. The clatter of their shoes, and studded hobnailed boots on the road killed the chatter of the high pitched women's voices and the slurred ones of the three warriors that followed up the rear. The fog was thick and there was a ghost at every twist on the road as Paddy lifted his hat whenever he met one. The church was cold and damp with the midnight mist as it drifted in the twin double oak doors. It was not just going to mass in those days that meant something but it was the penance one offered up on the way to and from mass also in the winter cold.

Christmas morning in Ballinahowen was as usual a busy morning for the women getting the Christmas dinner ready. The turkey was in the black cast range in the kitchen from early morning packed with Madge's own home made stuffing laced with herbs from the side of the hill behind the haggard. By mid morning he had a tan worthy of two good days in the bog or a day in a curragh west of the Islands.

The twins made the home made vegetable soup while Kate and Madge got the Christmas Puddings ready as Mick and his father sat outside the door on two timber butter boxes peeling the golden wonders and the vegetables. The sprouts were small that year but the carrots were nearly all nine inches long. The dinner that day was a feed and a half and Joe and Mary joined them all for the grub too. Mary definitely ate for two that day, but she always had a good apatite anyway. They all sat around after the dinner and stared momentarily into a fine fire of standing turf in the heart in the parlour until little by little sleep overcame most of the elders. Mick, Joe, and their two good wives went across the hill and up the cliff tops for a long walk while enjoying a soft watery sun along with a soft winter cool, but fresh, breeze on their faces. Kate often noticed the distant look in her husband's eyes that afternoon as he stared west word to the wide open Atlantic. The following morning Paddy took his two sons fishing where they all bonded in the new curragh that had been built that summer by Joe. They caught a nice assortment of fish that day, hauled a few lobster pots with a few nice ones in them, but the catch of the day was two fine salmon well over twelve pounds in weight. As Mick and Kate once again hoisted their sails for the Queens country Mick gave his mother a hug and slipped a shot of notes into her apron pocket. As he shook his father's hand he showed him the famous fiver and said to him, "I still have it Da".

John and Peggie Collins spent Christmas in London with the family as John had a lot of paperwork to catch up on. Stefan and Aine spent the Christmas in London as they did not want to be apart and Stefan had to work when Kate was in Ireland. John and Peggie Collins invited them up home on Christmas day and they both had a wonderful time with the family. Tom, Pa and Bertie spent another Christmas with Cait and the husband and did a full rerun on the last year they spent with them, drinking the house dry, eating it clean and going out the day after and ordering a van load of stuff again from The Bone who was, as usual, spending the Christmas with his eastern European lover shacked up in some free house leaking water from the roof and vodka and Guinness from their bodies.

Slate Lath and Purlin arrived back in London that Christmas and had the dinner in a homeless shelter setup by the Salvation Army. They made a fine pair of soldiers as they ploughed their way through a half acre of vegetables and a yard or two of well cooked turkey. They had been following all piece work up in the midlands and the north of England making a ton of the Queen's greenbacks and drinking them as fast. Purlin and Slate Lath spent the rest of Christmas shacked up with the Twelve Apostles and their four Jewish tailors in their mansion up near Regents Park. It was rough and ready but they were in out of the cold and the beds were warm but it turned out to be a great craic and a laugh with the hierarchy.

CHAPTER 13

———— ∞ ————

WHEN THEY ALL were back in London the first week in January the word was out about the Twelve Apostles. They were after buying a whole street between them that had been partially levelled during the blitz. It had remained blocked off with a brick wall across the two ends of the road leading to it. It was in some state. Three large bombs had detonated one on the roadway, one in a back garden which didn't do much damage but the third one was a direct hit and almost fully demolished three houses. The street had been taken over by the Government who had re housed the survivors elsewhere in a new development. London was still reeling from Hitler's war machine but ten years on and 1955 saw some new changes and plans, as things began to improve.

Mick called over one Friday night to collect his rent with Kate, who called to see Dora one of the ladies living next to their houses only to find her a little upset. She told Kate that she was going into a home for aged ladies the following week and she would be selling her house to pay for her keep. She didn't like leaving her home but she was glad to have company where she was going as well. Like a bolt out of the blue she asked Kate if her husband would be interested in buying her house. She told her she didn't know but that he'd be in to see her in a few minutes and she could mention it to him. Kate opened the door when Mick called and she whispered about the offer Dora had made to her so he was forewarned. As they walked in the hallway to the living room she said "Tell her we will call back tomorrow before we meet John in the Black Cap". They talked it over that night and Kate decided to use some of the money she had made with John to pay cash for the place, although it was a place that needed a lot of work, especially up stairs where nobody had lived in years. Mick told her he'd get the place in shape in no time at all. She signed on the dotted line later that week and the deal was done with Dora. Before St Patrick's Day the other old lady passed away next door and her son in Canada put her place up for sale also. Kate bought that also but had to get a small loan from her brother John which he agreed to keep her weekly profits on the hotel produce until the end of September. Kate and Mick were doing well now and had five houses in a row and the end of 1955 would see the mortgages paid in full on them all. Kate and Mick worked hard that year making what they could and living on scraps to keep their own show on the road.

The Twelve Apostles jacked in the Isle of Grain and looked for their cards the middle of January. They tore down a gateway through one of the brick walls leading to their new site. Mixers and equipment appeared out of the blue as they started to clear the street. Every brick and block was chipped and cleaned down stacked to be reused and the old mortar discarded to one side for trunking, where needed. They picked 10 houses that had only minor damage and got them up for rent my the 1st of April that year. They worked like never before and hired Patsy Gallagher from Mayo to put the nosh together for them every day. Patsy was a hard wiry type but had never seen men work or eat like them. They were bordering on the inhuman. All day Irish songs rang out and there was rarely a word of the Queen's English spoken on the site only when a delivery man came with materials of one type or another. Patsy who had some Irish soon picked up the Connemara Irish and knew every word that had to be used on a building site by the commencement of summer. Patsy rarely saw a day off with the way the lads slaved seven days a week but then they were a decent bunch and gave him a handsome wage each Friday. One weekend was taken off it was the one after St. Patrick's Day that fell on a Thursday. They worked that day finishing early for evening mass, and also the Friday but then they took the Saturday and Sunday off to wet the Shamrock, and by God did they have some piss up.

Patsy disappeared on Saturday and went off to a soccer match down in south London somewhere. Bertie and Tom went with him and before the match they went off to a Café Tom knew for a good mixed grill with a wipe of bread and butter and a good hot pot of tea. It was a fine feed, liver, onions and mushrooms graced with a basket of fresh chips. Patsy was sick from drink the night before and beads of moisture coated his wide western forehead with a shiny plaster of cold sweat. As they headed for the tube Tom said to Bertie, "I think he's fucked he'll never last the day". When it came to drink Patsy mixed the stuff

too much and got drunk and fucked up, way too fast. As
they got on the packed tube Tom and Bertie went to the
left and Patsy went right. They turned around and took
hold of a leather handle hanging from above their head to
steady themselves. The next thing they knew as the doors
closed was that patsy left out a rasper of wind that put
people running from where he was as fast as they could.
It was then Tom and Bertie saw him take hold of his belly
and go white in the face. His loose light coloured brown
corduroy pants then took another salvo, but that went
wrong and a flood hit his underpants as he grabbed his
ass in a frantic bid to keep the gush at bay but alas it was
futile. That entire half of the carriage then relocated to the
other end. It was like the flight of the Jews into Egypt in
the Bible, panic had set in. The Paddy stood there looking
on as the seat of his light coloured brown corduroy pants
started to steadily go a darker shade of brown. The second
the train stopped there was a rapid rush for the door and
people got out fast and went into other carriages. Tom
and Bertie were weak with the laughing knowing what
had happened but they still had to wait for the next stop.
Other people who were about the join the last three of
them in the carriage changed their minds and went to
another having been hit with a strong waft at the door.
When they reached their stop the three of them made out
for the fresh air as fast as they could, running up the steps
out of the sewer. Bertie and Tom were sent off to get a
trousers and jocks for poor auld Patsy and soon had him
back in shape. He went into a toilet in a pub and stripped
and had a good wash with the water out of a metal cast
cistern. He washed out the pants in a sink, gave it a good
squeeze and put it into a bag and left. After the match
they headed back up to the Black Cap and to the safety of

their own kind. Mum was the word and Bertie and Tom kept the story of the day's events private. The lads rarely ratted on one another when misfortune followed them, it was just they way they were noble, decent and loyal to one another. Life in London with the Irish that time was sometimes unbelievable, sometime humorous but most of all, these kind of things happened, and quite often, at times. Whether they were sad or just lonely for home it didn't really matter they lived just as they wanted to in that moment in time.

Aine and Stefan celebrated St. Partick's Day that year together. They were courting now a little over the year and were getting very serious indeed. All eyes were on them to see if the mild mannered and quite Stefan would pop the question to Aine. News broke that early April when the Polish Embassy had made contact with him one morning at the hotel while working. The embassy informed Stefan that an organisation in Germany had located two ladies that may be his mother, and the other his sister. They were all living in a forest with some Jewish people from early 1944 to early 1945. If it was them they are now living near Prague in Czechoslovakia. The communist regime there were not being too helpful but we have people working there with the British who think they have located the two of them living in a village near Prague". Stefan's heart was pounding so loud that he thought he would get a heart attack. As soon as they had further information they would be in touch as for now they had to thread cautiously. As Stefan, and Aine walked up the street they were shocked stunned and shaking somewhat. Aine asked Stefan was he alright; he was in deep thought and was quite emotional. They walked for 20 minutes around Hyde Park and Aine did not speak but just wanted to be with him. The first thing he said was "Aine I have to go and find my mother and sister". Aine responded saying to him let the embassy deal with the matter fearing he may get hurt or that she may never see him again. The people from the embassy will be watching me in England because they will expect me to go to Europe. We must both leave for Ireland as soon as we can arrange some time off from work and I will go to Czechoslovakia from Ireland. Aine tried to protest but he put his hand up and said "Aine I have to do this for my mother and sister I last saw them marched off by the Germans in 1940 when I was only 9 years old". "I hid in the forest in Poland for three months alone and scared". They both left for Ireland within 24 hours and stopped in Dublin overnight. The following day Stefan arranged to leave Dublin that night at midnight for Rotterdam. He took Aine to lunch and handed her a letter with his will attached to it. He said "If I am not back in London by Christmas all I have is yours". He then placed a beautiful diamond cluster on her ring finger on her right hand saying when I get back you can put that on your left hand if you want me as your husband. Her eyes melted in her own cluster of tears as she held his hand and said "My Love I will wait for you, just make sure you return soon and may God and the Blessed Virgin guide your every move". Stay with your parents till at least July so I can get inside Czechoslovakia he asked Aine. She made her way to Galway by train that night and Joe collected her at the railway station. As they rounded the bend and down the boreen at Ballinahowen, Stefan sailed out from the north wall at Dublin port and south for Rotterdam working on a merchant ship.

That summer the construction on the street the Twelve Apostles bought was progressing well and all during the summer months they only slept on site about five hours a night when it was dark. The mixer ran for up to eighteen hours a day as yard after yard of concrete was laid out as the footpaths stretched farther up the street day by day. Lorries of lumber, steel, sand, gravel and cement arrived every Monday morning as did Patsy Gallagher with the food to keep the lads fed. The breakfast was fired up on the shovels yet again, the stew came out of the bucket and the bread was buttered on a sheet of five eight ply used as their table which got hosed down each night before they bedded down till dawn in half built houses with no windows, but this time it was their own. By mid August they had 16 houses rented and the greenbacks were starting to roll in. They were now beginning to earn more than they were spending each week. The sand was coming as a favour for a few turns that were done for a contractor. The steel was ordered and left at the site each week while they were at mass. No one saw who brought it but it was also for a favour done. Only one of the twelve knew where it was coming from. It was delivered each week by the Connemara Paddy that had been bladed by the black man that didn't like his Irish singing. He never forgot who stood up for him that night. He owed the lads and he was not a man to forget.

Meanwhile Tom, Pa, Bertie and Mick tore through trenches of clay shovel by shovel down in the Isle of Grain. The grub was still on the never, never with The Bone but every so often he would complain to the boys, but they always reminded him about his warm bath, saying that, they would all say it happened just a week ago. He would keep doling out the grub after that conversation and there would be no further moaning. He was thinking of another solution as he didn't like to be at the butt end of any scam. The baker that arrived with the big loves of brown soda bread every morning spent the weekend on the beer with the boys up in Kilburn, his drinking was legendary. He was a slip of a hoor but was often seen to down 24 pints in a night wipe his mouth with the sleeve of his donkey jacket and walk off home as straight as a dye. When it came to the women, that was where his weakness lay, lay being the optimum word. He was often found to be approached by a lady known as hairy Helena, known for her hairy upper lip and arms, some said she was Dutch. Paul the baker would drop his pants wherever he got the urge. He was not one for going home early, or small talk. One night down the West End all the lads were standing around when Helena approached Paul he gave her a few fags and a few notes. They went around a corner and in behind a van. Cries of passion and excitement melodiously shrieked through the midnight air as everyone said what a great combination an Irishman and a Dutch lady really were. While they were jeered on with cat calls and whistles two Bobbies appeared from the shadows and arrested Helena and Paul and gave them a night's lodgings before a Crown Court appearance the following morning. He was charged with nine charges and was got fined over £150 and got a month in the clink. When he got out he was known as the naked baker from then on. Helena was taken off the streets and deported after she got a good fine. That is what angered the boys from the Auld Sod most of all. The comfort of her hairy arms were now gone forever.

Aine was at home when Mary gave birth to a fine strong baby boy the 31st of May 1955 and he was christened Joseph Patrick after his father and grandfather. As Joe looked at his son that morning he wondered when he would be twenty one would there be a living for him in his native land or would there be nothing facing him only the boat to America or to England. There was the joy of birth in Ireland in those days but with it also came the agony of immigration that all too soon often followed.

Aine received a letter from Stefan the third week in July to say that he was staying in a place called Freyung on the German Czech' border and that he had been in twice over the frontier but had yet to see his mother and sister. He reminded her to keep sending the Irish post cards from home to Mick and Kate at the hotel as a cover. Aine had not forget she had penned one every ten days to a fortnight as her fiancé has requested, Each card was intercepted by the British foreign office en route to Mick and Kate which kept them very happy and thinking that they were running the entire show. They in turn kept the diplomats in the Polish Embassy at ease also. A letter Stefan also wrote and signed that had been given to Aine before he left Dublin was posted from Galway as agreed the first week in August to the Polish Embassy in London telling them that they were in Ireland on holiday and asking them if there was any news of his mother and sister yet. All the decoys were now in place as Stefan continued his quest. Aine decided to stay in Ballinahowen for now as she didn't wish to arouse suspicion by going back to London yet and besides her father Paddy who was a shrewd auld hoor said she'd be better off at home for now. As the summer waned in Ballinahowen and the evening shortened across the cliff tops and out to sea Aine heart was becoming a little despondent as she wondered where her man was, and if he was safe and had he found his mother and sister. She knew Stefan as her man in civilized London but knew nothing really of his past in Europe before they met. There was no talk of the All Ireland Hurling Final in the Joyce house or indeed the football either all thoughts in the house and in the rosary each evening were for Stefan and his family. Wednesday morning the 28th of September Aine went to the village for a few messages for her mother with Niamh and as they neared the post office the postman stopped and said "here you are Darling" as he handed Aine a wire from London. It was from Kate in the hotel and read **"Collect my sister, mother and brother at the station in Galway this evening off the eight o'clock train".** Aine sank to her knees she had a feeling what it meant, but for now she was living in hope. She rushed to the post office and sat on a bench outside the door and read the wire a few more times. She knew that Kate had no sister and that her mother was dead and if John was coming, it would be his first time in Ballinahowen. She went into the post mistress and asked her to put a call through to London to the Lancaster Gate Hotel. Three times she tried but could not get a connection. Being in Ballinahowen was no different from being in Australia when it came to phoning London. She made back for the house with the wire and asked Joe to take her to Galway after dinner. They didn't say a word to mother or father and Niamh and Eilish said they would keep an eye on them at home.

Aine stood on the platform with Joe but the train was late as eight came and went. At twenty to nine they could see its light down the track. Aine's heart started to beat hard in her chest, at the thought of what was the train was bringing. The usual blast of steam was let off as the train halted and the doors flung open. Aine started to run as Joe followed his sister down the platform. Through a strong fog of steam and western drizzle she saw a tall bearded man with his arm in a sling and two ladies in tweed winter coats helping him as he carried two small bags. It was his shape but was it her man. As she got close she stopped to look closer. It was not his walk or his physique, he was stooped and in pain, but he had the eyes of her fiancé. They hugged and kissed a dozen times as the two ladies looked on and smiled. Stefan had lost weight and she could tell he was weak. Joe took the two bags and put Stefan's arm around his neck to support him. The younger lady then spoke and said "I am Remka, sister of Stefan and this is my mother, I am sorry my English is not good". Aine took them both in her arms and hugged them as they both cried with relief. They knew they were now safe. Aine then said to Remka you are safe tell your mother we will take care of you. The road home that night was a long one as it was dark and wet and Joe had to drive slowly as Stefan was not well and had some injuries. Aine sat in the back of the car with Marja Stefan's mother and his sister Remka and held their hands all the way home to the Joyce household. As they turned into the Joyce yard Paddy came to the door as he was just about to turn into bed. He had stayed up late thinking that Aine was over in Joe and Mary's place. Madge was in bed chatting with the twins as they talked about the things that mothers and daughters do. When Paddy saw the car load of people he knew there was something up and called out for Madge and the girls. They all rushed down stairs he went straight to Joe and said "where is Aine" not seeing her in the back in the dark. As Joe stood out he said "It is Stefan, his mother and sister they are with us". As they walked through the door the twins put on the kettle and got some food ready. Sefan was pale and his jacket was wet up near the left hand shoulder. Marja and Remka were ok but thin and gaunt and were in good need of some food and rest. Stefan took Aine's hand and said thank your parents for me and passed out into Paddy's large chair that hugged the warm black range. They took him to Aine's bed and put him lying down. He had a wound to his shoulder from a bullet Remka told Aine. As soon as Madge saw it she sent Eilish on her bike for Nurse Mannion a mile up the road. The nurse dressed his wound and said it had been well taken care off but it needed to be washed and dressed. She put a poultice of hot bread on the wound and said she call again tomorrow. Stefan came round as the hot bread touched his wound he flinched and thanked the nurse. There was no sleep in the Joyce house that night. The Woychek family were fed and bedded and received the traditional "Cead Mile Failte" in Connemara that night. Joe took Eilish and Niamh up home to his place as space was tight. Aine sat up that night with Stefan caring for him and making sure he was comfortable. As he slept she thought of how nice he was with a fine black beard. His clothes were rough and torn and she thought it different as she had never seen him in anything but a suit before, never mind half naked in bed. As the dawn rose it plastered the eastern sky in a collage of colours. The cock crew and woke her out of a doze she was having on the chair next to the bed. Everyone slept late that morning and the cock crew many a time between dawn and midday. Madge woke first and when she came down to the kitchen Niamh and Eilish had a fine table of food prepared for the breakfast. They had a bowl of fresh boiled eggs piping hot on the table with a good half pound of home made butter laid out. A warm bowl of creamy porridge also bubbled slowly on the range. They had come down home early knowing there would be needed there that day. Two large cakes of brown soda bread were hot out of the range and left up turned on the cake rack to cool. Marja and Remka got up and helped in the kitchen Paddy went into to check on Stefan and woke up Aine who was asleep sitting on the armchair next to his bed. Her left hand was clasped to his and on her ring finger was her engagement ring sparkling in the sunlight as it shone through the bedroom window. Paddy was a man of few words as everyone knew. He helped up his daughter, his first pet and the apple of his eye and asked her was she alright after the night. As Stefan opened his eyes he went to sit up slowly and thanked Paddy for his hospitality only to be met with naught but An cupla focail gaeilge. It was a true case of east meeting west as Aine smiled while her father congratulated them both on their engagement. She translated for Stefan as he looked at her ring finger and saw she had put it on her left hand. It was her way of saying she would be his wife. While he slept she had become his Fiancée without he knowing it. As Paddy went to help Stefan up he ushered his daughter out of the room. Aine laughed at her father as she knew he didn't want her to see Stefan half naked yet. That was Paddy Joyce for you he was a man of modest sentiments. He got Stefan dressed and helped him down stairs and sat him on his own chair beside a good warm range in the kitchen. Paddy then had the pleasure of turning to Madge saying in his native tongue. Madge you better go over and congratulate Aine and Stefan on their engagement.

Straight away all the women in the kitchen surrounded the newly engaged couple kissing and hugging Aine and looking at her ring. Stefan shook all their hands as he sat there so very proud of the choice he had made for a wife. Remka also explained that she would soon have another daughter to her mother in Polish. He was waited on hand and foot by all the women Marja helped him with his breakfast as it began to emerge what had happened while they were escaping from Czechoslovakia. Stefan had been shot in the left shoulder and had been bitten and ripped by dogs. He killed the dogs and hid with Marja and Remka in the woods until they were safe, they made for the German frontier during the night and walked about 25 miles back to his flat in Freyung. There they tended to his wounds and took out the bullet with a knife and burned the wound closed. The Poles had learned how to survive the hard way and if something had to be done it was taken care of. They left the next day and travelled to France where they got a cargo boat to Dublin.

Aine Madge and the twins made their three guests feel welcome in Ballinahowen. They wanted for nothing. Mick knowing that Stefan and his mother and sister were by now in Galway wired £50 to Aine to help with their keep. Kate sent over clothes and some ladies stuff in a large brown paper parcel plastered with English stamps. Joe and Mary bought them two new winter coats and gave one he had to Stefan as he began to walk out a bit as his shoulder healed. To strengthen his arm Stefan helped his father in law to be, around the farm with fencing and with bagging the turf for sale. They hadn't a word between them but Stefan picked up some Irish and Paddy had the odd word of Polish also. Stefan's sister Remka struck up a good friendship with the twins and they took her dancing a few nights to the local hall. They thought her more English as time went on and she in turn began to teach her mother also. They all spent their time well while in Galway learning English and helping around the farm and house. Paddy never had a much help as he had that year and he was often hear to mutter in Irish also that his ears were ringing all day long from the constant chatter of all the women. As Stefan recovered well and started to build himself up with a few Guinness here and there and some good wholesome food he went to sea fishing with Joe and his fellow fishermen and became a dab hand at it. It reminded him of the times he went fishing with his father as a boy out on the Baltic Sea before he got shot during the invasion of their homeland in 1939. The long and the short of it was he was hardy, and never shied away from work, and if anything he revelled in it.

They all stayed put there till Christmas and as usual Mick and Kate arrived on Christmas Eve on the early train into Eyre Square, in Galway. Joe who was still keeping the twins in his place by night bought a new double bed and bedded down his newly married kid brother and his wife. Stefan and Aine's engagement was celebrated in true Connemara style that Christmas. Stefan put away bottle after bottle of the best poteen in Conemara that Christmas as Aine began to see a very new side to her Fiancé. She saw not only how homely he had integrated with her family but how his mother and sister had done so as well. Both families had been trust together in a time of strife and tribulation and it helped to cement a long lasting friendship.

Mick, Kate, Aine, Stefan, Marja, and Remka left for their return to London in late December in order to get Marja and Remka settled in with a job and accommodation in London. They were looking forward to their new life in the city and the opportunity to make a decent living. Kate had a Job fixed up for Marja as a chambermaid in the hotel the day after she arrived back and she got a job as a waitress for Remka in the Café where Mick and herself frequented. Stefan slotted back into his job as Kate's assistant and Mick donned his donkey jacket and brown corduroy trousers and joined the boys once again back down in the Isle of grain.

CHAPTER 14

———∞∞∞———

THE STORIES BACK on the building sites after Christmas
were no different from the last few years. The drink
flowed; the turkeys were devoured with fine wipes of ham
and stuffing made from home made recipes. Life went on
much the same for those that went home for Christmas they
were missing the Auld Sod, for most of January. Parents
at home were getting older and there was always news of
a funeral somewhere between Cork and Donegal. Some of
the lads that went home were not able to come back as they
were often needed at home when the father would pass
on. The antidote of true love was so often supplied from a
lady who was paid for her services and moved on again.
She left no cake of home made bread on the table when
she left nor did she wash Paddy's shirt that he so often just
picked off the floor and pulled it over his head and headed
for another day's slavery in the rain, and the sharp winds
that supplemented the biting winter cold that always hit
London each winter from across northern Europe. Their
time rebuilding the crown was often funny and filled with

laughs but so often the humour was short lived and only took them as far as the next wintry shower.

Kate and Mick received the deeds to their houses between the first week in January and the end of February. John's weekly handshake started to grease Kate's hand every Saturday once again in the "Black Cap". Cash was always the order of the day and by having it allowed the Paddy freedom of movement from job to job and shire to shire, it was their security in a very foreign land. Mick and Kate made a good living out of the houses also and never had a bed empty in any of their houses for more than a few days. They were also making good money from their jobs and were putting away a fair polackan every week. In four years together they were building their bridge back to Galway little by little.

St. Patrick's Day fell that year on the best day of the week for a good pissup, a Saturday. Mick and Kate had a job to do that morning before they met John, Peggie and the children at the "Black Cap". They had a few drinks there and then went off to the Greek that Mick knew where he was putting on a feed of bacon and cabbage and Irish stew that day. The place was packed with Irish when they arrived and stuck in the middle of them all was Bertie, Tom, Pa and Patsy Gallagher. The craic was a hundred percent and they ate their fill until they could eat no more. Kate took Mick's hand at the table and said to John and Peggie that they had found out that morning that she was expecting. John and Peggie congratulated them both and said well at last I will be an uncle. They all headed up to "The Brighton" pub and celebrated the good news. Peggie and Aine found a corner with the kids and had one hell of a fine chinwag. Young Katie who was now a very pleasant eight year old sat between her mother and her aunt absorbing every word that passed between them as she was starting to take on the Irish ways of a real auld woman. John and Mick stood across the way next to the bar counter toasting one another's good fortune. John had done very well indeed for himself since he got Kate's business and also the business from the Isle of Grain. They both talked about their aspirations for the future and when they might venture back home and try and make a start. John and Peggie were thinking of going back and opening a supermarket somewhere around county Limerick, as they were all the go in England and it was the up and coming kind of shop he felt. Mick said himself and Aine were thinking of heading back to Galway in a few years, but not to Ballinahowen, but to somewhere near the city where he could build a shop and petrol pumps and maybe buy a place nearby that they could turn into a small hotel. He also had a life long dream where he would like to open a few tourist shops where he could sell sods of turf to the yanks. They both laughed as they finished another pint of porter. They all headed home that night half groggy and boozed but there was Sunday to recover and as usual they would all meet in the dining room of the hotel the following day for lunch.

Kate and Mick went to ten mass that morning and went back to the hotel for a while before lunch as Kate had a little work to prepare for the week ahead while Mick went back to their apartment and read the Sunday papers. Aine and Stefan had taken the train to Scotland for the weekend to see a bit of the country. Marja and Remka had settled in well since Christmas, and like Stefan, had no fear of long hours or hard work. Kate called Mick who had dozed off while reading the papers when it was time to go and meet John and Peggie. Just as they were leaving their apartment she heard the phone ring from the reception desk. It was John telling her that they would not be making it to lunch that day as they had just received news that Brian, Peggie's father had got a heart attack during the night and he was holding on but the prognosis wasn't good. Peggie and John left that evening for Ireland and Mick and Kate went up to their house to take care of the children till they returned. They caught the night boat and made it to Adare for lunch time Monday. They were met at the door by Peggie's sister Anne from Dublin. Brian was weak and had a strong glaze in his eyes. When he saw John and Peggie next to his bed he raised his hand to welcome them both as he said "John look after my little Peg she has always been my sweetheart". In reply John said "I will of course Mr. Noonan, I will" John then said he would give Anne's husband a hand with food in the kitchen and left Margaret and her two daughters alone with Brian and the priest Fr.McCarthy who arrived a while earlier. As dusk cast its shadow on the multi paned windows of "Brook Hall" that evening Brian Noonan succumbed and faded away from Adare and this life. Peggie came out of his room and cried endlessly on her husband's shoulder sobbing like she did many a time when a school girl. She had missed many years with her father but was so glad to have made her peace with him and her mother before he had passed away. The Funeral was a small affair in the village as Brian Noonan was laid to rest that Wednesday morning after ten o'clock mass. Family and friends went up the Dunraven Arms afterwards for a meal and then it was back to the house with Margaret. She was a strong sturdy lady and kept insisting she would be alright at home alone. Despite her comments Anne and her husband packed her into the car the following morning and took her back to Dublin for a holiday. Peggie and John caught the St. David out of Rosslare that night and made their way back for London. They slept most of the way down to London in the train as it had been a tough few days on them. The children were glad to see them both although little Katie protested when told to go to bed that Friday night a bit earlier than her Aunt had insisted upon during the week. They were all a pleasure to look after that week, John and Peggie had reared a good family so far and they were very respectful to one another as well as their Aunt Kate and her husband while they took care of them. Peggie was glad to be back and found that the children took her mind off the events of the week.

Kate and Mick worked hard the next few months and as Kate's time drew close she eased back at work a little and left Stefan take the reins. Stefan had started a degree at night in London in business and economics and studied hard that year. Marja and Remka went to English classes also and started to get a good grip on the language. Aine spent a lot of time with Kate and Mick the weeks leading up to the birth of their baby. Kate gave birth to a beautiful baby girl on Tuesday the 10th of July 1956. She weighed 7lbs 1oz and had he mother's black curly hair. They all said she had Mick's roguish eyes. Mick wired home to Ballinahowen with the good news. Kate and Mick decided to call their daughter after Kate's mother and gave her the name Noreen. Kate and Noreen left the hospital the following Saturday and headed back for the hotel. Kate took a few weeks off work and eased herself into the ways of motherhood. Kate and Mick doted over their new arrival as did all their friends and relatives. They christened Noreen in early August at St James's Church in Reading where they married just a year and a bit before. All Mick's friends on the site dropped him a few bob for his daughter to give her a start in life. They put the money to one side for their daughter and added a few green backs every week to her fund.

The Bone and the lads down the Isle of grain started to splinter that year and went to all different sites all over London and some went up to the North of England as the word was that there was a job to be got on every street corner. Tom, Bertie and Pa headed off by train one Saturday and made for Newcastle upon Tyne. They spent till Christmas 1957 up there and made a lot of money going from job to job doing nothing else only piece work. They followed the gas lines from place to place and had a laugh for ever yard they dug out and backfilled. Wine women and song were part of their social life and the weekends were filled with fun and frolics. There were serious about some women and less serious about more but they always treated them well and drank their way through every weekend. They all hit back for London and settled in a nice flat in Kentish Town in early December of 1957. The first night down in Kilburn they went for a few pints in the "Rifle Volunteer" pub. When they walked into the bar they were met with a wall of Kerry fellas. There were a few of the Rodgers, and Jackie Ryan, and the O'Brien brothers from Tralee. Jackie was behind the bar serving that night and stayed there in the run up to Christmas that year. None of the Tralee fellas were charged for their drink he took care of them all but that was his family's way. You would hand in a pound note for drink and get back in the change the price of the next round. There were schools of 31 and 45 going on in all the bars in Kilburn that Christmas for turkeys, hampers and boxes of whiskey and everyone was trying to win a bird. There were the O'Connor's from Dingle who were also as tough as nails. One of the O'Connors was bedding a lassie from west of Tralee known only as Mary who owned five houses. She worked hard for them over the years doing bar work with some of the roughest types a woman you could ever encounter. The word on the street was that the O' Connor fella from Dingle was there for the cash and the good time. One night Mary his woman came home early and found him in bed with a Jamaican woman after she was tipped off about her man who was seen walking up the road with what a friend described as a tall shadow of a woman. She fired him out the bedroom window and down into the garden into the middle of a cluster of rose bushes. When the word went out that night Patsy Gallagher said that the roses there might have had a few thorns but O'Connor was the biggest prick of them all. Mary then caught the Jamaican woman and beat her down the stairs naked with her clothes in her hand and up the street till she could get her coat on and ran away. The naked baker got picked up again that December for another lewd act in a car that he found open on the side of the street. He was fornicating with another lady, who knew the streets better than the crowd that drove the black taxis, in the back seat without as much as a strip of fabric covering either of them. A police paddy wagon pulled abreast of the car and shone a torch into the car revealing the two naked bodies. There were both hauled out and naked and ran into the back of the police wagon. The naked baker ended up doing a stint

in the clink for three months and got out the 6th of March
1958. He was fined £200 that time and missed Christmas
that year. The Twelve Apostles completed their street that
November and had made a princely sum wheeling and
dealing over the last few years. They had reconstructed
thirty eight houses and had filled them to the brim with
Irish families and single men trying to make a living in
the Queen's country. They took the deeds of three houses
each and all started to build their fortune from there. They
for now lived in the other two renting out their thirty six
for the time being. The Bone and Patsy Gallagher had met
two English women in mid 1956 and settled down in the
one with them. Life for The Bone had picked up a
step or two after he left the Isle of Grain and had saved
a clean fortune. He and Patsy bought a big restaurant
and a pub next door and served nothing there ever only
Irish dishes for the lads. Tuesday was the stew day and
Thursday was the day for the Bacon and Cabbage and
you dare not ask for meat on a Friday as they only sold
fish there that day. They both did well there The Bone ran
the restaurant and Patsy took up minding the pub.

Slate Lath and Purlin had appeared too that December
and had been missing for almost two years by the time
they did. They had gone off whaling up in the artic ocean
and berthed every so often, in the North of England for
a few weeks at a stretch. They were weather beaten and
looked about ten years older from the harsh winters they
experienced up north, but they had been to Norway,
Iceland and they thought they may have stopped once in
Greenland also. They had seen more of the world than
most of the lads who dug and dug in old blighty.

Tom, Bertie and Pa were back in London to go working now on the flyovers that is where the money was going to be for the next few years. There were bridges to be built also and they were all told to report for work on the feast of the Epiphany the 6th of January 1958. A day all the Irish Catholic women knew as little Christmas or small women's Christmas.

Tom and Pa made home for Tralee that Christmas and painted the town green with the Queen's greenbacks. Tom gave his mother the usual handshake and took care of all the needs she had that Christmas. The free range turkey and home cooked ham made him miss home in a way that he daren't think about as he knew he had to make his way back after the season was over. He complemented Rita as usual for the good Christmas dinner and left it at that.

Kate and Mick hit for Ballinahowen that Christmas and all the natives there doted about Mick and Kate's Noreen. Paddy and Madge had invited Stefan and his family and Aine home also that Christmas but Marja and Remka declined and stayed in London, they were putting a life together there now and wanted to experience what a Christmas in England was like. Stefan and Aine made the trip to Galway and walked the very footsteps Mick and Kate did a few years before, across the cliffs where they too planned their lives.

Stefan knew there was no hope of ever returning to his beloved homeland under communist rule so he and Aine now were to look to other options in maybe England or Ireland. In her heart Aine hoped she could come home one day to a better life, she had never settled in London, it was a job and a way of life there and there were times she thought only for meeting Stefan she would have already gone back home. Stefan had to complete his degree and they both needed to put some good money together. For now it was London and the certain hardships it brought for them both, besides Stefan's felt an obligation to look after his mother and sister who were still only learning English and trying to make a life for themselves' in London.

The twins wanted to go back to London with Aine and Mick that year but this time Paddy and Madge put their foot down firmly and said a straight no. Eilish was working in the village in the shop attached to the Post Office and Niamh was working in a draper's shop in Spidal. They were pretty annoyed with their parents but Mick and Aine took them aside and told them to give it another year and see how things faired. They did as they were told this time, having concern for their mother was a factor in their decision as they did not wish to upset her.

Peggie called Anne in Dublin Christmas morning from London on the telephone to wish them all a very Happy Christmas in the capital. Margaret was in Dublin with her for the holidays. As Peggie spoke to her mother that morning she thought there was a distinct weakness in her voice. She seemed to have lost heart since Brian died and was not really making progress in dealing with her grief. Peggie spoke to Anne and she suggested that maybe a break in London may do her some good, but she said she was not really up to the journey.

Aine, Stefan, Kate, Mick and little Noreen all left for London the last few days of December1957 and looked forward to what the New Year had in store for them. The trip back was cold and miserable like every trip back to England always was. The St. David was laden with sick, sad and sorry people. The Irish had a very unique way of showing what was in their hearts when they had left the Auld Sod to their back. They always planned to return home and soon, but alas it did not always work out.

The big black taxi took them all back to the hotel from Paddington Railway Station. The all settled in that night and slept well after their long journey from Galway. Kate and Stefan had a busy New Year's Eve ball that year and worked hard all night making sure all went off without a hitch.

Kate was in line for her usual rise again that year and it was an extra few pound each week for the home fund for herself Mick and now Noreen. Mick was still raking in the rent on the houses and was doing pretty well on the job also. He was made a foreman that January and got a company van and a good bit of a rise and he was able to put his shovel to rest for now at least. They met Peggie, John and the children that Sunday the 5th of January and had a good session. Peggie and Kate spent most of the day chatting about Peggie's mother Margaret whom she was very concerned about. For now she was in good hands with her sister but if she went home to "Brook Hall" Peggie wondered how long she would cope there alone.

Chapter 15

T HE WORK ON the bridges and flyovers was a totally new way of life for Tom, Bertie, Pa and Mick, who was now a foreman and with a van that was often seen in places all round London that it should never have been.

The weather that winter was a killer the frost and ice was hard and there were frequent snow storms that plagued those working outdoors that year. The four lads were working on high exposed places where the icy winds went through them no matter what they wore. There was one answer and one answer alone that winter and that was to work fast and hard to stay warm, besides it was all piece work and the faster you worked the more you clocked up on the time sheet. Mick filled The Bones shoes when it came to looking after the lads on the rolling site. His methods were somewhat more refined and he got catering equipment for the cooking not like the Bone with his bucket. His stews and bacon and cabbage had more flavour too but when it came to the breakfast the shovels were produced as they were quick and there was no waiting around. The rashers and sausages and puddings never tasted better than they did that winter. Tom, Bertie, Pa and Mick often sat down for the grub those weeks with the snow piling up between the fry on the piece of timber they used as a plate. It was more often almost frozen by the time they had it eaten. There was a Dublin fella there with them those months who had been christened the "Boody Man" because of the way he would emerge out of the blizzards with a hooded black duffle coat when the siren would go off for the dinner. He was a howl and he fired jokes off his tongue day after day like shovels of concrete as they hit the casing for the bridges. He kept the lads amused in the cold and was the life and soul of all the many get to gethers they had that winter. By the last week in February the weather eased a little and there was a mobile canteen set up in a lorry and trailer. When the lads saw it coming they all fucked the boss saying it was too shagging late now as the spring was around the corner. From there on Mick sourced all the food through John Collins and started to make a tidy profit as the stuff was coming right as usual.

There were seven Mayo lads working on the flyover and had come over as the weather broke from the home country that March. They were a mighty crew and hard work to them was more like fun. They were all between nineteen and twenty four and there were four brothers in the bunch. Their father and uncle had been over working near Birmingham during the war and they had both been killed one night during a bombing raid by the Germans. When the weekend came they owned London in their own minds. They would head for Patsy Gallagher's place and soak their bodies in drink of every nature every Saturday.

It was then out on to the street and they accused everyone of killing their father and uncle and bate all around them. There was rarely a weekend that passed where they did not get thrown in the can for a day or two and got the shit kicked out of them in the process. They would always appear back the Tuesday each week on the job like a company of soldiers who had just stormed the Normandy beaches. They were always bruised and battered from Bobbie's batons and from all the Scotch fellas they thought were Germans because of the strange way they spoke. One Monday morning one of them by the name of McNulty came to work with a parcel of meet dripping blood. As the breakfast took off he had ten sheep's hearts wrapped in the daily mirror. Everyone that day though the paper was alive and maybe had sustained injuries with the lads the night before. Mc Nulty lit a fire and got a length of high tensile steel and slapped the ten hearts down onto it and set it up over the fire to try and cook them. He turned them a few times and they all got a right good tan but they were far from cooked after the twenty five minutes on the spit. He offered them around and three more Mayo lads ate them with him. They started to devour them one by one until they had them all eaten and they 70% raw. The blood dripped down their faces and onto their clothes as they devoured them one after another. With their bloodshot eyes stitched together with red thread they looked every bit the image of Peter Cushing's actors in the vampire movies up at the Granby Cinema chasing scantily clad females through the woods at night. No one else mentioned food that day as they made their way home in Mick's van.

The tea would be eaten and Tom Bertie, Pa and Mick had started to do the odd trip in the van for John Collins up to the north London boundaries with the countryside to a small village. Each night they pulled into a yard and Mick's van was filled with brandy whiskey and often lots of other contraband. As they would pull out John would pull in to pick up the meat, poultry, vegetables and of course the spuds. They would all head back to a warehouse he had down in the city and unload the night's loads. This went on right through 1958 and all the lads trebled their wages that year. The Bone became one of their best customers that summer and Patsy nearly off loaded all the drink. There were Paddies drinking the best of French brandy that year and the best of relabelled whiskey that nobody ever asked where it came from. Bertie decided to get a van with some of his profits also and started to haul drink and food to more of the Irish and Greeks he knew he could trust up the north side of London. The Boody man and a fella from Cork City known only as the scaffolder started doing a run up to somewhere in Oxford for eggs and poultry. They built up quite a reputation for the pale blue duck eggs that they always had a plentiful supply of. They were kind of strong eating but once you got used to then they would bury the rashers deep into a Paddie's belly wrapped in a fine yoke. 1958 saw a huge standard in how the Paddy changed his diet and Kate even introduced Mr. Parks one morning to a good wholesome duck egg. He never asked Kate where she was getting them from as he was afraid she would tell him something he didn't really want to hear. They slowly but surely became part of the breakfast at the hotel. There was a tendency to steer clear of the duck egg brigade on the sites and it was often wondered how the gas company never recruited the fellas in question for their profound abilities.

London was ridden with scams those years and it was a wonder how the hoors, with their cockney accents in the shops ever made a decent bob. The black market was alive and well as the Paddies lined their pockets those years. The Bobbies and the CID boys never stopped hunting the Paddies that year but then they were kind of used to dealing with them as they had the trickery passed down to them since the days of the old R.I.C at home. The Galway and Mayo crowd were a dab hand at it as they were well used to the Poteen runs in Connemara. The terrain was different but all they really needed was the cuteness. Every Monday morning there was a new story of a chase and a van load that had been caught. Bertie painted the name of a contractor on the side of the van and was never stopped or even checked and he often moved more than most of the boys around the city. They all said they should write it down as it might make a good book someday. Some did and lost the notes, more committed them to memory backed up with a laugh or a funny incident to help them to remember later in life. They in time turned out to be the best stories as they were always told from a humorous perspective.

The big shock that year on St Patrick's Day was that The Bone and Patsy Gallagher were getting married, although not to one another. They were marrying two English girls who were sisters and who had been living with them over the pub and restaurant for some time. They were half Irish as their father came from Bohola in Co. Mayo. The Bone used to tell everyone that it was the top half of his one was Irish and that Patsy got the one with the Irish bottom. The women would laugh it off every time it was mentioned as they had their father's wit. Their mother was a timid creature and English from somewhere down around Bath. She was always appalled at the Irish jokes and being a kind of half breed Catholic, who only sometimes went to mass and confession, she would bless herself when the profanities would be launched in her direction. This always got a good laugh as she was left handed and would always make the sign of the cross with her left hand. The Bone was a good governor in the pub and took no shit whatsoever from the boys when they were inclined to get out of hand. Patsy always went next door for a pint and the Bone came out to him for the pigs head or the salted spare rib. Patsy often said to the newcomers not to irk The Bone as when he lost it he was crazier than an out house rat in a fit. They more often than not took his advice and kept their distance from him. During April that year the two lads were out the back area of the pub and restaurant clearing rubble that had been there for the last few years since they did the two places up. There intention was to put a corrugated iron roof over the double open yard and have the reception there. When their mother in law to be heard this she lost her temper for the first time ever with them. She called the boys and girls aside and gave out reams to them about their idea with her usual timid soft voice. The Bone and Patsy told her it would all be alright and that it would be a fine setup before the wedding the first Saturday in August. As the two boys walked out Patsy asked the Bone was she crying or was she just squealing as she sounded, like a fucken Banshee. That breed of Irish man that time rarely took any notice of what a woman had to say unless she had him on a promise or she had him filled to the brim with porter for her own ends. The Bone and Patsy cornered two right women they were hard grafters and would work from seven o' clock in the morning getting out the breakfasts in the restaurant and they were both often seen to leave the pub after midnight after they had the cash counted. They knew the value of the men they were marrying and respected their drive and determination in getting on in life, more often than not by hook or by crook. Once the money kept coming in they kept counting it. The crowd that called into the two places usually self destructed on food and drink so the money was always mounting up.

As the summer broke open the four lads were making savage progress on the concreting having a shot of bridges to do as fast as they could keep going. Only for Mick's stews and the drums of bacon and cabbage the lads would have fell in a heap many an evening. The lad's hands were worn to a thread and many a man on the site was hooped like a bicycle wheel, bent over so much that he could almost bite his toenails. As the flyover was passing through an urban flat land the craic was going well the lads spent the day cat calling and whistling at the women who paraded around their balconies and gardens in the bathing suits lapping up the sun. The Boody Man made a date for every weekend from the flyover and met some of the finest of women as he crossed the East End on his own aeroplane of 30 nt concrete.

The highlight of summer 1958 was of course the wedding of Patsy Gallagher and The Bone to the two half breeds with the Bohola blood in their veins. The wedding was a total showcase of Irish culture laced with Irish humour, and garnished with the greatest cross section of food and drink. The wedding was held in the "Church of Our Lady Help of Christians" up in Kentish Town. The Elephant

O'Hara didn't spare a penny for the girl's day out he covered the church in flowers and greenery and made it look like Tarzan's own jungle. Johnny Weissmuller would have been proud of his efforts. No one had ever seen the Bone or Patsy in a tux before and they looked well indeed. Some of the lads said that day that they had to cut the corduroy pants off the two grooms with a welding torch.

The two brides turned up at the church 20 minutes after midday sporting two fine dresses made by their aunt in Bohola. They looked every bit the picture of beauty but there wasn't a shadow of a doubt but that you would know they had a good drop of Mayo blood in them. Their black curly hair was only to be found in that area of Mayo, that the Elephant came from. The two of them proudly linked The Elephant up the church and he handed one to The Bone and the other to Patsy, making sure he gave the right one to the right man. Purlin said out loud in the congregation that it was the first time he ever saw an elephant lead two women to their slaughter. The comment contributed to a large hum of laughter which rose almost above the sound of the music as the organist played "Here comes the Bride". The ceremony went off without a hitch and the four made all the usual pledges and promises for ever etc. Tom said to the boys around him that he hadn't heard of four slaves getting married since before Abraham Lincon took office as president in the states nearly one hundred years ago. That of course drew another fine howl of laughter from the bottom left hand corner. As they four signed their documents the congregation clapped, wolf whistled, and cheered and jeered aloud something the priest wasn't too happy with their behaviour in the church of Our Lady Help of Christians but after all it was the same as being down town in the Irish Embassy or on Irish soil. He didn't say a word though, in case there was a riot or a row. As they all headed back for The Bone and Patsy's place there was never such a mixed bag of cars, vans, pickups and the odd small lorry even graced the roads of London behind a wedding party. There were no flash cars or bullshit only rough necks looking as if they were heading down once more to the Isle of Grain. The mother of the brides spent the day giving out about her daughters having their reception in a back yard under a corrugated iron roof. Everyone that spoke to her bought her a drink and as it transpired by the start of the meal she was bordering on a good sleep. She made it through the speeches and as some of the lads but, "she was laid to rest" in one of the backrooms down stairs for a doze and to give her time to regain the composure of a true subject of Queen Elizabeth. The meal was mighty and there was everything from black pudding to, crubeens, pigs head, Irish stew, even though it wasn't a Thursday and the finest wipe of flowery spuds that ever graced the table of Irish men in London. During the course of the meal there was nothing only wise craics, and when the speeches commenced it was then the real hop balls started. Drezna was there and shouted at the Bone "Hey you Boney why you not marry your Russian woman, were you afraid? You would hear a pin drop while she took a fine masculine swig from her two pint bottle of vodka. It was all in good spirits and she meant well. She had many a good night with the Bone and as she told the lads she prepared him for marriage Russian style. There was Shepherd's Pie, fish or every description and even Haggis for the Scotch crowd. Nobody was left without and The Bone himself had a feed of pigs head for the main course. The soup had been a cross between vegetable, fish soup and tomato and some said that with the red texture on it, that the fish most probably had not been even gutted. Kate and Peggie, coming from somewhat refined backgrounds thought the entire event to be uncouth and half wild, but then Kate's own wedding was not much better only that she was too busy at her own wedding to notice all that really happened. As the rain hammered down that evening on the corrugated iron roof and as the drink started to flow Peggie found Mrs Elephant O'Hara and she wedged down between the toilet bowl and the wall in the Ladies and she after peeling down half a wall of freshly put up tiles from the day before with something like porridge instead of grouting. The girls muttered and laughed between themselves as Peggie recounted more than once that she had found her with her dress up around her waist and she showing off the her charms that had kept the Elephant happy many a night. She was covered in tile grouting and her hair was all wet as she had also tore the pipe down from out of the metal cast cistern high up on the wall over the toilet bowl. Her two daughters took her up stairs in their wedding dresses and made her presentable again. When the Elephant was told, all he said was "She was never wan for holding her drink anyway". This time it gave him a chance to say to her that she made a pure buffoon of herself at her own daughter's weddings instead of it always being the reverse. Mrs Elephant had lived a tough life with the husband but in his own rough way he was a good as gold to her and always took care of her needs. He had worked at every sort of job, at sea, down the mines, in the trenches on the building sites, and wherever a bob was to be made you would find the auld beast.

A few weeks after the wedding Joe wrote to Kate and Mick to tell them that Mary was in the family way yet again and that a good piece of ground had gone up for sale on the eastern side of Galway City and that there was a 25 bedroom old folks home next to it. He said that the land was going cheap and that the old folk's home would be closing down next year as there was a new one being built. If he was still interested it might be the right time to move with the place, especially where it was. Kate, young Noreen and Mick went home the first week in September and bought the piece of ground. There was just a little less than two acres in the plot and it went for handy money. They bought the place for cash and got planning permission to build a shop and petrol pumps there in time. They had made their first move and it was a good one. Before they left they put in a bid for the old folk's home for when it might go on the market. The manager there said it would be late 1959 or maybe early 1960 before it would become vacant. Mick and Kate had a good look around the building and it was in fair disrepair but nothing Mick said a few months of labouring wouldn't put straight. Kate always laughed at Mick's casual approach to the hardest of work. She had seen him renovate five houses almost single handed and just took it in his stride.

The last Tuesday in September and only after being back from Galway two weeks she was called to Mr. Sheelswell's office. As she entered the room a very solemn Mr Shellswell told her that he had just received very bad news. He told her that Mr Parks had been knocked down that morning while he had being going down the street for the Financial Times and that he was alive but seriously injured. He was awaiting further news from the hospital. Kate began to cry and was very moved by the news. She suggested that they both go and see him but My Shellswell said that he was in intensive care at the moment and that he could not receive any visitors for now. Just like saying the King is dead, Long Live the King Mr Shellswell asked Kate to take over the position temporarily as Assistant Manager for now, until Mr Parks returned. He also suggested that Stefan take over her full duties for now, again on a temporary basis. She told Mr Shellswell that she would take care of all he asked and to please notify her of any change in Mr Park's condition. Mr Parks had always been like a father to Kate ever since she started at the Lancaster Gate Hotel as a young lady of sixteen years of age. He was always kind, polite and mannerly to her. Since her marriage to Mick he was the perfect gentleman to her husband also. He had never married and his life and soul was the hotel. He loved the buzz about the lobby and the fuss in the dining room where he ate his dinner at a corner table for the last thirty two years. Kate and Mick went to the church that evening and said their usual rosary for Mr Parks that he would be alright. They were able to visit him after ten days as he was improving from his injuries. Mick slipped him two handy naggings of Jameson, it being his favourite tipple with a coy wink and said no singing now after lights out hear! It was the first time since his accident that he smiled and gave a chuckle, even though it caught his ribs. He was released from hospital the tenth of December into a bad rainstorm. Kate and Julie ushered him to a big black beast of an Austin taxi and made back for the hotel. Mr Parks said on his trip home that if he had been in any other city in the world the day he was knocked down he would be dead by now. It was the first time they had ever seen him without a tie while wearing his suit. He felt odd himself also but then Mr Parks was that kind of English perfectionists that took pride in his appearance. For now he was convalescing and was told to stay off work until at least the 1st of February 1959 to regain his full strength.

As Christmas neared Anne contacted Peggie and John to tell them that Margaret was with her again was feeling ill and was admitted to hospital that morning. John and Peggie left that evening and caught the night boat into Dublin. They went to see Margaret the following morning and spent all that day with her. Anne and Peggie spoke to the doctor who told them both that their mother was in good health but seemed very depressed and had lost the will to live. She had never got over Brian's death and it had kept chipping away at her. For a robust confident Lady she had deteriorated very much this last year. She looked gaunt and old although only in her sixty sixth year. John went back after a week but Peggie stayed on in Dublin with Anne and her husband. Margaret passed away on the 18th of December 1958 just under twenty one months after her beloved husband Brian. John and the children met Peggie in Adare the following day at lunch time. They waked her that night and "Brook Hall" was filled with twelve of Peggie's and John's friends from London. None of them including Mick, Kate, Noreen, The Bone and the wife, Patsy and the wife, The elephant and the wife, the Boody Man, Slate Lath and Purlin had not forgotten all the perks which Peggie and John had passed their way. Patsy's eyes became slightly twisted at the wake and the Boody Man started telling yarns. Anne and her husband were not overly impressed but then they were of a slightly different stock. She was removed to the church on the Saturday evening the 20th and laid to rest the following day next to Brian whom she had married forty three years ago. They all went once again to the Dunraven Arms Hotel and laid on lunch for all the mourners. After lunch Anne and Peggie were taken aside and spoken to by a gentleman in a pin striped suit he was their father's solicitor from Limerick City. He asked them to call to his office the following morning if possible as Brian and Margaret has asked that their last will and testament be read within a week after the last one of them becoming deceased. They complied with his wishes and met with this gentleman the following morning at ten O'clock. Anne had been left all her parent's money but for ten thousand pounds, which amounted to a very princely sum indeed. Peggie was left the sum of ten thousand pound and also "Brook Hall" with one stipulation, that husband John and she occupy it with within two years of the last one of them passing. Otherwise it was to be sold and the proceeds of it divided between her and her sister Anne. The two girls parted on good terms respecting the wishes of their parents and their feelings for one another. All the London mourners relocated around Ireland that Christmas as John, Peggie and the children stayed on in "Brook Hall" and became legal residents of the property in March of 1959. Peggie gave her own daughter Katie a Christmas that year like she had known as a young girl. The smell of the free range turkey and ham filled Brooke Hall once more and the flamed lit Christmas pudding glowed on the lavish dining room table that day. Peggie's heart was filled with emotion as she and John sat in front of the log fire that evening, she ached for her father and mother but she was happy she had returned to Brook Hall to make peace with her parents and she would now never forget that day she walked down the drive after leaving with John.

Ballinahowen was full of happiness and holiness again that Christmas. As Mick, Kate and Noreen arrived in Galway from Adare they met and collected Stefan and Aine off the train and headed on home. Mary looked the picture of health and she pregnant with her and Joe's second baby. Paddy and Madge were in good health the twins were still working and had boyfriends and showed little interest in London that year.

The Bone, Patsy and the two wives spent Christmas in Dublin and they all passed out a few times from drink. Patsy and the Bone spent St. Stephen's night in a Garda station after been arrested for fighting in a pub. The following morning after they were released the four of them headed for the boat to Hollyhead.

The pain and the anguish of the Irish continued as it was soaked in their laughs and happiness. Some still ached for the smoke filled kitchens that they had left behind with the smouldering turf now like the London smog. At home they could go out and breathe soft south westerly breezes to clear their lungs, but here there was no escape from the smog, hardship, and the loneliness of the bed sit and dingy basement flat.

CHAPTER 16

⸺◦⦿◦⸺

MR. PARKS WAS back at work the second week of February and was feeling quite well despite the harrowing injuries he had sustained in his accident. On the morning of the 9th he strutted into the dining room for breakfast with his usual carnation in his lapel. As he headed for his corner table Aine placed a double pot of tea on his table with some piping hot toast to get him started. She poured his tea and greeted him with a strong Cead Mile Failte, Connemara style, but in his native English tongue of course. It wasn't the language she used but how she delivered her words with her traditional Irish smile. As he placed his napkin on his lap he complained about the cold. He ordered a bowl of Aine's special porridge which he had become accustomed to over the last eighteen months. She always laid out the golden speckled brown sugar atop of it for him and poured a decent helping of good quality cream over it all, coming from an Irish source down the market. Seeing that everyone's favourite hotel gentleman was started she would head again for the kitchen to collect his scrambled egg, made of course from the mystery blue duck eggs.

Kate emerged from the kitchen with her own breakfast tray and joined him. They laughed and joked about how the Irish kitchen staff, were the making of him. Julie dropped by and welcomed him back to work also, with a fleeting smile. The red carnation was always an indication of how you knew My Parks was working, and not on a day off.

Tom, and Bertie were still on the flyovers that winter and were feeling the winter cold in more ways than one. Pa had gone home that Christmas but still hadn't returned he said he'd definitely be back Paddy's Day for the annual wipe out. Bertie confided in Tom that winter that he had a feeling some of the lads including John Collins were being shadowed by the C.I.D. from Scotland Yard. They discussed the whole story and Tom said the best thing to do, before scaring them was to shadow the yard boys themselves, but in borrowed car. They two cleaned up well and borrowed a car from the Bone and kept an eye on the route John and the lads were taking into London from the north. They watched the convoy for four nights changing their habits and being quite ghost like. Their prognosis was that the heat was coming on the lads ok. The food stuff was being bought but there was a case of revenue not being paid maybe. The drink was an entirely different story most of it was being smuggled. The last Friday night in February there was a meeting held in The Bone's wedding hall, he had a good stash of drink from the four corners of the globe there. It was the Aladdin's cave. John's warehouse was the danger. He had a fortune tied up there and was building up a huge stock to ship back to Ireland as he and Peggie were planning to return later in the year maybe August, but definitely before the winter bit home, they wanted to be settled into Brook Hall. That weekend at five each morning John's warehouse was cleared out with the lorry and stashed in The Bones place. They even had it swept out and rented to four Indian fellas by Sunday night. John sold the lorry, and took the heat off his back. He had four large building vans bought before the end of the week and headed for the same supplier and took different routes back into London from then on to throw the C.I.D. off his scent. On the run up to St. Patrick's Day John's old warehouse was raided and they yard boys found nothing but clothes stacked to the ceiling. Their leads had been scattered and there wasn't a sign of any of the Irish lads. From then on the Irish lads had to be extra careful as the heat would really be stepped up now.

Pa arrived back the 16th of March 1959 and was almost flat broke. He was back on the flyover again the following Monday morning and was teamed up with the Boody Man. Their laughs could be heard all day long and they two hammered and sawed the shutter timbers for the concreting. The scaffolder was under a bridge one morning, relieving himself, after a breakfast of beans black pudding and sausages. Out of the blue he noticed a little Labrador pup sneak in after him and start wagging his tail he was followed by a woman who was calling out his name. As she came into the tunnel she was treated to a display of the full moon at eleven O'Clock in the morning. Bertie, Tom, Pa and the Boody Man all cheered as they saw the Lady running out shouting help. The Police landed at the site within the hour, as they expected, but alas there was no identifiable ass to be found on the site. The lads stood there smiling at the Police telling them that they though he must have been a night of the road or something. They said the lady had made a complaint about a builder flashing his rear end. She was sitting in the back of the Black Mariah with a face like thunder. The Boody Man got a good look at her and recognised her from around the area. When the Police had left he said to Tom and the lads that she was no stranger to the attributes of a builder's ass and had comforted many a one over the years. The Scaffolder had to lie low for a while and stay away from the Beans, Black pudding and sausages.

They all worked like dogs that year as there was just enough work to get them all to Christmas left on that job. Tom was then going to head up to the North of England where he heard there were a few other major Jobs going to start. Pa met up with his wife to be that summer and she was a fine Irish Girl and a lovely person. Bertie met an English woman late that year also and settled down long term with her. The two lads stayed on in London that November as Tom took the train north and to a new site.

Towards the end of the year Mick got a note from the old folk's home in Galway to tell him that the building would be going up for public auction in early January 1960 and he would be told of the date as soon as it was fixed. Kate was a little reluctant to buy but Mick said he thought it a good idea to sell the houses in London and start shifting the cash back home that Christmas. She knew he was serious and that the writing was now on the wall for her life in London. When Mick Joyce made up his mind about a deal he always moved with the speed of a bullet. Her heart skipped a beat, the tears glazed her eyes and her palms became moist. She was twelve years in London that July and had always prayed they would go home. Mick had another idea. He sat his black curly haired wife down and told her "I will buy your hotel for you". We will hold the houses another while. She pondered on where he would get the money for it. He slid out his trunk that night that his treasure was stored in and opened it. They sold the lot to a buyer who was represented by a tall ginger haired man that November and made the cost of the hotel twice over. He would have it repaired and stocked with all they needed to open the hotel and still have a little change left over. The week before they both headed for Ballinahowen Kate surprised Mick with the news that she was pregnant with their second baby. He gleamed into her eyes as she scolded him saying you'll fill our hotel in Galway with all our own customers before you're finished Michael Joyce. He laughed with joy as he hugged his Kate close to him.

John Collins headed for Ireland and Adare with the family that Christmas and never went back as he could feel the back of his neck getting warmer every time he saw the C.I.D. boys pass by. He put Sean, Padraig and Peggie driving a lorry full to the brim with everything he would need to get started in Adare. He led the posse with another lorry with young Kevin. Katie who was now 12 travelled with her mother. There were several occasions while heading for Fishguard that John though he would be pulled over but he just kept saying rosaries all the way till he reached Rosslare. Once he was on home soil he gave a gasp of pure relief. They all had a good breakfast in a nice hotel, as Peggie and the two hardy boys who drove all the way from London needed it. Young Kevin and Katie had slept most of the way and were full of beans. They all left Wexford that morning at nine and struck on for County Limerick. Kevin was all questions for John about what business he would start up once they got home. He told him it would take about a year to get going but that they would make a good start after Christmas. With all the talk Kevin soon fell fast asleep again. As John closed in on Clonmel he decided to stop there for more food and a rest for the drivers. He thought of the time before he left for Boston as he wondered would Peggie get a chance to follow him. They had a hard life starting off and her mother and father had treated her very unfairly, but alas that was water under the bridge now. He had done well after the war in England and he had four trunks full of the Queen's taxes in the back of the lorry he was driving. They were packed with green backs. He also had three cases of American dollars, courtesy of Harry Truman also. Peggie and John had roughed it but they would never see one of their children leave for the St. David. They were hell bent on setting them all up once they got fixed up and settled in at Brook Hall.

Slate Lath, Purlin, The Boody man, and the Scaffolder all went off whaling that winter up in the Artic Ocean and made enough to stay drunk for an entire year. The ice filled their veins instead of blood and by the time they got back to London in the spring of 1960 they were like a crowd of explorers back from the South Pole. They were weather beaten, they were haggard looking, and they all had aged fast. Slate Lath looked some show with a beard and his bushy curly hair. He looked like a ragged mop standing up side down. Some of the lads used to say on the sites for weeks after he returned that if you stood a bottle of milk next to the Slate Lath that he would freeze it to ice for you. They all had these black circles around their eyes and for years after and they often looked like the walking dead as they headed up to mass on Sunday morning.

The Elephant O' Hara died a few weeks after Christmas, some said, it was a heart attack brought on by drink and hard living but he had the big dreaded C since early July that year. The Little Banshee was heart broken and went off down to Bath after the funeral and took up living with her two spinster sisters. The Bone and Patsy got hammered thinking about the loss the Elephant was in their life. When it came to the Banshee's departure all they said was "All the best". One night a few weeks after the sad event Patsy picked up and Irish Press someone left in the pub and he saw a few pubs for sale, in it, in Dublin. He got thinking! He cornered the wife that night as she rounded into the bedroom. Hey me darling did you ever think of going to live in Ireland. She Said "the old man often dreamed about going back to fucken Bohola but the mother was never keen on the idea I think she was afraid she'd find more in Ireland like him" she laughed. There is fuck all in Mayo my love but what would you think about going to Dublin? Are you and the Bone hatching a plan again? I saw two pubs for sale in Dublin in the Irish press tonight and it made me think that maybe a move home would be a good thing. Well you know what they said in the Bible where a man goes so does his wife and she will lay with him by his side. He said "what about you laying on top of him now?" as he grabbed her bottom. Oh that too Patsy Gallagher she said with her rye smile. That smile continued all the way between the sheets and it was the night they made a small Paddy Gallagher that would, when born, take his first gulp of Irish air. Patsy and the Bone headed for Dublin that week and bought a pair of pubs each. They would need some work but all it would take for them to get going was a string of fucks some swear words and a wipe of the Queen's greenbacks with a ball of a temper thrown in. They drank their way over and back on the boat and were like two sick pigs by the time the hit London.

Kate Mick and Noreen met up with Aine and Stefan in the large yard behind the hotel and piled into Kate and Mick's new car. They were making their first trip to Ballinahowen by car from London. It was cold, damp and so foggy that all the way down to Reading one could hardly see the car just ahead of you. Aine and Kate snuggled little Noreen between them in the back seat as the road rose up behind them. Stephan and Mick chatted about Christmas in Ballinahowen and that they would have to get in some fishing. The journey was uneventful and the new car went well. The pulled into the yard at home in Ballinahowen the following evening as another wintry watery wave of sun rested on the Atlantic horizon out beyond the Islands. The entire family gathered that night around the Joyce fireside after they buried a good swipe of salty sparerib. Stefan had got very used to the Irish diet from Aine and he was delighted with the feed and after a few half ones of poteen he kept complementing Madge on the fine meal she graced her fine oak table with. The women all decorated the house on Christmas Eve morning while Paddy, Joe, Stefan and Mick made for the pier at daybreak. They checked the nets that Joe had cast the previous afternoon. They caught four fine salmon one that was smoked over the fire and two others were poached Joe took the other one up to Mary along with a pair of lobsters and a bag of white trout. That night in the kitchen Madge quizzed her young lad saying "I see you have done more harm again Mick". "How do you mean Ma" was his reply. Madge was not a woman to be fooled. As Mick smiled he said yes God willing we will have another little Joyce next year. May God bless you all she said and took her son in her arms, as she said "It is time to try and get home soon now if you can England is no place to bring up a family my son". To her delight he left her in on a secret and said "I'll be home Ma before another Christmas will pass. We have a plan and we are well on course with it". As Mick walked out into the parlour behind his mother he walked over to his girl from Limerick and announced their good news to the family. Niamh said how nice it was to have both Kate and Mary in the family way together. Joe slagged his baby brother and Kate saying and I thought you had television to watch at night in London, I must have been wrong. The house shook with laughter. At half eleven they all headed for midnight Mass as usual and prayed for the year ahead to be as good as the last. As Stefan sat next to Aine while the consecration was starting he handed her a note in Polish. She whispered what is that? He told her to turn it over and as she did written in beautiful Old English Script were the words. "I want to Marry You soon". Before the consecration was over they had planned a St. Patrick's Day wedding for Ballinahown. Aine blushed a dozen times before they left the church. Over Christmas they booked there wedding for St. Patrick's Day and arranged the reception also. Aine and Stefan had to go back to London on the 28th of December but Mick and Kate stayed in Ballinahowen until to 7th of January when the auction was on in Galway for the old folk's home. They bagged the home as there was only two other bidders and they ended up getting it for about a thousand pounds less than what they anticipated they would. As they drove back to London the planned that they would be home to see their new baby born in Ireland. Their deadline was the first week in July. Kate was all talk about her plans for the hotel and Mick never shut up about building the filling station and the shop. There was a lash of ground between the two of them but it would be a hoor to get his hands on it as it was owned by one of the fellas who bid against him for the old folk's home. Maybe in time he could fire up a bit of an auld tigeen there. It would be handy to have the whole lot side by side.

Tom settled into a cold rough winter up North that year and worked hard. He never went home for Christmas that year. He missed the Turkey with Rita's home made stuffing and home cured ham. As he awoke Christmas morning he felt a lump in his chest and a grinding pain shudder across his heart. He was in good old blighty nearly eight years now and wondered about his past and future and would he ever be able to merge them together. He had made and squandered three fortunes since he left Tralee. He often thought of himself like one of the cowboys of the old Wild West in the books he used to read in bed at night wandering the plains of the mid western United States. He had some money put aside from chances and a bit of roguery. All he knew for now was he could not keep going like this. He was 26 that Christmas and had lost his heart to a few special girls but nothing came of his efforts in that area. Behind the rugged hard appearance that got him through each day concreting, and learning more about engineering than just being a hired hand in the living hell of construction he was a decent sensitive man that had a warm heart entombed deep within his mighty body of pure tool steel. As he toiled up north that year and well into the summer of 1960 he ran scams of every description smuggling and shipping stuff down to the lads in London. The boys in blue and in ordinary clothes were often no more than a yard or two behind his cunning skills. He kept on the move and did not lodge in any place for too long. Yes he was that drifter who moved week by week through his cowboy novel stopping in saloon after saloon and lassoing every chance he encountered to make a fast greenback. He often thought in the years after if it were not for the author of those cowboy novels he could have been caught more than once. One evening as the pressure was creeping up on him and the net was closing he decided to disappear with just the clothes on his back and head south. His pockets were laden with cash and he had to get to London to put it into safe keeping. He got back to London to find that Pa had left for Ireland and had got married. Bertie was still in London and had broken up with the English girl he had kipped up with. He said they had a flaming row one night after she caught him while drunk kissing an old girlfriend. Tom could see his heart was aching but there was no going back he said. The Bone and Patsy had gone to Dublin to do some work in their pubs while they left the two wives in London to run the businesses. They were due to sell out to two Welsh fellas in September.

That January after the auction in Galway Mick and Kate decided to get back to London and start to look for buyers for the houses and to hand in their notices at the hotel and also for Mick's Jobs. Kate met with Mr Shellswell and Mr Parks in late January and handed her notice in for the 1st of March 1960. She was heading for Ballinahowen with

Aine and Noreen to help Aine prepare for her wedding on St. Patrick's Day. Mick went back after the wedding to sort out the houses and tie up all the legal stuff.

The marriage of Paddy and Madge's eldest daughter Aine was a proud event for them both. She had met a good man and he was a devout Catholic who said more prayers each day than a lot of priests. Their plans for now were to remain in England near Stefan's mother and sister as he was all they had from a time in their lives they yearned for some days and wanted to forget others. Ballinahowen came alive that St. Patrick's Day with 1960s style. Paddy and Madge had saved for this day for a long time gave Stefan and Aine a prime plot of ground down at the end of the land where they could build a house and gaze out over the Atlantic with a fine view of the pier and the stony strand in the foreground. The reception was held in Galway and the family had a day to remember. Remka and Marja cried most of the day as Madge did a few times also. The men said it was probably the result of consuming the contents naggings of HOLY WATER! They honeymooned in Scotland a place that Stefan and Aine had always found great peace and happiness. They got back to work the 4th of April and moved into a nice flat not too far from the hotel. Stefan promised Aine that when he finished his degree that Christmas he would try and see if he could get a job in Ireland.

Mick headed back to London leaving Kate and Noreen at home in Ballinahowen. He had two of the houses sold quickly and got a good price for them from an Indian fella. He had a brother coming to England in April and he said he might buy the other three. Mick was hoping as the money was good and they were the next Paddy trying to make a killing in England.

The Bone and Patsy relocated to Dublin that September with the women after selling out everything in London. They filled three lorries and took two of them full of drink back to Dublin. As Slate Lath and Purlin said their goodbyes and headed off for the docks to try and get a berth on a wailing boat for the winter. Purlin said there was more spirits in the lads lorries than up in heaven. They were turning a sad moment into a laugh as usual. They disappeared for the next four years and met Bertie once around 1964 looking weather beaten, old, and haggard from hard work in the icy north. They told Bertie they had worked in a fish factory somewhere also for a year. They were not sure was it Greenland or Newfoundland. They parted after a few pints that evening and no one ever heard of them again. Some said they were gone back home to Ireland but it was thought they went down with a ship in a storm north of Iceland in the late sixties.

Mick Joyce sold the other three houses that April and had the legal matters all signed over by May the 20th. He filled a Lorry and headed home to Galway that weekend. His thoughts were wide and varied as he travelled home that Saturday. Eight years in England had changed his life. It had made him a very wealthy man and he had met and married a wonderful girl who was Irish to the core and would be a good woman at his side for the rest of his life. Ireland was showing signs of coming alive and the business prospects were looking good. As he rattled along to the boat in his black Bedford twin wheeled lorry he had next to him the shovel he took to London with him

back in fifty two. It had a fine rounded top to the spade
and as he glanced at it he could see the breakfast and his
beads of sweat that had worn its handle like the oar on a
curragh facing the Atlantic Ocean. He loved that shovel
it had dug every shovelful he ever handled and was really
an extension of his arms that had made him a very wealthy
man indeed. His shovel was his pride and joy but his father's
fiver was his true treasure. He had arranged to meet Kate
and Noreen in Galway as Kate had rented a house about a
quarter of a mile from the old folk's home. His eyes lit up
as he looked down from the lorry window which was held
closed with a small timber wedge, in the front garden he
saw his pregnant wife and his little daughter. He stopped
for a minute and just looked and stared at his life before
him, he had never felt this happy. He drove into the yard
next to the house that would be home for the next year
or so. He leapt out of the cab and ran to his two favourite
girls. The last two months had felt like two years, but alas
he was really home. Mick sat down to a fine Irish stew that
evening with the freshest vegetables in it he had tasted in a
while, and as for the beef, well it was real beef it was Irish.
As Kate laid out a decent slice of apple pie and a good
dollop of real fresh cream from the dairy down the road
she placed an envelope in front of him as well. Suspecting
trouble, as she looked serious, he opened it with a knife. It
was a deed to the plot of land between the old folk's home
and the plot they had bought for the filling station. Mick
sat staring at his wife in amazement and asked her "how
did you get it?". I just called to the farmer and he sold it
to me. He said it wasn't much good to him without the
building next door. He wished Mick and herself well and
sold her the acre for five hundred pounds. Michael Joyce
was stunned he thought to himself she is some piece or

work. Mick marked out the filling station and shop and the house next door that week and contacted the bone and Patsy in Dublin. He asked them if they wanted a start. He also sent the same message to a few of the Twelve Apostles who were at home in Swinford in Mayo. Before the last Saturday in May he had a team ready to start on the Monday the 13th of June. The Bone and Patsy arrived on with the Boody man and the Scaffolder who had called to Dublin for a weekend but stayed for two months on the piss picking up work here and there in Dublin. The six religious from Mayo arrived as usual with a stare in their eyes and gunning to get started. It was like old times they were all together again like brown's cows. They all sat around the table that Sunday, evening before, The Bone started to fuck all the Connemara boys out of it, as it was all Irish once more. Kate had bought a huge saucepan that she could boil about fifty spuds in as the next few months was going to be hard going cooking the food.

She hired two young girls to give her a hand with the cooking and the laundry with the lads. Mick Joyce Junior was born Friday morning the 1st of July 1960. He was a fine lad and had weighed in at 6lbs 12ozs. None of the crowd could figure out who he was like but one thing for sure was that he was from the west of Ireland. The twins came to Galway while Kate was laid up to help with the cooking and cleaning and to size up the Lord's Apostles.

CHAPTER 17

J OHN AND PEGGIE Collins had settled in well to Brook
Hall and Kevin and Katie had adapted well to school in
Limerick. John, Sean and Padraig had tucked in well that
year to work as a team and had built a fine supermarket
that was the talk of west Limerick. John and Peggie
had reared a good family and had thought them the true
values of helping one another in life. They gave good
construction employment in the area and the Bone, Patsy,
the Scaffolder and the Boody Man all came down to help
them open before Christmas that year after they wrapped
up in Galway with Mick. When Peggie and John finished
the supermarket, like Mick and Kate they setup a petrol
station also to one side of the supermarket. From the word
go it all took off like a hoard of stampeding asses from west
Clare, and they were a good wipe of them to be found up
that part of the west. The deal was then after Christmas
1960 Mick and Kate would get the lads back up as they
had the hotel and the house to get organised.

As the summer opened up east of Galway City, Mick and Kate's petrol station and shop was up to wall plate and the roof started by the end of July. The weather was up and down but weather never worried the lads. The only thing they crowed about was the fucken snow and the frost driven with the easterly winds. The ceiling joists and rafters were being nailed down faster than they could be thrown up onto the roof. All it took for the next batch was a roar and a fit of fucking from the Bone and the rafters were seen flying through the air. It was like old times up in the East End of London the craic was non stop and they laughed all day every day. One of the Apostles fell off the roof while the tiles were going up with the laughing and was laid up for a two weeks with a few broken ribs and a bruised groin. Yes his balls ended up a fine shade of black and blue. Niamh was nursing and feeding him while he was laid up and she being one hell of a rogue told him that she would put some cream on them or they would never heal otherwise. He swallowed the bait and she ended up telling the whole God damn parish the story. At least everyone knew his name from then on he was christened "Blue Balls". Despite the craic about his jewels they took up going out together and were doing a steady line as the year drew to a close. Everyone said it was the cream that did the trick. Mick and Kate had the shop stocked and open for the 1st of October 1960 and they asked Niamh and Eilish to stay on and run the shop. They hired a couple of other girls and two young lads to sell the petrol. By that stage Eilish was also doing a bit of smiling at another of the Apostles from Swinford and he often came up from Adare that fall where he was working down at Peggie and John's place. After they were finished the shop and petrol station they turned their eyes to the old folk's home and the foundations for their own house. Mick planned what he would do in January 1961 when the lads arrived back after the Christmas. Niamh and Eilish ended up marrying the two Apostles in early 1963 and they all moved back around Swinford somewhere.

Christmas 1960 Aine, Stefan, Marja, and Remka arrived home to Ballinahowen. Aine and Marja were gaunt and very sick from the smog in London and had planned not to return after Christmas and to try and settle in Ireland instead. They were both so bad that they had to go into hospital before December was out where they remained until the end of January 1961. Marja worked for Mick and Kate temporarily in the shop with the twins and rented a nice cottage nearby. Stefan having qualified with a Business Degree before he came to Ireland got a good job teaching in one of the schools in Galway. Mick and Kate promised Aine, Marja and Remka a job in the hotel when they opened it up. Aine and Stefan rented a place in Galway and settled in well to the Irish way of life with the clean fresh North Atlantic air it brought with it. Every weekend Aine and Stefan headed for Ballinahowen as Stefan followed his hearts desire, fishing from the Galway shoreline in his curragh. His job was a means to an end and gave him a good living but he found it hard working indoors with the Galway fresh air outside the door. However for now he had Aine to look after and he kept his head down.

Tom and Bertie met up in London again that Christmas but it was not the same all the friends had moved on or were on the missing list. Some were doing time in the clink for a variety of misdemeanours. More were shacked up with English girls in council flats all over London and some were just shacked up. Tom and Bertie spent the Christmas in Caits place but this Christmas the bread was not cut with a saw and Bertie didn't fall into the bath. They reminisced and laughed their cheek bones off their faces as the tears of laughter nearly cut channels down to their cheeks and jaws. Bertie stayed in London that January and Tom left for a good job down in Southampton as for him now the North of England was a hotbed of danger and he dare not venture up there again.

He started with Chivers Construction firm in Southampton that January and was not slow in making a name for himself with his knowledge and skill in the business. By June he was promoted to foreman and by December that year he was being lined up for a new job in the Bahamas to be followed by one in South Africa, and another in Canada to start in 1964. His passport and visa was got and all the travel arrangement were made for January 1962 but the Friday evening before Christmas he called into the head office and asked for his cards and the pay coming to him. The boss and his assistant spent the day trying to talk him out of it but his mind was made up and the cowboy had read another chapter and had saddled up his horse and he was on the move yet again. That evening he walked out the gate cards in hand, two weeks wages and a fine Christmas bonus to buy him his ticket home to Tralee and to a fine turkey dinner from Rita. He met Pa's brother during Christmas who told him Pa was living in County Louth where his wife was from. After Christmas he made back for London and got a start on the job Bertie was working on. They worked together on a motorway until they both fell out over a woman in late January 1962. They had a flaming row and never spoke to one another again. Tom started up to his old antics again smuggling off the docks and running scams around the city until the heat started to come at him from all sides. Everywhere he went his friends were running their hand down their lapel which told him the coppers were watching him. He phoned his brother Andy in Ireland the end of March and he fixed him up with a Government job up the midlands. He collected what he was owed and bailed out of London for good on the 18th of April 1962. He started work a week later in Ireland on half the wages he was on in England. However it was a secure number and had a pension going with it years down the road. He met Mick Bertie's brother years after in Tralee and asked him about Bertie. He told him he settled with an English girl in North London in 1963 and never returned to Ireland. One morning in the mid 1990s he was prayed for at Mass in Tralee. Tom found out that he had passed away that week in London. Although they had not met in almost thirty years his heart ached for his old long lost friend,

Pa came back to live in Tralee with his wife and family and settled down there in the late 1970s and worked on my house as a mighty fine chippie in the 1980s. The craic was a laugh a minute that time too as I got the full low down from him about Tom and his cunning stunts and what they all got up to in London.

Stefan ended up buying a trawler and packed in the teaching to go fishing. Aine gave birth to twins on the 1st of May 1962. They were blessed with a boy and a girl. Stefan insisted on calling his daughter Anne after her mother and they called the young lad David after Stefan's father. They built a fine home on the plot overlooking the pier and made it their nest. Marja and Remka went to work in Mick and Kate's hotel in Galway and learned to speak English as good as any native. Remka met a teacher that Stefan had known in Galway and they courted until July of 1963. One month before they were due to wed Stefan went to sea fishing with his crew and spent three days out in a stormy Atlantic. They had to spend a night behind one of the islands as the swell was too great to bring home the trawler. They all prayed that night on the boat and in the church in Ballinahowen and Aine was beside herself with worry. There were five husbands and fathers on board and they were a day overdue now as the storm still raged. They were all experienced seafarers and knew the Atlantic currents and swells. Those days a man in a long black coat and a beard was seen kneeling and praying on the hill overlooking the harbour. He too was awaiting the return of the trawler. From time to time he would disappear in the driving Atlantic mist and be seen yet again rosary beads in hand. He was not a local and only a young boy playing, the son of one of Stefan's crew was asked by him when the boat was due back. After three days and nights of prayer and storming every saint in heaven the wind abated and the trawler made for the shelter of the pier. Every family in the parish congregated on the pier including Aine. As the five wind swept fishermen stepped foot on dry land Stefan kissed the ground and made the sign of the cross. Aine hugged her husband, her love and the father of her twins. She asked him never to go to sea again and he smiled, took her by the hand and made up the pier through the crowd and he fatigued beyond belief. As he slowly moved through the crowd he heard a voice say in his native tongue "It is good my boy to see you have not lost your faith" Stefan stood riveted to the ground wife in hand, as he gazed into the eyes of the man with the long black coat and rough grey / black beard. Who was he? Then he said in Polish "father is it you" and he told him it was. David had been captured during the war and spent fourteen years in a Soviet Gulag. Stefan told his father back at the house that his mother and sister were alive and living in Galway. He also told him that Remka will be getting married in four weeks. Stefan drove with his father to Galway that afternoon and he met his darling Marja and his beautiful daughter Remka. Stefan made his way back to Ballinahowen that evening stopping every so often to keep his eyes open, as he had not slept in four days. David, Marja, and Remka stayed in the cottage and talked about their life since they were parted in Poland all those years ago. They told him how they were living in Czechoslovakia and that Stefan had been shot getting them into Germany. They told him how they had lived in London for the last few years and now were in Ireland for good. Stefan slept all the next day from chronic exhaustion and when he awoke he thought he had been dreaming. Aine, Stefan and young Anne and David piled into the car the next day for a real family reunion in Galway. David met his two grand children and met a more relaxed Aine than he had two days ago. Stefan's father told him when he was released last year by the Soviets he made his way south to Persia and Cairo where he worked on a boat that took him to Spain. From there he travelled to London to look for work. When he registered at the Polish Embassy he was told that his wife and maybe his daughter were living in London and got their address where he spoke to the lady of the house they had lived in. She told that they were gone well over two years ago to Ireland to a place called Ballinahowen in Galway.

Mick and Kate had their third child on the 18th of December 1963 and they christened her Julie after Kate's friend who had come back to Ireland that year and settled in Dublin with her new husband. They kept in regular contact for years after and well into their old age. Mick and Kate had their last child on the 1st of May 1965 a fine strong sturdy boy. The Bone and the wife stood for him at the christening and The Bone suggested they call him after him. Kate said "by the way what is your real name" He replied "The Bone". The wife then said tell her you gawmougue. She then said in her half English half Bohola accent it is Ignatius O' Brien or better known as IGGY. The cat was finally out of the bag. A loud cheer rang out in the church and the baby was christened without undue delay, but not Iggy.

Tom never married although as he often put it "He had many a close shave". As he drove down to Galway one evening in late 1973 to attend a work colleague's retirement function he stopped for petrol and twenty players at a petrol station. The wind was driving the sheets of rain across the windscreen he noticed a woman walk into the shop with a girl. As he followed them in he watched them shake the rain off their coats he noticed the familiar step. The woman turned and there before his eyes was Kate Joyce. They stopped and looked and looked again. "Is it you Tom" she said as Mick rounded the corner and said how are you doing my friend. They spent the night together in Mick and Kate's place rehashing over old times and the fun they had in London. Tom moved off the

233

following morning for Kerry where he started a new job some months later, they never met again.

In 1978 Mick and Kate's son Mick Jnr, who spent every summer at sea with Stefan since he had been fourteen signed on for a degree course in Marine Biology at UCG and started to study his life's passion. After a few days he noticed a girl called Sinead, who was also doing Marine Biology, at a party one night and took up dating her. As they years went by they became close and worked hard at their courses together she often went home with him and he many a time with her to West Cork. They had been nurturing a secret from their parents that would be out soon. They got engaged the night before they were both conferred with their degrees and had been planning their lives together now for some time. They thought the conferring to be the perfect opportunity to bring their two families together. All the officialdom was over by lunch time the families met afterwards. Young Mick Joyce introduced his parents to Sinead's parents as he said "Mom and Dad please meet Jack and Mary Barry from Castletowbere". Kate hugged Mary Barry and Mick Joyce grasped Jack Barry's mighty hand once more in his life's circle, a circle that would soon be complete with the marriage of their two children. It had been twenty eight years since they last met on Mick and Kate's honeymoon in West Cork. The years of hard work had showed on them all but like they all promised none of their children had taken the boat abroad.

David gave Remka his daughter's hand in marriage to her husband one month after he had found her, Stefan and his wife. The wedding was held in the hotel and it was the first one they had there. All went off well as Kate, the expert, took charge for the day. The newly weds settled not far from Mick and Kate's place and lived a long and very happy life together. David got a job in an engineering firm working ten hours a day for four days a week. He spent two other days at sea always with his son whom he loved dearly for finding his loving wife Marja and his little Remka. Like God David always rested the 7th day of the week in his presence and also in the treasured company of his dear wife Marja.

The Bone and Patsy never stopped the skulduggery. They worked the Dublin docks for drink and every sort of contraband for years after and retired two wealthy gentlemen. The Boody Man and the Scaffolder set up their own business in the seventies and ripped off half of Dublin and many said almost the entire city of Cork. They two made it good on the back of Her Majesty, good old Lizzy as the used to affectionately refer to her as.

Tom returned to Kerry to live in 1974 and took great care of three elderly relatives including his mother Rita who lived up into her ninety second year. He also took care of, and saw, his two brothers Pat and Andy get stricken with cancer and saw them both buried, one either side of the millennium. Tom still lives to this day where he grew up, not far from what was the green field that Bertie, Pa and himself kicked football together. He now drives to Mass and doesn't trot behind his mother as she used to lead her flock of young chicks to mass at half six on a Sunday morn' for seven mass. He is now stricken with the curse, that so many a ghostly immigrant brought back with them from the trenches of London and the blizzard swept flyovers of old blighty. His bones now suffer the pain and anguish of arthritis waking him in the dead of the night causing him pain and suffering as he wonders will he stick it out in bed or get up and wait for the dawn he so often faced out into with arms of steel and the strength of an ox. The one guiding tilly lamp he has brought with him since his small little legs trotted down to mass every step of the way was his iron clad faith and his devotion to the Blessed Virgin. She guided him throughout his life and kept him safe when the moment in time demanded it. He lived a lot of his life in a tough hard way at times, but she brought him to his mother's door when he was most needed to properly fulfil his one and only true destiny, to care for those he loved and earn the graces of God and Our Lady in the process. Almost sixty years have now passed since he boarded the train at ten to two, for the boat to England. He now lives a comfortable life surrounded by nieces and nephews. May the wisdom he has always bestowed on us be remembered many years into the future and may he always live in our hearts.

May God Bless You!

EPILOGUE

⬥

AS A RACE of people the Irish Nation go back in early history to a few thousand years before Christ. They have always been a resilient people and were able to take the rough with the smooth. For seven hundred and fifty years they fought with our closest neighbour for our freedom which we finally gained in 1922. It was time to put our heads down and make something of ourselves as a true free people. America had opened Ellis Island to us and had welcomed us to come to their country and build it up from the raw humble sod. Many an Irishman fought during the world wars under the banner of the crown against tyranny and oppression and many had lost their lives doing so. When England called upon the Irish again to help them to **"rebuild their crown"** we packed our bags and the boats and again went East to London, Birmingham, Bath, and deep into the coal mines to etch out a living and a crust of bread.

The forties, fifties, and sixties we exported the brawn to the towns and cities of blighty. We exported many a man who did not know, nought but their native tongue. Many an Irish girl followed their brother, sometimes their father and often their boyfriend making a life for themselves across the Irish Sea never to set foot on Irish soil again. Each year that passed they made plans to return and go home and find a job. Some followed their dream and went home to whence they had come from only to find the old street or townland changed beyond belief and only knowing an odd school friend who they might meet casually on the street corner. Fate worked well for some who worked hard and decided to return home no matter what. An opportunity could never be missed or a chance never passed up as that was the money that bought the final ticket home when all was done.

Many left with the shirt on their backs and more with just the Aran sweater the boots and the corduroy pants wrapping a morsel of food in the sports page of the local paper be it the Kerryman or the Donegal Democrat. Some slept rough on park benches for the first two weeks until they got their first pay packet. Many more bedded down in rat infested bombed out buildings without sanitation, running water or sometimes a pane of glass to glaze the rotting frame of an old 19th century window. The paved streets of London at one time had been the central hub of the British Empire were hard underfoot and not like the soft green hills and fields of home. They had to be trodden for a while but the soft green grass always beckoned the Paddy to one day return.

By 1950 we had our freedom as a nation no more than twenty eight years and we were nothing but children learning to walk the pathway of life. We were exploited for the work we were prepared to do and the hardships we were willing to embrace. Our ways were sometime uncouth and brash but it was our way of laughing through those years, something that kept us all going. Yes there were the notices on shop doors that said "No Irish Wanted" where an Irish child would not be sold a bottle of milk or a loaf or bread. Flats and houses were often not rented to the Irish families as they may keep the landlord awake at night with the cries of a child dispossessed of it homeland and destined never again perhaps to set foot on the sod where they were born. So often it all rang out with the stories of a bygone age when our country was still subjugated.

For those who stayed or for those who returned they took with them well into old age, if God blessed them with years, the pangs of arthritic pain and discomfort, the anguish of their minds as the cramped themselves into a one room bed sit or a dingy council flat five stories up where the lift rarely worked. Many woke up in the mornings with their heads on a pillow six inches away from the cooker or the fridge. Their last thought at night before their eyes closed was of the green field next to the house, or the patch of ground up the road where they kicked a ragged leather football. Many returned in the sixties and the seventies and brought their hard earned money with them and did well for themselves. As they went on their knees each week before Confession, Mass and Holy Communion they thanked the almighty for lighting their route back home.

When we grew up it was in the shadow of the rosary said around every fireside in the evening. We thanked the lord for getting up from the table with food in our stomachs.

We were always thought about the famine when our population was halved and decimated in the dykes and ditches of our precious land. The Ireland that emerged out of that age was not an Ireland graced with the pin striped suit, or the house on a hill, it came from the salt of the earth, the donkey jacket and the wellingtons with the turned down tops to let in the cool breeze to dry the soaking wet feet of the Paddy. Where we are at now was hard fought for and even more hard worked for. Lest we ever forget where we came from let us drop a prayer down through our hearts for the Paddies when we think of, what we were, and what we have now become.

3440387R00136

Printed in Great Britain
by Amazon.co.uk, Ltd.,
Marston Gate.